# DUG IN TOO DEEP

"Don't you wanna dig in that hole?"

"Luther, all I want to do is get the hell out of here."

"Mr. Alan . . ." he began, and the sun flashed on something in the corner of my eye. I wheeled toward the far side of the clearing, and before I could react, I glimpsed a second flash, but this one was accompanied by a loud crack.

I fell to the ground and in my peripheral vision saw Luther fall, too.

Then I heard tires spraying gravel across the clearing, and I rose onto my hands and knees. All at once I wasn't aware of the cold, only of the sweat drenching my body. I pulled myself to my feet and realized my legs were shaking.

"Luther, you can get up. They're gone."

I saw with horror that there was no movement from the form on the ground.

*Other Alan Graham Mysteries by*
**Malcolm Shuman**
*from Avon Books*

ASSASSIN'S BLOOD
THE MERIWETHER MURDER
BURIAL GROUND

# PAST DYING

## AN ALAN GRAHAM MYSTERY

# MALCOLM SHUMAN

**AVON BOOKS**
*An Imprint of HarperCollinsPublishers*

AVON BOOKS
*An Imprint of* HarperCollins*Publishers*
10 East 53rd Street
New York, New York 10022-5299

Copyright © 2000 by Malcolm K. Shuman
ISBN: 0-380-80486-7
www.avonbooks.com

First Avon Books paperback printing: September 2000

Avon Trademark Reg. U.S. Pat. Off. and in Other Countries, Marca Registrada, Hecho en U.S.A.
HarperCollins® is a trademark of HarperCollins Publishers Inc.

Printed in the U.S.A.

WCD   10  9  8  7  6  5  4  3  2  1

*This book is for Dave Miller, M.D.,*
*dedicated healer and faithful friend*

# ACKNOWLEDGMENTS

The author is grateful to his editor, Jennifer Sawyer Fisher; to her assistant, Clarissa Hutton; to his agent, Peter Rubie; and to the unsung copyeditor who saved him from so many embarrassing errors. He is especially grateful, however, to his friends in Louisiana: Paul Lemke, Esq., Jack F. Owens, Esq., Mrs. Joy Trunzler, forensic anthropologist Mary Manhein, aka "the Bone Lady," and Tom Wells, historic archaeologist and expert on metals. Their assistance and kindness can never be adequately repaid.

# ≡PROLOGUE

*December 1833*

    *The man on the tan horse looked out over the river at the steep bluffs on the other side. The ferry that had taken him across was already halfway back to the east bank, where the failing sun had painted the clutch of hovels at the base of the bluffs a deceptive gold. Someone looking across could get the idea the riverside settlement was a promised land, the man thought wryly, instead of a trap where whores and card sharps picked a stranger's pocket until he was lucky to get out with the clothes on his back.*

    *He'd been there many times, as well as in the mansions on the hills beyond the bluffs. He'd been wined, dined, had met the daughters of the gentry and had played cards with their fathers and brothers. They'd listened to his stories of land for the taking, in Louisiana, Arkansas, and, most recently, Texas, and some had invested in his schemes. They'd been awed by the stories of the brawl just upriver, on the sandbar, where, six years ago, he'd killed a man with his big knife, and by the tale of how he, his brother, and a few other men had outfought a band of savage Indians on the San Saba River in Texas. His brother had even published an account of the fight in a magazine called the* Saturday Evening Post. *That, together with local accounts of the sandbar duel, had made the horseman a local legend. Just two years short of forty, and the son-in-law of the vice governor of the Mexican State of Texas y Coahuila,*

1

*James Bowie should have been at the crest of his power and enjoyment of life.*

And yet, no sooner had he reached the United States on his trip east this summer than it had all turned to ashes.

First he'd learned of the death of one of his brothers. Stephen's life had been troubled and he had not gotten along well with his other brothers, but he was still blood and it hurt to know that Stephen was no more. Then, in New Orleans, his older brother, Rezin, who'd been with James on the San Saba, showed James the news of the Supreme Court decision: It had invalidated the Arkansas land claims James had so feverishly put together. The Court said they were forgeries and the people to whom he had sold them could not claim what was not theirs. In a flash James's hope for a fortune had evaporated, leaving him not only with worthless paper, but with a reputation as a dishonest speculator. And if these were not enough, the steam mill machinery for Rezin's plantation had never worked right, frost had killed the crop, and many of his brother's slaves had died of cholera.

If for no other reason than to leave the scene of disaster, James and Rezin had departed for the East shortly after his own arrival in Louisiana from Texas. They'd visited New York, where Rezin had been treated for his deteriorating eyesight, and then they'd gone down to the nation's capital, and tried to convince people at the Treasury Department to assist them on a financial claim against the government. But it had not worked, and all that had come of the trip was the story in the Post.

Perhaps it was his lowered resistance, or the effect of the old bullet and sword wounds from the sandbar fight, but soon after James got back to Natchez after his visit east he'd come down with malaria. In his delirium, as he tossed and turned, he called for his wife, Ursula, in faraway Texas, and gave incoherent orders for his last will and testament to be drawn.

But despite the debilitating fever, despite the lung still weak from the sword wound, despite the recent defeats, one after the other, his fever had finally broken and he had survived.

And it was on a dismal day early in November, while he

lay in the house of his friend in Natchez, gradually regaining his strength, that the news came from Texas.

His wife and her parents were dead, taken by cholera.

He sank bank on his pillow, eyes closed, and willed death to take him.

And death, smiling as always, refused.

So he made plans to return to Texas.

Stay, his friends had begged: Wait until your strength has returned.

But he'd shaken his head and continued to pack his few things.

At least take the steamboat to the mouth of the Red and then up to Natchitoches.

But he'd told them there was a man he wanted to see in Lordsport, along the land route.

Then start tomorrow, they'd advised: It's too late in the day, and on the trail after dark even you could fall prey to robbers.

He wasn't worried. No wilderness could be as dangerous as the place he'd just been. And, besides, he was well armed: a pair of pistols in his belt and a heavy knife in a scabbard. If the gunpowder was wet or the flint failed to strike a sufficient spark, the blade wouldn't disappoint him.

So now he plodded forward on the wagon road. By dark he could make it to the inn on Tiger Bayou, and if there was no place for him inside, he could always sleep under the stars. He'd probably be more comfortable on the ground anyway, he thought, mindful of the vermin-infested lodgings that travelers had to endure along the Louisiana roads.

The rocking saddle lulled him, only awakening him to pain when his mount stepped into a rut and jarred his body. He was dimly aware of the sunlight waning and the sudden onset of darkness. He was not as far along as he'd planned.

Well, no matter. He could pitch camp wherever he wanted.

He raised his head to the sky and counted the stars in the Dipper, then took in the broad band of the Milky Way. The Indians called it the Spirits' Road. Sometimes, truth be known, he felt more at home among the savages than he did among the blue bloods of Natchez and the Creoles of New Orleans. You knew where you stood with Indians.

*And there was always that story about the tribe in Texas that guarded a mine full of gold. He'd failed once in finding it, but maybe if he set out again it would tear his mind away from the sorrows that weighed him down.*

*Suddenly, as he stared into the blackness of the sky, a blaze of light illuminated the firmament. The horse started, gave a whinny of fright, and the man tugged the reins.*

*It was a falling star, plummeting downward. As its flame extinguished the man tried to figure where it had touched earth. Maybe near Lordsport, on the Cane River. Or maybe even farther west, in the unclaimed land between the United States and Mexico. Or maybe in Texas itself.*

*He'd seen many falling stars, but never one this bright, and though he was too hard-headed to have much room for superstition, he had to wonder if it was a sign: Was the star telling him that he was headed in the right direction? That his restoration, indeed, lay to the west? Or was it a message from the Dark One, who'd refused to take him so many other times: a signal telling him to come back to Texas, that this time he wouldn't be refused.*

*That's how I imagined it over a century and a half later, after the woman called about the thing in the river and people started dying.*

# ONE

I told the Corps of Engineers I didn't do UFOs.

"Neither do we," Bertha Bomberg said. She was the Corps representative who oversaw our archaeological services contract with the New Orleans Engineer District and in general made our lives miserable. "But this woman saw something and she's called everybody in the world, from the sheriff to the Division of Archaeology to her congressman and now she's calling the Corps of Engineers, because the thing fell into a bayou and she figures we ought to have some jurisdiction."

"I agree. Why don't you go up to Lordsport and talk to her?"

"Because, Alan, I would have to sign out a government car and explain to my supervisor in the Planning Division what I was doing and I wouldn't get authorization because it's in Vicksburg District, anyway."

"So you want me to go, instead."

"You're working on that highway project just a few miles outside of town. I thought it would just be—"

"—simpler for me to take time off and charge it to the Department of Transportation and Development," I said. "Hey, that's neat. Why didn't I think of it?"

"Don't be sarcastic, Alan. Next year . . ."

"I know. Our contract is being reviewed."

"I'm glad you understand. Besides . . ." She sighed. "I hate to see a taxpayer feel like they're not getting any response.

5

We're here to serve the public and this lady can't get anyone to listen to her."

Bertha Bomberg, public servant, was a face I hadn't seen up to now.

What else could I do but go?

I left the next morning, enduring Marilyn's tsking because I'd promised to try to hold down costs, and the highway department had already threatened an audit. I headed north up 61, to St. Francisville, recalling, as I passed familiar landmarks, the Tunica Treasure business that had brought Pepper and me together two years ago. Yesterday she'd laughed when I'd told her about Bertha's strange request.

"Just consider it a civic duty," she said from the other side of the shower curtain as small droplets of spray found their way around the barrier to settle onto my face and arms.

"I'm not feeling very civic-minded," I told her over the sound of the shower. "Especially when I have to leave you alone here for two days and nights."

We'd grown appreciably closer since our initial less-than-promising meeting. I was, in fact, on the verge of getting her to give up her apartment for good and move in. Now I had to go do La Bombast's work for her.

"I'll be okay," she said with a laugh, stepping out of the shower. Before I could lick my lips she'd whipped a towel around her, and I sighed. "I have my courses to teach," she reminded me.

"And that's another thing," I complained. "You come back from a summer in Mexico, on a dig, and not three weeks later that so-called anthropology department at the university snaps you up to take the place of that historical archaeologist who took off in a huff."

"But I thought you'd be glad: Marilyn never felt comfortable having me around. I was threatening to her sense of power. And poor David never knew what to make of me. This way, I don't compete with anybody."

"But that whole department is a nest of leches."

Her hand reached out to touch my face: "Poor Alan. Still insecure. What can I do . . . ?"

I told her and she did.

Now I was thirty miles away, resenting the fact that tonight, and probably tomorrow night as well, I would be sleeping on a bunk in a houseful of raucous archaeological crew people instead of in my own bed with the woman who I was still worried might burst like a bubble if touched once too often.

The season didn't help: It was a dismal January day, three weeks after New Year's, when everything from the sky to the very air is gray, and the excitement of the Christmas season has evaporated, leaving only a stack of greeting cards, a few pine needles on the floor, and the knowledge that ahead, at the end of the gray tunnel of winter, lies the furnace of summer. I hated summer almost as much as the dreary days after Christmas.

And I hated all the nights I was away from Pepper.

It was ten o'clock when I reached Natchez, and a fine rain was falling. Outside it was just above freezing and the weather forecast said the front extended west all the way to Texas. The crew would be inside today, processing artifacts, because it was too nasty to accomplish anything in the field.

I passed the sign pointing to the Grand Village of the Natchez, now a state park, and a few minutes later, at the hospital, arced left, toward the river. Ahead, high on the bluff sat a Ramada motel, and at the base of the hill, at water's edge, was a re-creation of Natchez Under the Hill, which, in the days before the Civil War, had been a sinkhole of depravity for river men, gamblers, and loose women. Nowadays, there were tourist joints and a gambling boat. These days losing your money didn't require having your throat cut.

Once over the bridge I was in Louisiana again, and into the flat floodplain of the Mississippi River, rich farmland that produced cotton and soy beans.

By the time I reached Ferriday, twenty miles west of Natchez, the rain had become a drizzle and I had the heater turned up full.

I hadn't told David I was coming because I wasn't sure how to explain what I was doing: UFOs weren't exactly the kind of things we were in business to investigate. Better just to come, talk to the woman, and explain afterward.

What had Pepper called it? A civic duty.

The rain stopped just after eleven, in time for me to see the brooding, rugged hills that loomed over the Cane River plain and shadowed the tiny community of Lordsport. Ahead of me was the old truss drawbridge that marked the entrance to town. The bridge was the reason we were here to begin with: The state was going to build a new one to the south, bypassing the town, and there was a major archaeological site in the way. We were excavating the site, but I had to wonder what the bypass would do for the town itself: Once a thriving steamboat port, it had been left moribund by the development of roads in this century. Though it was still a parish seat, once a bypass was in place there would be little reason to go there at all.

I slowed for the narrow bridge, with its bare two lanes, and glanced down at the water: gray as slate and as cold as Bertha Bomberg's heart—except that I'd just experienced a kernel of heretofore unobserved humanity in said heart, which was why I was here.

Then I caught myself: It wasn't warmth—La Bombast just didn't want to be bothered.

Ahead, after a scatter of houses and shops, was the old brick, four-story courthouse that dated from 1930. I found a parking place next to a white sheriff's cruiser and pulled in.

I went up the brick steps and into the old building, passing the four cases of archaeological artifacts that had been salvaged from the various mounds and sites in the area. One of the cases was empty, and I supposed another display was being prepared. This was probably the only parish in the state that had a sheriff interested in prehistory. I knew this because he'd once worked for me. I took the elevator down to the basement floor, and went through a doorway with a painted sign that said SHERIFF'S OFFICE. A sixty-ish deputy was leaning over the counter, talking about deer hunting to a man in camouflage fatigues. When I asked for Sheriff Scully, the deputy straightened up from the counter and ambled into one of the offices at the side. A minute later Scully himself came out, a six-foot, two-inch, straw-haired man in his early thirties whose face broke into a grin when he saw me.

"Alan. So she finally got you." He laughed, sticking out a hand as the other two men watched idly.

"She?" I asked.

"Ethel Crawford," he said. "That's why you're here, isn't it?"

I glanced at the two onlookers, who seemed interested in my answer. "I got a call from the Corps of Engineers."

"Course you did. She wouldn't leave me alone so I told her to call the Corps, that maybe one of the archaeologists digging on the bypass would be able to help."

"That was thoughtful, Jeff."

Jeff Scully shrugged. "How the hell else was I gonna get to see you again? David said you've gone into hibernation, don't hardly go to the field anymore at all." He winked at the other men. "Something about some research you're doing with a female archaeologist."

I cleared my throat. "David's got a big mouth."

"Hey, I don't blame you. If I could find a woman that would have me I'd stay at home, too." He eyed my middle. "And she must be a pretty good cook."

"About this Mrs. Crawford," I said, sucking in my stomach. "Why is this something the local sheriff can't handle?"

The two onlookers started to chuckle and it was Scully's turn to sigh.

"You don't know Miss Ethel," he said, lowering his voice. "She wants a scientist, not a cop. I couldn't talk any sense to her."

He came around the end of the counter and grabbed his windbreaker from the coat stand.

"I'll be back in a while," he said to the deputy and guided me into the hallway.

"I saw one of your display cases was empty," I said. "Getting ready for a new exhibit?"

Jeff Scully shook his head. "Somebody ripped it off," he growled. "From the damn courthouse, can you believe that? It was the only display we had about the history of the town. I put it together after you helped me assemble the cases with Indian artifacts."

"What was in it?" I asked.

"Some old coins, a plat map of the town made by Judge McGraw, a replica of a Bowie knife . . ."

"A Bowie knife?"

"Yeah, some of the Bowie family lived in Cane River Parish a hundred and fifty years ago and Jim Bowie and his brother Rezin came through every once in a while, so we figured a Bowie knife was a good thing for the display."

"Was any of it worth anything?"

"Not much," the sheriff said, disgusted. "And what burns me is they broke in at night, when the only way in was the basement door. Whoever did it had to go right past the office with a deputy on duty. Naturally, nobody saw a damn thing. I fired the night deputy and said the next one I caught sleeping would go to jail for malfeasance. But that didn't get the stuff back. Sometimes I don't know why I even let 'em talk me into running for this office. I was happier before, as a horse doctor."

"Any suspects?"

"Normally I'd be looking at Jacko Reilly. He used to account for ninety percent of the crimes in this town. But he did us a favor a couple of months ago and took off for greener pastures."

We went out through the back door, past a trusty in an orange jumpsuit, huddling inside for warmth. Scully pointed to a white, unmarked car.

"Where to?" I asked.

"Library," he said. "That's where we'll find Miss Ethel. This'll make her year."

I closed the door of the cruiser. "Is this lady reliable?" I asked. There was something about his tone of voice.

"Miss Ethel? Solid as a rock. Oh, there was the peeping Tom last year, and the ghost she saw at the old Parker place the year before, but . . ."

I groaned. "Jeff, if this lady's—"

"Just kidding," he said with a wink and backed into the street. "You form your own opinion."

# ▰Two

The library was a one-story, tan brick building across the street from the courthouse. Water dripped from the oaks in front and we stepped over puddles on the walkway. The four or five people huddled at the reading tables looked up as we entered.

A fat little woman with short, gray hair headed for us while we were still wiping our feet on the mat.

Jeff jerked his head in my direction: "Miss Ethel, this is Dr. Alan Graham. He came up from Baton Rouge. The Corps of Engineers called him. He's an archaeologist."

The little woman's blue eyes lit.

"You've come to find out what fell in the river," she said, sticking out a hand.

"I don't know if I can help you," I said. "But I'll do what I can."

"He's an expert," Scully pronounced, and I restrained an urge to kick him hard.

Abruptly, the librarian turned to the shelves, from whence a younger woman with brown hair and glasses had emerged.

"I'm going out," she told her assistant. "I'm going to show Dr. Graham here where the thing fell into the river. I'll be back later on." She looked up at the sheriff. "Well, let's go."

We went back out to the car and I took the backseat, letting Miss Ethel sit up front.

"Now we have to pick up Jeremiah," she said.

"Miss Ethel—" Scully began but she cut him off:

"He saw it, too. You know where he lives. I know he'll be there. He has nowhere else to go on a day like this."

"Who's Jeremiah?" I asked.

"They call him Hawkeye," Scully said, "because he's got one eye. Local humor. He's a black guy, fishes in the river, and picks up cans and bottles for recycling."

"He was in his boat when it hit," the librarian explained. "He heard it, too. He's a witness."

"Yeah," Scully drawled.

Jeremiah Persons, AKA Hawkeye, lived in a tumbled-down shack just across the river from the town. A wisp of smoke curling up from his chimney was the only sign that anyone might be alive behind the cardboard-covered windows. A shopping cart sat untended in the yard, and a stack of old tires graced one corner of the lot. Beside the house lay the stubble of a garden, its furrows sloppy from the rain, and the yard itself was a quagmire of mud and water.

Scully stopped just off the main road, on the last firm ground, and tapped his horn a couple of times. A few seconds later the front door opened and a face peered out.

Miss Ethel swung open her door and got out, oblivious of the wet.

"Jeremiah, put on your coat and come out here. We need to talk, you hear?"

The door shut and we waited. Three minutes later the door opened again and a form emerged. It wore an army field jacket and a leather cap with ear flaps. The figure slogged through the mud to the car and Miss Ethel rolled down her window.

"Get in," she ordered. "We're going to show Dr. Graham where the thing went into the river."

Jeremiah Persons climbed in beside me, saying nothing, and the sheriff backed gingerly onto the roadway, then started forward again, toward the bridge.

"It was about ten-thirty at night," Miss Ethel said, "the day after Thanksgiving. I was driving back from Ferriday, visiting my niece. It was a clear night, almost no clouds."

The iron trusses loomed in front of us.

"I was right where we are now," she said. "I had my window down, because the air conditioning doesn't work in the Chrysler anymore, and it was about seventy degrees. I was thinking what a shame it's always so hot around Thanksgiving."

We started up the bridge.

"You can stop here, Jefferson," she declared.

"But . . ."

"Just put on that flashing light thing and direct traffic around us while I explain to Dr. Graham."

"Yes, ma'am."

Jeff Scully stopped in the center of the span, put on the emergency brake, started the blue flasher lights on the dash and rear window, and forced himself out of the vehicle.

"Just stand over there and make sure we don't get hit by a car," she ordered, then turned to me.

"I was going about twenty. I never go faster than that when I go over this old bridge. And that's when I heard it."

"Heard what?" I asked.

"Well, it was a loud *whoosh*, with a little bit of a whistle. Like to scared me to death, I tell you. And then it hit the water." She pointed to a spot just downstream. "Right about there."

"I see," I said, staring out at the gray surface.

A car crept past and Jeff Scully waved it on.

"It made a loud splash and there were big waves."

"Was there a moon?" I asked.

"Not much of one. But I could hear the waves hitting the banks. I was so scared I slowed down and stopped right in the middle, where we are now."

"Did you see a trail of fire or anything?" I asked. "Or hear an explosion, like a sonic boom?"

"No. I heard just what I told you. But whatever it was has to have been big, to have kept the water splashing against the banks for so long afterward."

"Yes, ma'am."

She rolled down the window and called out to Scully. "All right, Jefferson, get back in and drive us under the bridge so Jeremiah can explain where he was when it happened."

The sheriff nodded wearily. "Yes, ma'am."

We drove back into town and made a U-turn at the base of the bridge and then went back across to the other side. At the base of the bridge ramp was a shell road that turned back toward the water's edge, and we followed it until we were almost under the bridge itself. The librarian sprang out of the car, and I heard Scully groan as he opened his door.

"Come on, Jeremiah," she called, "show Dr. Graham where you were when it happened. And don't slip on these rocks."

Jeremiah Persons hobbled forward, squinting from his good eye, as water dripped onto us from the metal girders above.

"There," Jeremiah said, pointing.

"Where?" I asked. All I saw was the gray surface.

" 'Bout halfway out," he said. "It come down there."

"You saw it?" I asked.

"Saw the waves," he said. "Heard the splash. 'Bout knocked me outa the boat."

"You were fishing?"

"Checking my trot lines . . ." He hesitated, sneaking a glance at Scully.

The sheriff shook his head. "Go ahead, Jeremiah. I'm the sheriff, not the game warden. Besides, if I arrested everybody around here who fished without a license, they'd have to build a new jail."

"Tell Dr. Graham what else you heard," Ethel Crawford ordered. "Tell him what it sounded like."

"Loud," the old man mumbled. "Like a train. Or maybe a sire-een."

I saw Scully's brows rise.

"How far were you from where it hit?" I asked.

"Maybe fifty feets. Maybe a hundred. Waves come over the side of the boat."

Scully folded his arms: "Jeremiah, when you're out alone in the boat, maybe you take a little something to keep you warm, eh? A bottle of that Nighttrain, maybe?"

"Nah, suh, not that night," Jeremiah Persons said.

"No?"

"Doctor said don't drink it when I'm taking medicine. Well, I was taking medicine that night 'cause I had a headache." He brought out a small bottle and showed it to me.

"Interesting," I said, because I couldn't think of anything else.

"What are you going to do now?" Miss Ethel asked.

I shrugged. "Don't know there's anything I *can* do. There's no way to find out what's down there without spending a lot of money. Now, if the sheriff wanted to drag the bottom . . ."

"If it was space junk," Scully said, "or even an asteroid, it most likely buried itself in the mud. Dragging probably wouldn't find it anyway."

"Space junk?" Miss Ethel asked.

"Something from a rocket launch or a piece of a satellite falling back into the earth's atmosphere," I said. "People would be surprised if they knew how much of that stuff falls around us all the time. Mostly it burns up in the atmosphere, but sometimes a chunk of metal makes it through. Or it could be something off an airplane. I've heard of pieces falling off in flight."

"I called NASA," Miss Ethel declared. "They said it wasn't theirs."

"They may not know. It could be from a Russian satellite. I'm not sure what can be done."

I started toward the car but her voice caught me.

"Jefferson said you had some kind of metal-detecting machine."

I gave Scully a dark look. "Oh?"

"I told her about the magnetometer," Scully said, avoiding my eyes. "That your crew had done a mag scan of the river where the new bridge is supposed to cross, half a mile south of here, and since you had the machine up here already, and had a boat and all, that maybe . . ."

The thought of a boat trip in the rain, on a half-frozen river, with the wind cutting through my jacket, was not appealing.

"Well . . ."

"Probably wouldn't take but an hour or two," he said. "I mean, since you already have it here."

David was going to hit the ceiling.

"I'll see what I can do," I said.

\*        \*        \*

When we'd dropped off our two guides Scully gave me a sheepish grin.

"Sorry, Alan, but it's an election year. I can't afford not to get involved. Even if it's a batty old librarian and a one-eyed drunk."

"And get *me* involved," I said dourly. "If I'd have known you were going to turn out to be a politician . . ."

"Didn't," Scully said, pulling into his parking place. "All I ever wanted to be was an archaeologist. That's why I worked for you that summer ten years ago."

"Twelve."

"But not many people make a living at it. So I went to vet school and became a veterinarian. I would've been happy but then people started reminding me about my father and how he was sheriff for twenty years, and they expect me to help 'em."

"So you agreed to run because of your father."

"That was the beginning. It was really thanks to Jacko Reilly, though. Folks wanted to be rid of him. But now he's gone and what am I going to do for an encore?"

"Beats me. Why didn't you drag the river before you got me up here?"

"Because there's nothing down there. But do me a favor: Run the mag and make the old lady happy."

# ▰▰▰ THREE

"You're going to *what?*" David Goldman demanded.

We were seated at the kitchen bar in what had once been a farmer's house, about a half a mile west of Lordsport, off Highway 20. There was a drink in front of each of us, thanks to the bottle of Dickel's I'd brought with me. A fire blazed in the gas space heater on the far wall, and on the closed-in back porch the other four members of the crew were washing artifacts.

"Bertha didn't leave me much choice," I told him.

David scowled.

"But that means you have to pull somebody off my crew, and I'm trying to finish on time, since you raised hell last time about my being a day over the budget."

"*Marilyn* raised hell," I corrected. "That's her job. Saving money and keeping clients happy."

"Forget about the archaeology," he mumbled.

"No clients, no archaeology," I said. It was a discussion we'd had before.

"Besides," I told him. "I'll run the mag and have Jeff run the boat. You aren't using the rig now."

"It still pisses me off," he protested. "Where does Bombast get the nerve? Flying frigging saucers!"

"I had to make it up to her," I told him. "She's been short-tempered with me ever since you caught her call last month and told her to say hello to Larry and Curly."

"I couldn't help it."

"No."

I finished my glass and went onto the back porch, where three people sat around a pair of zinc wash tubs, scrubbing bits of pottery. On the right, with tattooed biceps bulging under the sleeves of his dirty T-shirt, sat Gator, a sometime student who could sniff out an archaeological site like an Indian. Seated across from him was a small, dark-haired man who looked dapper even in faded jeans. L. Franklin Hill was our computer guru, but he was also a born field leader. Separating them was a tiny, pixie-ish woman, Meg Lawrence. In her third year of college, she was taking a semester off to do archaeology, over the protests of her parents. I'd promised her father I'd make her go back to school at the end of the summer.

"I hear we're going hunting for a flying saucer," Gator said, grinning, his uneven teeth giving him a jack-o'-lantern look.

"Who said?" I asked.

David shrugged. "Jeff Scully was talking the other day."

I looked at David. "So this wasn't exactly a surprise."

"I figured you'd say no."

"Bullshit," I said. "You knew I wouldn't be able to say no. You guys are enjoying this."

David looked away. "Well, you don't do fieldwork nearly as much as you used to," he said. "We didn't think it would hurt."

"We had a bet," Gator said. "David said Pepper wouldn't let you go."

My face must've reddened because Meg shook her head.

"Don't pay any attention to these guys, Alan. They're just a bunch of juveniles."

"Apparently," I said, turning around and almost colliding with the Mahatma, our New Age crew member, who could be as maddening as he was good-hearted.

"You find it?" the Mahatma, whose birth name was Dean Callahan, asked.

"What?"

"The UFO."

"Go say a mantra, Dean."

"You know, this could be a vortex. I feel a vibration whenever I get close to the water's edge. And when we ran the mag it kept giving false readings . . ."

"You see what I'm cooped up with?" David asked. "It makes even *your* company seem good."

"The rain's supposed to stop tonight," I said. "I'll run the mag tomorrow and leave you people alone."

It was ten-thirty in the morning before we got the boat into the water. True to predictions, the rain had cleared out, leaving a dry, cold wind that, after an hour, had sawed my face raw and left my hands numb. While Jeff Scully manned the outboard in the stern, guiding the boat, I sat in the bow, watching the read-out from the magnetometer, which was little more than an arrangement of electrical coils in a three-foot-long torpedo-shaped tube called a tow fish that trailed behind the boat on a cable. Powered by a battery, the magnetometer would pick up any underwater concentration of metal. The "anomaly," as such disturbances were called, would be reflected on the paper printout moving across the face of the control unit at my feet, which was a metal case with knobs and a track for the moving paper.

I looked back at Jeff, and he shook his head. We'd just made a pass parallel to the west bank and another approximately down the middle of the river, and as yet there were no unusual readings. I knew what Jeff was thinking because I was thinking it, too, and every time I opened my mouth to tell him we'd done enough, I glanced over at the bank where my Blazer was parked with the boat trailer. There, at the foot of the water, bundled up like a mummy, Miss Ethel watched expectantly, as she had for the past hour.

Neither of us wanted to tell her the bad news.

"I guess we could go along the east bank," Jeff called over the sound of the outboard. "Then nobody can say we didn't do everything we could."

I nodded, and the boat swung around to head downstream. The bridge passed over us, an iron shadow on slate gray water.

She still wasn't going to be satisfied: She'd probably want divers.

We were at least two hundred yards downstream from

where the object was supposed to have hit. What bothered me most was the possibility that the mag might actually pick up something: There might be old boat motors, tire rims, all kinds of junk, buried in the mud forty feet down. They would all show something on the printout. How could I explain to the librarian that I wasn't about to pay a diver to check out every squiggle on the paper?

Jeff started the transect, heading toward the bridge. I watched the paper feed out of the printer.

A line of four-digit numbers, roughly the same. Nothing.

The bridge was a quarter mile ahead and the wind was straight in my face, so that tears ran down my cheeks.

What the hell was I doing in the middle of a river, on one of the coldest days of the year, when I could be warm and snug at home, next to Pepper?

Wishful thinking, because she'd be in class now, spewing out theory to a bunch of groggy students.

At least I *told* myself they'd be groggy. For all I knew she'd have them on the edges of their chairs.

Damn, what was wrong with me? Two years ago, B.P.—before Pepper, as David liked to say—I wouldn't have thought about staying inside. Maybe he was right. Maybe I'd let my feelings for her spoil me. Maybe . . .

I suddenly realized the numbers on the printout were larger than the numbers printed just before.

I looked up in surprise: The bridge was almost overhead, and our cars on the east shore were just opposite us.

The numbers went back to normal as we passed under the bridge.

I let Jeff make a circle and head back downstream, closer to the bank.

As we came even with the cars, and the place where Miss Ethel watched, I looked down at the printout.

The numbers were not as exaggerated as before, but the effect was there.

There was something metallic near the east bank.

I waited until we reached the bend downstream and had turned, then called out for Jeff to take first transect again. I wanted confirmation.

Once more the printout showed high readings.

I held up my hand and Jeff throttled back the engine.

The silence enveloped me, and then I heard the lapping of the waves.

"What is it?" he asked.

"There's something down there," I said. "Something big."

"Oh, shit," he muttered. "You mean she really *did* see something?"

I stayed over with the crew that night, because it wouldn't be until the next day that Jeff Scully could get a diver on site. Supper was excellent, a plentiful helping of pork roast, fresh green beans, mashed potatoes, corn on the cob, mint jelly, and homemade apple pie. When I'd finished a second helping, rinsed my plate in the sink, and gone back to my place beside the space heater, I felt my eyes trying to close. The crew members had driven to Natchez, looking for something to do, but David had stayed, to keep me company and to finish his field notes.

"Good food, huh?" he said.

"So hiring the Duprees to cook worked out," I said.

"More or less."

"More or less?"

"Alice Mae's a good cook. But the problem's Luther."

"Oh?" The Duprees were a father-daughter combo who'd been recommended by Jeff Scully, whose judgment I was quickly coming to doubt.

"Like I say, Alice Mae can cook but she has to rely on Luther for the food. Now, usually it's pretty good—venison, fresh fish, and the like, though I'm not too sure about where Luther gets it all. But I don't ask questions."

"So what's the problem?"

"The problem's Luther."

I looked down at my glass. "Oh?"

"They locked him up for drunkenness two weeks ago and the food went to shit. Alice Mae had to scrounge whatever she could, but the nearest real grocery's in Simmsburg, which meant I had to send somebody shopping with her. Now . . ."

"Now?"

"Luther got caught a couple of days ago by Mr. Pope, the game warden, for hunting in the wildlife preserve without a license. He bonded out, but Alice Mae's almost out of provisions, and if Luther gets put away for a long stretch . . ." He shrugged. "I'm scared the crew's gonna quit But I don't know anybody else around here who wants to cook three meals a day for an archaeological crew. "

"Jesus," I swore.

"Tell me about it," David said. "And now we've got a flying saucer."

"It isn't a flying saucer," I said.

"Then what is it?"

"How the hell do I know?"

He watched me get up and move to the kitchen counter, where the telephone sat. I punched in my home number and waited. Two rings, three, and then the answering machine came on.

Damn it, where was she? I tried the number for her apartment, which she'd insisted on keeping as a sign of her independence, and waited.

*"This is Pepper. I'm not at home right now . . ."*

I hung up. It was eight o'clock. She was always at home by eight. Well, maybe she'd stepped out for a six-pack of Cokes.

What was I thinking? She was a Yankee: She didn't have the Coke addiction of a well-brought-up Southern girl.

Chips, then?

But why eat chips when she could get *real* food at a place that served short orders and beer and played music. A place like the Chimes Bar, near campus. Or, even worse, the Alligator, ten miles out in the country, on a lonely road . . .

I felt my heart throbbing and started to pace.

"Not home, huh?" David asked. "Well, she probably found some young stud, closer to her age."

"Screw you."

He poured another five fingers of whiskey into my glass. "Have another drink."

\* \* \*

The next morning the diver came. He was a skinny young man named Elvis, with a scuba tank instead of sideburns and guitar. He parked his Ranger near my Blazer and the sheriff's cruiser and slipped into his wetsuit.

"Little bit warmer today," he said, and Jeff and I nodded. The front had moved through and the temperature was up to a pleasant sixty degrees.

"Aren't you worried about radiation?" Miss Ethel asked.

He gave her a perplexed look and turned on Scully.

"What you say was down there?"

"Dunno," the sheriff said, looking in my direction for help. "Alan took the mag reading . . ."

"Maybe a chunk of meteorite. Or some space junk," I said. "Or something that fell off an airplane."

"I ain't going where there's no radiation."

"There isn't any radiation," Scully declared.

"How do you know?"

"The mag would've showed it," he blurted and dared me to contradict him. I looked away quickly.

But the diver, surprisingly, didn't take him up.

"I'll see what it is," he said. "But if I don't like it I'm not gonna stay down there long."

"Aren't you going to take a camera?" Miss Ethel asked.

Elvis shook his head. "You can't see anything down there with the mud. You have to feel your way. So it better be something that feels right."

Miss Ethel glanced around nervously. "That boy from the newspaper's supposed to be here."

"I'm sure he'll come," Scully said. "I think I heard he had a birthday to cover first. Old man Gibbons turned a hundred."

Jeff and I cranked the boat down off the trailer behind my Blazer. Once it was in the water, we held it as the diver climbed in and I followed. Jeff shoved the craft into the stream, and I yanked the starter cord of the outboard. I nudged us into the middle of the river, about where the mag had shown the anomaly, and pointed. Elvis nodded, fitted his mask over his face, and went over the side. I watched his foam turn into bubbles and then moved upstream a few yards. I threw the anchor—a concrete cinder block on a rope—over the side, and cut the engine.

Traffic rumbled over the bridge, and I caught a glimpse of a blue car reflected in the muddy water. When I looked up, the blue car was crawling down the shell road toward the place where the other vehicles were parked. The car pulled up beside my Blazer, and a tall, blond young man with a camera got out.

The press, I thought, here to immortalize every second of our embarrassment.

I wondered if I could just drop into the water like Elvis and surface a hundred yards away, out of sight.

Miss Ethel was already giving him an earful, and he was dutifully jotting it down on his pad.

Something gray and bullet-shaped exploded from the surface twenty yards downstream, and I recognized Elvis's head. He saw me and treaded water while I let out anchor rope, drifting down to where he floated. He grabbed the gunwale, and I helped him into the boat.

"Well?" I asked.

He pushed up his face mask. "Like I said, it's darker than a well digger's ass down there. And almost as cold. Get me back on land."

Jeff helped him out of the bow as I guided the boat up onto the shore and Miss Ethel rushed forward, accompanied by the reporter.

"Did you see it?" she demanded.

"No, ma'am. But I sure felt it."

I heard her suck in her breath.

"I'm Tim Raines, editor of the *Weekly Trumpet*," the young man with the camera burst out. "Can you tell me what you felt?"

"Well," Elvis drawled, "it had windows."

"Windows?" the librarian asked. "You mean it was some kind of *craft*?"

"Yes, ma'am."

"What kind?" the reporter asked, eyes big behind thick glasses. "I mean, could you find a hatch or anything?"

"No, but there was a door." He held up a small aluminum object. "And I'd say from this key, it was General Motors."

He turned to Jeff. "Sheriff, I think we need a wrecker with a grappling hook."

I heard Scully groan.

"Right," he said, walking over to his car for the radio.

It was noon when the wrecker arrived, and by then a small crowd had congregated on both sides, to watch. A thin, grizzled man in an army field jacket and an orange hunter's cap was introduced to me as Snuffy Stokes, the mayor. Chain-smoking and clearing his throat with a sound like a chain saw, His Honor watched impassively as the diver disappeared under the surface to attach the grapple.

"Who'd drive their car down here," he asked nobody in particular, "when the bridge is up there?"

I didn't like the look on Jeff Scully's face, pale with tinges of green.

"Unless they just wanted to get rid of their old car," the mayor went on.

"No," Jeff said. "They didn't want to get rid of it."

The diver reappeared and climbed back into the boat, which I'd let one of the deputies handle. He waved an arm, and the wrecker driver started the winch.

"I don't care," Miss Ethel said as the water bubbled and frothed. "It was *not* a car that fell in."

"Yeah," the mayor said, as the front bumper broke the surface, "but a car's what you got."

I watched as the vehicle, smeared brown with mud and trailing a filament of fishing line, was hauled slowly up onto the shell bank, where it sat with rivulets of water pouring from every opening.

It was a red Firebird, six or seven years old, with the windshield intact and the tires in place. The driver's side window was down, and I saw Tim Raines peer inside and then draw quickly back.

"My God," he gasped, the camera falling out of his hands to swing limply at his neck. "There's a body in there."

"But who . . . ?" Miss Ethel began.

Jeff Scully shook his head, not bothering to look.

"Five'll get you fifty," he said, "it's Jacko Reilly."

# ▰ FOUR

I drove home the next morning. It was Friday, and I wanted to spend the weekend with Pepper. Besides, I couldn't take many more days like yesterday.

The car and body had no sooner been pulled out of the water than the reporter had started snapping photos. I knew what was going on in his head. A small-town weekly didn't print much real news, and here was a ticket for a young reporter to get out of a backwater and land a spot on a big-city newspaper. There was no telling how we'd all be misquoted.

And then there was Miss Ethel Crawford, telling all who would listen that we'd looked in the wrong place, because the splash she'd heard certainly hadn't been a car. But her protests were lost in the uproar, because something had been found, regardless of what she'd told us, and a body inside a car was more newsworthy than a claim of something that, at best, had only been heard. As for Hawkeye, when a deputy went to his cabin during the afternoon the old man wouldn't come out, insisting through the closed door that he hadn't seen anything.

To make things worse, the meal that night was a disaster.

Luther Dupree, a scrawny, gray-haired man with a game leg, ladled skimpy helpings of an unidentifiable stew onto the plates, along with a single slice of two-day-old bread.

"Armadillo?" Meg asked.

"Old shoes," Frank Hill suggested.

Only the vegetarian Mahatma seemed blissfully unconcerned.

26

David's eyes caught mine with an "I told you" look, so I shoved back my chair and went out to where Luther was making for his truck.

"Luther, we've got to talk," I told him, as he opened his truck door. It was just after twilight, and a cool breeze was ruffling the leaves of the pin oaks and hickories. "The crew's complaining about what they ate tonight. I wasn't so happy with it, either."

The little man nodded. "I know, Mr. Alan, I know. If that game warden had of been doing his job instead of following me up on the preserve, I could of had something in time, but Alice Mae didn't have no money and by the time I got shut of them bloodsuckers at the courthouse it was too late. I tell you, Mr. Alan, somebody's got to do something about this country."

"Damn it, Luther, it's not our fault you can't obey the law. We gave Alice Mae money."

"You gotta see it like it is, Mr. Alan. Up here the law ain't like it is in the city. Old man Pope, the game warden, has had it in for me ever since I beat him on that rare species fishing business three years back, made him look like a fool. Now he ain't got nothing better to do than try to get even. Alice Mae spent the money to get me out."

"Our crew has to eat."

"Don't I know." The little man shuffled miserably. "And I'll do my best if they'll just let me." He shook his head. "But it's only got worse since Jacko Reilly disappeared."

"Jacko Reilly?"

"He used to keep 'em all busy, Jacko did. Breaking into camps, selling dope—oh, they's a hell of a lot of dope in this parish, Mr. Alan—even selling treasure maps like he did to that poor stupid bastard in Jena. I pure hated to hear Jacko was gone. Now all they got to do is bother folks like me."

I sighed. "Luther, you'd better figure something out."

"Yes, sir." He climbed into his truck, slammed the door twice before it would lock, and tried to start the engine. The motor groaned, and I was heading for my Blazer and the jumper cables when the engine caught, the lights flickered on, and Luther made a quick semicircle in the yard, then lurched into the gravel drive.

I didn't know whether my talk with Luther would do any good or not: A lifetime of shiftlessness doesn't go away that easily. But I felt sorry for Alice Mae, a gangly girl in her mid-twenties who seemed to have little going for her and needed the work. And I didn't know who else we could find to cook. So I crossed my fingers.

The last straw occurred half an hour later when, after three futile attempts to reach Pepper, I heard the front door open and turned to see Jeff Scully in the entrance, a brown paper bag in one hand. At first I thought he'd been drinking, but by the time he was inside I realized he was sober.

The crew quickly found reasons to retire to their rooms and David went to the kitchen cabinet and got out a bottle of whiskey.

"I don't guess you got room for another crew member," Scully cracked, claiming one of the stuffed chairs.

"Tired of being sheriff?" David asked, sitting down in a folding chair and handing us each a drink.

"Tired of little old ladies who think they see flying saucers," Scully declared. "Tired of bastards like Jacko Reilly who get themselves killed in my parish instead of just leaving to bother some other parish."

"Nobody's sorry he's dead, are they?" I asked.

"His old man will be, if the news travels as far as state prison. Ten or twenty women who thought he was a life form. His cousin Chaney, who just happens to be running against me."

"The old sheriff?" I asked.

He nodded. "The one I beat three years ago, when folks in this parish said they were tired of Jacko and his carrying on."

"They won't be sorry he's dead," David said. "They can't hold that against you."

"You don't understand," Scully said, running a hand through his sandy hair. "The Reillys are all over the parish. They hate each other ordinarily, but let something happen to just one of 'em and they swarm. Right now they're swarmin'."

"You didn't kill him," I said. "All you did was find him."

"They don't see it that way," he said. "They want to know why I couldn't protect him. It's Chaney Reilly who's telling 'em all that crap. One of my deputies told me before I came over here. Chaney's saying I spent all my time harassing poor Jacko, who was just a little wild, but not a bad boy, right? And then somebody murdered him and I not only didn't stop it, I didn't even know it happened."

"Who says he was murdered?" David asked. "Maybe he was drunk and missed the bridge."

Scully shook his head. "His lights were off. We found that out when we looked at his car. And so was his ignition. Somebody turned off his lights and engine so as to not atttract attention and then rolled him into the water." He hiccupped. "And old Doc Carraway, the coroner, found a cut mark on one of his ribs and a nick in one of his vertebrae where a knife point stuck. Looks like somebody stabbed him with a pretty big knife. Way I see it, somebody did the parish a favor. But the way *they* see it, I might as well have done it myself."

"No weapon?" I asked.

"Nah. And not much of Jacko, just his body and the junk that was on the car seat, from his pockets." He coughed. "Actually, there *was* something kinda funny there."

"Like what?"

"Well, what it was, was all coins—nickels, dimes, pennies, a couple of quarters. A money clip with some threads of bills in it, mostly rotted."

He reached into his pocket then. "And this."

He opened his big fist and I found myself staring down at a tiny gray-colored wedge with what appeared to be writing on it.

"Looks like part of a coin," Jeff said. "But somebody cut it up."

*Rex,* the writing said.

"It's two bits," I told him.

"A quarter?"

"A quarter of a Spanish peso coin. The coin itself weighed an ounce, but each coin could be divided into halves, quarters, or even eighths. Silver pesos were used as money in this country until well into the last century and were recognized by the

U.S. government. Somebody cut this peso into quarters."

"But where did Jacko get it? He's got to have stolen it from somebody."

I shrugged. "You're asking the wrong person."

"Well, I can't ask anybody around here."

"Sounds like you need an expert," David said smugly.

Scully smiled. "Kind of what I was thinking. Somebody who knows metals, knows about coins, knows about historic artifacts."

I started to get a weak feeling. "Don't look at me like that."

"Why not? Isn't that your job? Don't you have experts who can tell you about historic artifacts?"

"That's true," David said. "You could take it back with you. Pepper can clean it up and check out some collectors who might know if anybody around here had a hoard."

"I thought that was a job for the State Police Lab."

"If I could trust 'em. But they worked with Chaney Reilly for twelve years. Take the damn thing, Alan. Please."

I shrugged again. "If you want."

"Good," Scully said, handing me the silver piece. "If you can find out who owned it, we may have a chance in hell."

I took the piece gingerly, got a small polyethylene artifact bag from the porch, and dropped the coin fragment inside.

"I'll do what I can," I told him.

Scully took his drink in one gulp and rose. "Thanks then. Tell everybody in Baton Rouge hello. Goddamn, why did I ever come back here when I could've got nine dollars an hour working for you and having fun?"

"Sheer greed," I said and watched him head for the door.

I reached Baton Rouge just after noon. I checked in at the office and found, to my relief, that there were no disasters, no crises. Marilyn, my tiny office manager, who had come as a student ten years ago and never left, actually informed me that a check had arrived and we were solvent, although, she pointed out, it would only allow us to pay off a small part of our overextended credit line, and we badly needed more work to materialize. I nodded, thanked her, and said it would, because somehow, magically, it always did, though the wait was always excruciating.

A couple of students were sorting artifacts in the lab, which was in reality the living room of what had once been an old house. A red-haired, muscular graduate student, who gave us twenty hours a week, was busy writing at one of the computers. I tapped him on the shoulder and went back into my office, which was a bedroom that had been partitioned.

He stood in front of me, waiting, a smirk on his face. I wondered if I was unzipped or whether the smirk meant Blackie Rector had scored the night before.

I set the paper bag with the silver piece on my desk.

"I have here a valuable artifact," I told him. "I want you to guard it with your life."

"What is it?" he asked, still smirking.

"Two silver bits," I said. "It comes from a murder scene. Sheriff Jeff Scully wants us to clean it up and tell him whatever we can about it."

"Business must be bad," Blackie said, brown eyes twinkling behind his glasses. "Couldn't he at least have given you fifty cents?"

"Jeff's a friend," I said. "He worked here as a student. He used to do your job, back when we could afford skilled help."

"So what do you want me to do with it?" he asked.

I got up and went to the wood cabinet in one corner of my office. "I'm going to lock it up in here. Make sure nobody tries to open this."

"Will do."

"By the way, seen Dr. Courtney lately?"

"So that's why you called me in here. Don't you have her phone number?"

"Don't be a wise-ass."

"Haven't seen her," he said. "Since last night, anyway."

"Last night?"

"She was at the Chimes when I stopped by for a modest libation about seven-ish, after an afternoon of mental calisthenics connected with the statistics portion of my comprehensives."

I felt my muscles tense. "I take it she wasn't alone."

"It seems to me she was holding a colloquy with a male member of the anthropology faculty."

"Who?"

"Do I have to answer?"

"Yes, damn it."

"I fear it was Captain Hook."

*"She was with Ellsworth Hooker?"*

"Alas. But it was a public house. There was nothing untoward going on. And he didn't have his hand in her blouse."

"How long were you there?"

"Not long. Seven or eight beers."

"So they were there half the night?"

"I don't know. I don't remember much after seven or eight beers."

I gave him a withering look. "Go back to your computer."

For the next few minutes I applied myself to the paperwork in my plastic in box. There was a request for a speaker from a small museum in one of the Florida parishes, and I'd probably agree to come out of a sense of duty. There was a copy of a letter from the IRS threatening to levy if we didn't pay withholding taxes that Marilyn had already deposited. Her handwriting at the top told me what she thought of the IRS and said she'd handle it. And there was a note from Sam MacGregor, my old professor who'd gotten me started in this game, advising me that he and Libby were back from a trip to China and would be happy to see me. I'd call him later on. Finally, there was a trio of résumés from out-of-town archaeologists whose projects had ended and now needed work. One was from California and had done all her work in the Southwest. I put her letter in the "not likely" file. The second was from a recent graduate of a small college in Georgia who had extensive field experience in the Southeast. I put his résumé back in the box, making a mental note to give him a call. Finally, there was one from a graduate student at Louisiana State University, advising that she would be free this summer, had experience, and could produce a recommendation from the noted expert on the French Paleolithic, Dr. Ellsworth Hooker.

*Hooker.* My hand started to crumple the résumé and then I caught myself. No reason she should suffer because of my aversion to the man. She was probably too young to know his sordid reputation—the two ex-wives, the alleged affair with the wife of someone at the Geological Survey, rumors of wife swapping.

But, damn it, *Pepper* wasn't too young. The man's reputation was an open book.

I called my house and her apartment. No answer. Then I called the Department of Geography and Anthropology, but the secretary hadn't seen her since her class this morning. She tried her office but there was no response.

Maybe, I thought, I should try Hooker's archaeology lab. It had nice big double doors that could be locked and flat lab tables where . . .

Stop being a paranoid fool.

I dawdled for the rest of the day and then, suddenly aware that I hadn't eaten, left early and walked up to the Chimes Bar. It had become the standard watering hole for the archaeology crowd since the Library Bar had shut down, to my infinite regret. The Chimes made good hamburgers and also specialized in imported beers, and maybe if I took my time she'd come in, because it was Friday afternoon.

But half an hour and most of a hamburger later she still hadn't appeared. I was on my way to the bar for a third beer when the door opened, spilling daylight into the dingy interior.

"Alan, what are you doing here?"

It was Esmerelda LaFleur, our historian, who taught part-time at the university and did research for us on the side. Her red hair blazed in the sunlight, and in the instant before the door closed I had the impression of a gangly scarecrow.

"Why *shouldn't* I be here?" I asked.

She gave an exaggerated shrug. "You've been out of town. I'd have thought you'd head straight to Pepper when you got back."

"I have to find her first," I said dryly.

"Oh, no, has she disappeared?"

"I can't find her," I said.

"Maybe," she said, rolling her eyes, "you ought to try your

house. That's where she was heading when I asked her to come here with me ten minutes ago. She wouldn't hear of it. Something about a homecoming for you."

I planted a kiss on her cheek and was out the door before she could say another word.

I'd ask about Captain Hook later.

# ≡ FIVE

It was *much* later and we were lying upstairs in the big bed when I told her what Blackie had said.

"Of course, he was drinking," I said and waited.

Pepper turned over to face me, her skin ivory in the dimness.

"I have to confess, Alan: Ellsworth's leaving his mistress and we're running away together."

My heart stopped momentarily, and then she started laughing.

"You should see the look on your face." She put a hand on my cheek. "You're priceless."

"I don't think it's funny," I mumbled.

"Look, dummy, I happen to teach in that department. It's a temporary position. But they're making noises about my staying on."

"You want to work with that bunch of philandering, spiteful, petty—"

"Just like any other group of human beings," she said softly. "And the answer is, why not? It keeps everybody happy: David doesn't feel like I'm crowding him and Marilyn can have you all to herself."

"There's nothing between Marilyn and me, never has been."

"I know that, but she's always been jealous of having your attention. She simply doesn't want to share power with another woman."

I couldn't argue that.

"As far as Ellsworth Hooker, he wanted to talk to me about writing an article together on theory for *American Antiquity*."

"And he thought your thought processes would loosen up with a little beer."

"Hey, he's a full professor . . ."

"Only because he's been there forever. He got chased away from a *good* department. This one picked him up on the rebound."

"But he *is* here and now he's in a position to help me or hurt me. Alan, I have to be polite to the man. Even if he is a creep."

"You really think he's a creep?"

"Of course."

I exhaled. "You know, I tried to call you for two nights in a row."

"I was at the library the night before last. And I went there again last night after I got away from Hooker. I saw Blackie at the Chimes, by the way: It's a wonder he could do any work today. He was pretty stoked."

"Blackie can hold his own," I said.

"Yeah. It's just poor Alan I have to worry about." She touched my lips with a finger. "Poor thing, up there in Lordsport, chasing UFOs."

That's when I told her about Jacko Reilly and the Spanish coin.

She sat up suddenly, the sheet falling to reveal the soft globes of her breasts.

"Where is it?"

"Locked up in the office."

She was already putting on her clothes.

"Let's go see what we have."

"Right now?"

The bedside light went on and she must have seen my disappointment.

"Hey, we've got all night," she said, fastening her jeans. "But this sounds really interesting."

"Interesting," I repeated, watching her breasts disappear as she slipped a T-shirt over her torso.

"Let's go. The sooner we start the cleaning process the sooner we can get back."

It was just after nine, a Friday night, and a loud student party was going on in the old house next to the office. Our tiny parking lot, which had once been a backyard, was filled with cars I didn't recognize and I double-parked, blocking a couple of them in. Not that they were likely to move before morning, anyway.

We went into the office and I got the bag with the silver piece out of my cabinet. I handed it to Pepper and followed her out to the lab, where she turned on one of the high-intensity lamps clamped to one of the lab tables. She placed the piece on a sheet of white paper and picked up a magnifying glass. Bending low, she studied the design and then, with a pair of tweezers, turned the fragment over.

"You're right. It's a quarter of a Spanish peso. See the design here?"

I bent over and squinted.

"It's incomplete," she explained, "but it looks like part of a pillar next to the coat of arms. It's called the pillar design and it came in early in the eighteenth century, if I remember right. In fact, I think we have part of the date here: Seventeen something or other." She stood up.

"Value?" I asked.

She shrugged. "Hard to say, but my guess is not all that much. Silver isn't worth what it used to be and this is only a fragment of a coin, so the coin isn't valuable to a collector."

She reached into her bag and took out a camera. "I'll take some photos for documentation." She went to the light table and placed a small ruler below the artifact, to give an idea of its size. She clicked off several shots from each side and then turned off the lamp.

She recorded her photos in a small note pad.

"Let's weigh it," she said and placed it on a laboratory balance. She wrote the weight in her notebook and then put the notebook away.

"I'll have to check it out in the coin books I have in my

office at school. It may be possible to find out more from one of them."

"It can wait till tomorrow," I said, moving behind her to put my hands on her hips.

"But now I'm curious," she said. "Don't you want to drive over and get them? Won't take but a minute and—"

"No."

She let herself relax back against me and gave a deep-throated chuckle. She turned around and looped her arms around my neck: "I guess mere silver really *can* wait."

"Yes," I agreed smugly, replacing the coin in the cabinet.

The next day, Saturday, I slept late. When I awoke Pepper was downstairs, already dressed and seated in my study. She held up a catalog.

"I went out and got this while you were still asleep. They list all kinds of coins. I think this was a Mexican mint Spanish *real* or peso. They were minted between 1772 and 1821." She pointed to an illustration and I studied it.

"It does look like it," I said.

"Yup. What we got here is a real pirate coin."

"You mean 'avast there' and all that?"

"Sure enough. Although these coins were used all throughout Louisiana at one time. It's not odd to find one but it would be nice to know where your late friend got it." She closed the book. "Do you think he dug it up somewhere?"

"From what I've heard, digging would be a lot of work for him. But *somebody* may have dug it up. I wonder who collects Spanish coins in that area?"

"I don't know but I can find out."

I nodded, suddenly restless. "You know, you may have to testify if they catch whoever did this."

"No problem."

"I hope not."

"Something wrong?"

"I don't like having a piece of evidence from a crime scene in my possession. If something happens to it, Jeff Scully'll be up the creek."

"Why should anything happen?"

"Because Lordsport's a funny place. It's got a strange mix of people. I've never been in any place like it except—"

"—a small peasant village in Mexico, were you going to say?"

"Something like that. Jeff was one of the best field assistants I ever hired. You never had to tell him anything twice. And he was completely at home in the woods. I thought for a while he was going to change his major and become an archaeologist."

"But he became a sheriff instead," she said.

"Yeah. His father had been the sheriff for years and died when Jeff was in his teens. I think he felt like he'd be letting down the old man not to follow in his father's footsteps. So, even though he was a horse doctor and not a lawman, he somehow got talked into running for office."

"Well, he got elected, so he can't be a total failure."

"No. But, from what he told me before I left, that wasn't something he'd planned. He said it was Judge Galt's doing."

"Judge Galt?"

"The local political power. He said the old sheriff was a Reilly, and one of the Reillys, the late unlamented Jacko, was running wild, terrorizing the parish. So Galt very quietly decided to move his support to somebody new, who could put a lid on Jacko and his pals."

"And that's where your friend Jeff comes in," she said.

"Yeah. He told me he tried to get out of it, said he didn't have any law enforcement experience, but the judge was insistent. All the folks in the parish knew him because of his vet work and they remembered his dad. So what do you do when your neighbors and colleagues say they need you and you're the only one who can help?"

"You're saying he's in over his head."

"It's true he doesn't have any law enforcement background, but you don't need that to be a sheriff these days, so long as you have a good chief deputy. It's more like there's something eating at him."

"Why is he running again, then, if he's unhappy in the job?"

"Same reason he ran to begin with, I imagine: The Galt crowd's telling him they need him and his father's ghost is out there on the battlement telling him he can't quit."

"You make him sound like Hamlet with a badge."

"He may be."

I fed Digger, my mixed shepherd, and I was changing for my morning run around the lakes when Pepper caught me.

"You may want to call Sam," she said.

"Yeah, I mean to. I heard he's back."

"I wouldn't put it off."

"Oh?"

She was wearing a worried expression I seldom saw.

"I dropped by yesterday to say hello, and he wasn't looking good."

Now my senses were on the alert. "What do you mean?"

"It wasn't just that he was tired. There was a grayness in his face I haven't seen before. He tried to be his old self but he just didn't seem to have the same zest."

"Well, he's close to eighty. They've been gone for a month. The card I got from China said he'd been riding yaks."

"You may want to drop in," she said.

I nodded. "I will."

Sam MacGregor lived on the River Road, in neighboring Iberville Parish, in a restored antebellum plantation house. When I pulled into his drive just after eleven everything looked normal, no ambulances or accumulations of cars. Just the Olds that Sam drove and Libby's Toyota minivan.

I knocked on the door and Libby let me in.

"I'm so glad you came. He needs somebody to perk him up. I think he brought some kind of bug back from China. He just hasn't been himself."

Sam was seated in the parlor in his big stuffed chair, fully dressed, a magazine on his lap. He turned his head when he saw me and started to get up but I gestured for him to stay put.

"I hear you caught something in China," I said.

Sam shrugged. "Just Yangtze blood poisoning or some other unknown disease. I'll be all right."

I handed him a bottle of J. W. Dant I'd picked up at Albertson's.

"Maybe this'll help," I said.

"I hope so. If you don't mind, though, I'll put mine off until later." He called to Libby: "Pet, see that Alan gets something to drink." He turned back to face me and gave a little cough. "So what have you been working on lately?"

I told him about the project in Lordsport and then about Miss Ethel and her UFO. Finally, I told him about the car and finding the body of Jacko Reilly.

"Damn," he muttered, stroking his white goatee. "You always manage to put your foot in it."

"I have to help Jeff," I said.

"Watch yourself, Alan. There's nothing like these small towns for dirty politics and pure out-and-out treachery."

"You're not saying I shouldn't trust Jeff?"

"How much have you seen of him in the last five or six years? Power does funny things to people."

"Jeff's okay," I told him.

When I left, I thought Pepper had been right: Sam's usual enthusiasm was missing and his skin had a gray cast. It was a sobering thought that the man who'd gotten me started in this business, always stood behind me and given his support, might be mortal.

I was still thinking about our visit later in the day when my phone rang and I had a premonition it might be Libby, telling me something had happened. But I was wrong. The quavering voice on the other end, while female, did not belong to Libby MacGregor.

"Dr. Graham? Is this Dr. Alan Graham?"

I hesitated.

"Yes?"

"This is Ethel Crawford. I got your number from your business card. I hate to bother you at home."

*Not more about the damn UFO . . .*

"What can I do for you?" I'm afraid my tone was brusque.

"I think you better get back up here."

"To Lordsport?"

"Yes, of course. I tried talking to Jefferson but he was almost rude. You seem like the kind of person who'll listen."

"Yes, ma'am. Well, I did everything I could and—"

"This is different. You really need to come up."

"This is Saturday. I can't do it now. I may be up later in the week. What's this about, anyway?"

When she spoke again her voice was a whisper: "I can't talk on the phone, don't you see? You'll just have to come. Now."

"I can't come now, Miss Ethel. It's almost a three hour drive. I'll call Sheriff Scully and—"

"Never mind. I should have known."

The phone went dead. I stared at it for a long time. Pepper came in from the kitchen, where she'd been experimenting with my jambalaya recipe.

"Who was that?"

I told her.

"Do you think you ought to go?"

"And miss tonight's poker game? Look, you've been badgering me for two years to let you play and I've finally convinced the other guys and, believe me, it wasn't easy. If I bug out, it'll be like resigning from the group."

"You're such a gentleman," she said sarcastically.

"I try." I reached for my Rolodex. "Anyway, I'll call Jeff and tell him to go talk to the lady."

But Jeff Scully wasn't at home and his office said he was hunting. I told the deputy on duty to check on Miss Ethel and heard him groan.

"Sheriff Scully was just there yesterday."

"Just go by again today, will you? I'll square it with your boss."

"Sure," the deputy said without conviction.

I hung up the phone and turned toward the kitchen, to make sure the jambalaya would be edible.

It was total insanity to even think of dropping everything to rush up to Lordsport to listen to an old lady's fantasies about a UFO. Nobody would blame me for blowing it off. In a couple of hours my friends would be here for an evening of companionship around the card table, and after that I had another deliciously long night with Pepper. It would have taken dynamite to pry me loose.

In short, I stayed.

It was a big mistake.

# ▰Six

Sunday, after breakfast at ten, I drove to the office to catch up on some paperwork. When I got back, just before noon, Pepper watched me go to my study and then came and stood behind me.

"So what is it?" she asked.

"What's what?"

"You hardly said a word after you got up and nothing at all during breakfast."

"No?"

"No. Not since the poker game, in fact."

"Oh."

"Was it that big a deal, letting me play?"

"Not for me, but the others aren't used to having a woman. I'm sure they'll—"

"They seemed fine with the idea," she said. "You're the only one who acted upset."

"Well, it was my house. They couldn't say no. That's what made it so awkward. I mean, they know that you're . . . that you and I . . . that the two of us . . ."

"What's that got to do with it?"

"Well, what if everybody decides to bring his wife or lady friend or whatever?"

"Then the whole game goes to hell, is that it?" she asked.

"I didn't say that . . . exactly. It's just that it's a break in tradition. The guys are used to one another. And they curse a lot. It kind of throws them to have a lady. A person of refine-

43

ment, like yourself, and besides, you beat them."

"I won a little. But that's because stud poker's a game of skill."

"They aren't used to five-card. It threw 'em."

"At first you told me you were scared I'd embarrass you by calling spades wild. Now it's because I play real poker with five cards."

I knew it was a lost argument. The Saturday night game would never be the same. A tradition had fallen. What was there to say?

"I think I'll walk the dog," I told her.

When I got back an hour later it was early afternoon and there was a note on my computer.

HAVE GONE TO LIBRARY, WHICH ALLOWS BOTH SEXES.
I'LL BE BACK WHEN I GET BACK. JEFF SCULLY CALLED.
WANTS YOU TO CALL HIS OFFICE ON DIRECT LINE (318)
555–9701. URGENT.

No heart shape above her initials. No signature.

I carefully folded the paper, so that the next time we had an argument I could point out that not signing one's messages was childish. Then I dialed Jeff's number. He answered on the first ring.

I identified myself. "What's going on?"

"It's Miss Ethel," he said. "My deputy drove over to her place after you talked to him yesterday and . . ."

"And?"

"She was gone."

A chill passed through me.

"Maybe she went somewhere to visit a relative. Does she have family?"

"No husband, and only a niece in Ferriday. The niece never saw her. What I'm saying, Alan, is she's disappeared."

"Maybe she went shopping in Natchez."

"And stayed over? I doubt it."

"I'm sure there's an explanation."

"Yeah, and they all expect me to have it. I've already gotten a call from that newspaper fellow. And if that's not bad enough, I got a call from the judge. He wants things cleared up without bringing in the State Police. Alan, things have gone from bad to shit."

"Sounds like it."

"So what did she tell you when she called?" he asked. "Did she say anything about taking off?"

I repeated what I could remember of the phone call: "She said I should come up but she wouldn't say why. It was almost like she thought somebody was listening on the line."

"Hell," Scully swore. "I should've paid more attention. I thought she was just a crazy old maid."

"That makes two of us."

"What about the silver piece?" he asked. "Had any luck with it?"

I told him what we'd found out. "It may have been in some-body's collection. Are there any coin collectors up there?"

"Everybody's got knives and guns. But I don't know of any serious coin collectors. It's just as likely Jacko and his gang burgled some pawnshop or museum or private house in a four- or five-parish area. He got around. Trouble was, he kept com-ing back here."

"Well, he won't anymore."

"Speaking of coming back, are you going to be with the crew this week?"

"I hadn't thought about it. They're home for the weekend, but they'll probably leave for Lordsport tomorrow morning."

He sighed. "It's nice to have some sane people around. I swear, Alan, I don't know who to trust up here anymore. By the way, you didn't tell anybody I gave you the silver piece, did you?"

"Nobody but my people."

"Good. Hey, you remember that job we did ten years ago over at Tallulah?"

"Sure."

"The one where you fell out of the boat into the Tensas River?"

"I've tried to forget it," I said.

"Kind of lucky I was along. Those heavy boots would've dragged you to the bottom."

"Jeff, I was *standing* on the bottom."

"But that bottom mud was sucking you down. It's like a quagmire. I'm just glad I was there to give you a hand."

"Right."

"I remember you said you never would've gotten that job done if I hadn't been there. You were short of crew, everybody'd begged off at the last minute, and you'd promised your client you could get up there and start in three days."

"I'm grateful," I said.

"Yeah, we had a few beers when that was over. You know, Alan, you always were sort of a mentor to me."

"Jeff, it's getting deep."

"If I'm lying I'm dying."

"You only worked for me six months."

"Yeah, but I kept coming back to ask you questions and you were never too busy to listen. I had the feeling that if I ever needed anything you'd be there."

"Enough," I said. "Is it really that bad up there?"

"Alan, you are literally the only person I can trust."

"And you want me to come back."

"It's not like you don't have any business here. I mean, your company has a major project and you'd probably be up here anyway, right?"

"Jeff, what do you want me to do?"

"You can go places I can't because of who I am. You can ask dumb-ass questions and people'll just think it's because you're an archaeologist."

"Stands to reason," I muttered.

"You've had some experience in these things. There was that business at Desirée Plantation last year, and then when you got mixed up with the Tunica artifacts—Alan, you see things other people don't."

"Almost got me killed, too," I said.

"You'll be okay. This is my bailiwick. Look, I'll even have some groceries delivered."

*"What?"*

"I had to lock up Luther again, Friday night. The game warden caught him with a doe this time, big as hell, no excuses accepted. But it's only temporary—he bankrupts the parish

every time I lock him up: gets sick and we have to spend
thirty thousand dollars keeping him in the hospital giving him
medical tests."

My eyes wandered over to Pepper's note.

Well, why shouldn't I go back to Lordsport? I had business,
like Jeff said, and if she wasn't even going to sign her
notes . . .

"I guess I can manage," I said. "I can be up there tonight."

"There you go. Come to my house."

"Right."

I hung up, thinking about what I'd committed myself to.
Jeff was a friend, and I wanted to help him, but I was about
to step into a nest of rural politics. And besides, I was doing
it partly because I was miffed at Pepper.

But why should I be the one to worry all the time? Let her
do some worrying for a change.

I scribbled out a note at the bottom of her own:

*Gone to Lordsport, taking Digger.*

I threw some clothes and a toilet kit into an AWOL bag
and then loaded a box of Digger's dog food into the red
Blazer. I called David and told him I'd be up there when he
and the crew arrived and then checked in with Marilyn, whom
I caught at home.

"I don't think there's anything urgent I have to do at the
office," I said.

Finally, I took Digger himself, who happily leaped into the
vehicle and took a position on the passenger's side, beside me.

"You'd sign your notes, wouldn't you?" I asked, buckling
myself in. "If you could write, that is."

His tongue flopped out and I thought I detected a nod.

"Well, come on, then," I told him, starting the engine.
"You're going to love Lordsport."

The Scully farm was two miles south of town, on the river.
The place had belonged to Jeff's folks and he'd inherited it
when they died, just as I'd inherited the house where I lived,
but unlike his father, who'd managed the farm as an avocation

while serving as a state trooper and then sheriff, Jeff had let the farm operations go, preferring to lease the land for crops. Now, as I drove up the winding gravel drive to the old house set back in the trees, I wondered why he'd never married. The place, unlit and brooding, seemed as lonely as he was.

Of course, I was a bachelor, too. But my excuse was a short, unhappy marriage to a beautiful Mexican archaeologist, which had soured me on long-term relationships until I'd met Pepper.

Maybe he was having too much fun playing the field.

Yeah, Jeff Scully having fun.

I stopped in the yard, in front of the house, almost bumping into the birdbath in the dark. Digger trotted beside me, nose to the ground, and I tried to remember if Jeff had a dog. As if in answer a pale shape came bounding out of the darkness then, only to begin a series of angry yaps as it saw Digger. My dog, as affable as he was big, gave a couple of acknowledging barks in return, and the other dog quieted. I saw from its light color and the single light blue eye on one side that it was a Catahoula, a breed originated by the Indians and cultivated by the later European colonists for hog hunting.

Odd, the house was totally dark. Almost as if he'd forgotten I was coming.

"Digger, do you hear anybody inside?"

But the shepherd just nosed the walkway, as if he'd discovered some fascinating scent in the cracks of the concrete.

I went up to the door, opened the screen, and then saw the note:

*Alan—*

*Sorry I got called away. May not be back till late. I'll catch up with you tomorrow at your camp.*

*Jeff*

I put the note in my pocket.

Why should I be surprised? He was the chief law enforcement officer of his parish. He could be called out at all odd hours for wrecks, break-ins, robberies, mysterious deaths . . .

An image of Ethel Crawford flashed into my mind.

What if they'd found her?

There was nothing I could do about it if they had, so I let Digger jump back into the Blazer, got in myself, and left the dark farm.

I'd counted on eating off Jeff but now I had to make a decision: Drive all the way to the nearest town with a restaurant, which meant ten miles on a dark road, or do the best I could at the local convenience store. If the deli was still open, I might be able to get a meal there.

The convenience store was open, and a clutch of pickups crowded the small parking area. Across the street the old brick courthouse loomed against the dark sky and I thought of our erstwhile cook, Luther, safe in his basement cell. It was galling to think he was getting a better meal than I was about to.

The deli was closed, of course, and I bought a couple of cans of Vienna sausages, some crackers and a six-pack of Dr. Peppers. A couple of burly locals regarded me from the corners of their eyes but said nothing.

I drove across the street to the back entrance of the courthouse, where the sheriff's cruisers were parked, and went into the building. A trusty in an orange jumpsuit was buffing the hallway and stopped just long enough to let me pass through the doors into the main office where a deputy sat watching a small TV.

"Sheriff around?" I asked.

"Haven't seen him," the deputy said. "Need something?"

"It's not important," I said and went back out to my vehicle, where Digger tried to lick my face.

"I know," I told him. "You don't like being left alone in a strange place."

We drove back out through town, passing the Scully farm, and a few minutes later reached the house where the crew stayed.

It, too, was dark, and I went in and turned on the lights and then lit the space heaters, to chase away the chill. The crew's paraphernalia was still strewn about, and on the back porch there was a stray plastic bag of artifacts from the site. It had been overlooked in the rush to get home for the weekend, no doubt; I'd have to put it where it would be seen, because missing bags created problems in the lab.

I went into David's room and dropped my AWOL bag beside the bed. Digger looked up hopefully.

"The floor'll do fine for you," I said. "I don't think the bed's big enough for both of us."

I found a plate in the cupboard and opened a can of dog food. Digger ate greedily, and I turned around to open my own pitiful cans. Then I saw the phone on the wooden counter.

I probably ought to call, let her know I was all right. I reached for the receiver, then drew back my hand.

Why should I be the one to call? Why should I always be the one who worked himself into a frenzy when she wasn't around? Damn it, it was high time for *her* to show some concern.

Don't be childish. Is that what it's all about: Who'll blink first? If you really love her, you'll call and make up.

But it will wait. You're hungry. You'll think more logically when you have some food in your stomach, even if the best you can do is Vienna sausages and chips. And maybe she'll call while you're eating.

But when I was done the phone was still silent.

I got up, washed my dishes, and threw my cans into the trash.

I thought of trying Jeff again but decided against it: He knew where I was, just as Pepper did.

Digger went to the door and whined.

"Okay," I said, heaving myself up. I let him out into the yard and followed.

Another cold front was moving in and the wind bit into my bare arms. I went to the Blazer and got Digger's chain.

"Come here. You're a city dog. I don't want you wandering around out here and getting lost."

I snapped one end onto his collar and looped the other end around the pipe well in the yard. I'd let him stay out for a half hour or so and then let him inside again before I went to sleep.

Once back in the house, I warmed up for a few seconds in

front of the living room heater and then went into the bathroom, where an old four-footed iron tub confronted me.

Well, there wasn't anything better to do.

I drew a hot bath and was about to step into the tub when
I heard Digger barking outside.

A coon, maybe, or a passing possum.

Except that when he'd had a duel with the possum in the
backyard at home his tone had been different—angry that
something had invaded his territory. This barking was higher-
pitched, almost frantic.

I threw on my clothes, grabbed my jacket, and started outside, wishing I'd brought a flashlight.

"What is it, boy?"

He lunged toward the corner of the house and I started in
that direction, aware that I was stepping into darkness.

"Who's there?" I asked, just in case. "Is somebody there?"

I bent over, grabbed a stick from the ground, and felt ahead
of me.

My feet made a crunching sound in the leaves and I was
suddenly aware that Digger had stopped barking, his cries replaced by a low-throated growl.

I poked the darkness and felt the bushes part.

This was crazy. What if it was a snake? I could step right
on top of it.

Except that snakes were in hibernation right now.

Okay, a bear. Black bears weren't usually aggressive, but
poke one and it might surprise you. Or a rabid fox. That was
all I needed . . .

I was still pondering the possibilities when I heard a phone
ringing and realized it was coming from inside the house.

*Damn. Pepper . . .*

I turned, and in the instant my back was turned he lunged
out of the darkness, knocking me off balance, and I felt my
breath rush out as I hit the ground.

I lay in the cold, on the leafy mat, trying to breathe normally, vaguely aware of footsteps dying away in the night.

By the time I got back to my feet the phone had stopped
ringing.

I unhooked Digger's chain, brought him inside the house with me, and bolted the door.

Whoever it was had long fled. I'd report it to Jeff tomorrow. If Jeff ever came back.

# ▤ SEVEN

The next morning when I pulled in at Jeff Scully's house I smelled bacon frying.

He let me in, gave me a firm handshake, and watched as I released Digger to play with the Catahoula.

"I figured the least I could do was fix you breakfast," he said as I came inside. It was just after six. I'd called him as soon as I'd woken up and was gratified to find him at home. Now he took my jacket. "Come on back, it's almost ready."

I followed him through a living room decorated with hunting trophies and a gun case. There was also a piano, and I wondered if it had been left to him by his mother and whether he played.

"There was a pileup on Highway 20 last night. When it comes to the bad ones, I go myself. It's not my favorite part of the job, especially making the notifications."

"Anything more on Miss Crawford?"

He shook his head. "I put out an APB on her car but it's like she was beamed off the face of the earth."

He laid a rasher of bacon and a couple of fried eggs on my plate, and then ladled out a monster helping of grits.

"You may want to wait for the orange juice before you finish," he said, laughing, as I stirred my egg yolks into the grits and dove in. "But go ahead: There's plenty."

"You think somebody kidnapped Miss Ethel?" I asked.

"It doesn't make sense. She doesn't have any family. There'd be nobody to pay a ransom."

I downed the last of the eggs and grits and went to work on a piece of bacon.

"Have you considered whether this is a put-up job?" I asked between chews.

"You mean whether she took off on purpose?"

I nodded. "She got a lot of attention out of this UFO business. But when Jacko Reilly turned up, everybody forgot about her. Now she's the center of attention again."

"Yeah. It would help if she'd told either one of us what it was she wanted the other day."

"I was assuming it had something to do with what she thought she saw—or heard," I said. "But what if she noticed something we didn't when the car was dredged up?"

"You mean something that would be dangerous to the killer?"

"That's right."

"Always possible, but what?"

"I don't know. By the way, did you figure out how long Jacko'd been down there?"

Scully took my plate and returned it with another helping of everything.

"Last anybody admits to seeing him was around Thanksgiving, right after Judge Galt's big Thanksgiving family turkey smoking for the rest of the Galt clan. Jacko wasn't invited, of course, but he made sure to show up on the highway that goes past the judge's place and try to run a few people off the road. By the time I disentangled myself from the crowd and made it out to the highway he was gone, and as far as I know nobody saw him again until we brought the car up the other day."

"Was he married?"

Scully snorted. "After a fashion. He hooked up with a girl from Jonesville, Lisa Fowkes. Dad runs a gas station. Decent people. Pentecostals. Jacko got her right out of the tenth grade. Course, Jacko never finished the ninth grade. Can't say her parents were real enthusiastic about the match, but what could they do? Jacko moved her into his double-wide outside of town here and they settled down to marital disharmony. Then, two years after the baby was born, Carline showed up."

"Carline?"

"Yeah. Came home from prep school to visit her father in Lordsport. Naturally, since she was a cut—or two or three—above Jacko, he wanted her." Jeff brought his own plate to the table and sat down next to me. "You know how it is, Alan: There are some men that attract women purely because they're rotten. Here was Jacko, a high school dropout, crackhead, swaggering thief and bully, and some women just fell all over the bastard."

"It says something about that kind of woman," I said.

"Boy, does it. Anyway, pretty soon Carline and Lisa were pulling Jacko in both directions and taking up all his valuable time that he could've spent drinking and burgling and spotlighting does out of season in the hills. So he hit on a solution."

"I'm scared to ask what."

"It was brilliant: He brought 'em together, had 'em both pile into the back of that old Ford truck he used to have to haul off the hogs he'd rustled, and drove the two gals out to the town dump. Then he made 'em get out and told 'em to fight until there was a winner."

"So who won?"

"Lisa, the wife."

"So he put out Carline?"

"He made Carline ride back in the truck bed and let Lisa ride up front. Then he went back to his double-wide with Lisa."

"When was all this?"

"Early November, right before he disappeared."

"I guess both of the women have alibis."

"Who can say? We don't know which day he got killed."

"What about Carline? Where's she now?"

"Her father shipped her back to Mississippi. He told her not to ever set foot in the parish again without telling him."

"Then her father had a motive, too."

My friend nodded. "Yeah, but there's not a hell of a lot I can do about him right now."

"Why?"

"Because her father's Ross Flynn, the district attorney."

My fork froze halfway between my mouth and the plate as the news sank in.

"Damn, Jeff, just about everybody around here had a reason to do Jacko in."

"You said it. I guess you could even say Snuffy Stokes had a reason, because Jacko was a one-man crime wave and he wasn't exactly good advertising for the town."

"What about Jacko's friends? A guy like that has followers."

"Yeah, there were some numb-nuts that followed him around. His cousin Skeeter, fellow named Presley Hobbs, and four or five others that alternated between Jacko and the parish work gang. Wasn't exactly the mafia, but every burglary in a five-parish area got blamed on 'em. Drugstore gets hit in Winnsboro, must be the boys. Old man gets his head splattered in Columbia and his guns stolen, the red car down the block must mean our boy did the killing. Good for embarrassing the sheriff, if you know what I mean." He wiped his hands on a towel and waved me away from the sink. "Never mind the dishes, I have a woman coming in later to clean." He walked out into the living room and then through a door into the hallway. "Come on and talk to me while I put on my monkey suit for court."

I stood outside his bedroom, in the hall, and watched him stand in front of a mirror, tying his tie.

"Jeff, answer me something."

"What's that, bud?" He pulled the knot tight against his neck and reached into his bureau, coming out with a silver tie pin.

"While we were waiting for them to pull the car up the other morning, you knew what was coming."

He adjusted the tie and stepped back to look at himself.

"I had a feeling. Why would a car be down there in the middle of the river if there wasn't something somebody was trying to hide? Then, when I saw it was a red Firebird, I pretty well knew: There wasn't another like it in the parish, and Jacko loved that car. He wouldn't have deep-sixed it on his own." He reached into a closet for his coat jacket and slipped it on.

"Now I'm all dressed up for a hangin'."

I grabbed my own jacket, followed him out the front door, and watched him lock it.

"See you later on," he said, heading for the white cruiser parked to one side. "But in the meantime do me a favor . . ."

"Yeah?"

"Call that woman of yours so she doesn't go bothering me again late at night."

My heart leaped.

"What?"

"Pepper left a message on my machine last night. Said she'd called the camp earlier and nobody'd answered and she wanted to know if you were staying with me. I called the number she left when I got in this morning and told her I hadn't seen you but that when I drove past the camp, on my way home about five A.M., I saw your Blazer in the drive. That quieted her down some."

I remembered the ringing phone, right before I'd been jumped from the bushes.

"I'll call her," I said, feeling suddenly guilty, "but something funny happened to me last night." I told him about the incident and saw his shaggy brows arch.

"You didn't get any kind of look at 'em?"

"No."

"Well, you can come in and file a report, but unless they left some kind of physical evidence I don't know what anybody can do."

"I don't, either. I just thought I ought to mention it."

He nodded. "Sure. There haven't been any camp burglaries around here since Jacko went to shovel coal, but you never know when somebody's gonna start up. Folks have the idea archaeologists dig up treasure, so it must be stored at the archaeology camp, right? I'll have the patrols keep an eye out."

I drove back to the camp a hundred pounds lighter.

Pepper had called. She cared. She hadn't just blown it off and assumed I'd blink first. She gave a damn.

I pulled into the drive and let Digger run free, then went into the house.

I was dialing her number when there was a soft knocking on the back door.

"Just a minute." I replaced the receiver and went to the back door.

A tall, rawboned young woman was standing on the porch, shivering under a thin shawl, her arms crossed against the morning chill.

"Alice Mae," I said. "What are you doing out dressed like that?"

Alice Mae Dupree darted into the warm house, rubbing her hands together to get rid of the chill. She was thin, with a pinched face and the air of a beaten dog.

"I'm fine," she said. "I come in Paw's truck. Heater don't work but it ain't far."

"Sit down," I said, pointing to one of the kitchen chairs. "I'll get you some coffee."

She sat tentatively, as if the chair might collapse under her, and stared up at me with mournful brown eyes.

"Mr. Alan, I need help."

I took a seat in one of the other chairs and waited.

"It's about Paw," she said. "He's in jail and I don't have no money to get groceries, on account of he used up what Mr. David gave him for this week and I'm scared Mr. David—"

I nodded. "I heard about it."

She nodded, looking at the floor, her stringy brown hair falling over her face, and twisted nervously at the stem of an old-fashioned, clunky gold wristwatch that was her only jewelry. "Sometimes he drinks too much. Usually. And he don't have no thoughts about hunting laws."

"Well, I doubt he'll be in jail long."

"But what am I supposed to do in the meantime?" She leaned forward, eyes beseeching. "This is all we got right now, ever since Maw died and . . ."

I was beginning to understand.

"You want me to get him out of jail."

"If there's a way, yes sir. You're friends with Sheriff Scully."

I sighed again. "I'll do what I can."

She jumped up, threw her arms around me. "God bless you!"

God save me, I thought, coming up here and getting pulled into everybody's private problems.

She rushed to the sink, began putting the clean plates into the cabinets. "I'll have the place looking good for Mr. David and the others," she declared. "When you get back from town everything'll be clean and—"

I patted her arm. "I'm sure it will."

I left her to her cleaning and drove to the courthouse, where the nearest parking places were all filled. I found a space a block away, in the shadow of the bridge. As I got out of the vehicle I turned and looked out over the river. The brown surface was still and just across the water in a plowed field sat the lonely shack of Jeremiah Persons. The place appeared to be shut tight, and there was no smoke coming from the chimney. I wondered if the old man was home and where he went when he wasn't.

When I got to the courthouse the hall was crowded, mainly with local people, though here and there a suit with a briefcase indicated a lawyer. I went directly to the sheriff's office, where I asked for Jeff. After a wait of ten minutes in one of the hard-backed chairs, the same deputy who'd come with us to fish out the car swung open the gate at the end of the counter and motioned for me to come through.

I was shown into a large office with a window that looked out on the great hill that hovered over the town. Jeff sat behind an oak desk, below the stuffed head of a huge buck, hastily thumbing through a set of papers that looked like a pleading of some sort.

"Alan." He glanced up, surprised. "What's going on?"

I told him about my visit from Alice Mae Dupree. "She wants Luther out of jail," I explained.

Jeff Scully shook his head. "I don't want him in jail, either. He's about to bankrupt us. Still, the judge is a hard case. He'll demand bail . . ."

"How much?"

"I don't know. Maybe a thousand."

"How about recognizance?"

"Jesus, bud, you're pushing. Still, I don't reckon it'll help the parish for Alice Mae to go back on food stamps. Not to mention Luther's hospital bill after he has one of his attacks."

I waited while he chewed his lip.

"Okay," he said finally, "we'll see what Galt says. You keep quiet and let me do the talking, you hear."

He jumped up from the desk and opened a side door that led directly into the hall. "Come on, we'll use the elevator." He led me into the hallway, to the elevator.

We got out on the second floor and went into another hallway, with wooden doors on either side. Jeff stopped in front of one of the doors and knocked twice. A deep voice from inside told him to come in, and he motioned for me to follow.

I found myself in a room as big as Jeff's, except this one was walled with law books and the few bare spaces were decorated with framed parchments. I recognized the Magna Carta, the Constitution, and the Declaration of Independence. I did not recognize the two men who stopped talking to look at us as we came in.

The first man was forty, with graying hair and a limp mustache that drooped over the corners of his mouth. He wore a coat and tie and a pair of lizard-skin cowboy boots. When he saw us he set his glass down on the desk, next to an open bottle of Wild Turkey. Across the desk, in a padded executive chair, sat the second man. Stocky, well over two hundred pounds, he sported a Lincoln beard and, unlike the other man, was dressed in a sport shirt and slacks, and I saw a bead necklace nestling in his chest hairs. The glass in front of him was half full.

"Well, Jeff, to what do we owe this pleasure?" the man behind the desk drawled. His dark eyes narrowed slightly as he saw me. "And this is . . . ?"

"Dr. Alan Graham, the archaeologist who helped me find Reilly's car," Jeff explained. "Ross Flynn, the district attorney, and this is Judge Galt."

I moved forward and shook hands with the pair.

"We were just talking about the late unlamented," the judge

said and lifted a photo from his desk. He handed it to Jeff, who snorted and handed it to me.

"Jacko Reilly," he said.

I looked down and saw a broad face, close-set eyes, and a thin mouth with what almost seemed to be a smile twisting the lips, as if this were all part of some practical joke. A sign across the chest said CANE RIVER PARISH PRISON, and there was a number. I gave the picture back to the judge.

"Alan's got a problem with Luther Dupree," Jeff said. The other two men listened as he explained the situation. The judge stretched, yawning, and the D.A. shook his head.

"So you'd like to solve this *ex parte*," Galt said. He raised his brows and looked at the D.A., who shrugged.

"This is a state charge," Galt went on. "Shouldn't Wildlife and Fisheries have something to say about it?"

"We're only asking for recognizance," Jeff explained. "The charge stands."

"Seems like Luther's had a lot of recognizances," the judge said.

"But he's always showed up," Jeff said. "And he's employed by Dr. Graham here as a cook."

"Employed?" Flynn's eyebrows arced. "That's a new one for Luther."

"What you think, Ross?" Galt asked. Flynn shrugged.

"Done, then," Galt declared. "But since Dr. Graham is his employer, I'm going to make him responsible that Luther doesn't commit any other crimes and shows up for his court date tomorrow."

"Yes, sir," I said meekly.

The judge smiled. "You know, I recall a man down at Frogmore, Homer Potter was his name. Old Homer tried to rope a bull once. Folks warned him he wouldn't be able to hold on, but old Homer knew better. Looped the other end of the rope around his neck. It worked. More or less. Poor Homer. Hope that doesn't happen to anybody here." He squinted at Jeff.

I felt an invisible noose tighten around my neck.

"Any progress on the Reilly case?" the judge asked.

Jeff shook his head. "No, sir. We're still investigating."

"And Ethel Crawford?"

"No word."

"Strange business," Galt said. "I'm hearing a lot of talk."

The D.A. nodded. "People are talking about space aliens or some bullshit."

"Space aliens don't stab people in the chest," Jeff said. "Whoever did this was as human as we are."

"That worries me more," said the judge. "People won't blame you for not finding a space man. But if they think there's a killer in this town . . ."

"I'm doing the best I can," Jeff said.

"That's all a man can do," the judge agreed. "Reminds me of the time, after I first come on the bench, when I sentenced Beau Bedgood to forty years for armed robbery. He looked at me and said, 'For God's sake, Judge, I'm already forty. That'll make me eighty when I get out.' And I told him, 'Just do the best you can.' And you know what?" He squinted at Jeff: "Old Beau's still up there, doing the best he can. Good luck, gentlemen."

# ▰ EIGHT

Half an hour later I stood in front of the courthouse with Luther, the cold wind stabbing my face.

"Mr. Alan, I don't know how to thank you. If there's anything I can do . . ."

"I'll think of something."

We started across the street, the little man half running after me.

"I heard Jacko had some silver with him."

"Oh?" I turned to look at my companion.

Luther gave a toothless grin. "It's all over the courthouse. Ain't nothing secret there."

"Any idea where Jacko would've gotten silver?" I asked.

Luther shrugged. "A silver mine, maybe?"

"Around here?"

"Well, not a mine, really, a hoard."

I stopped next to my Blazer. "What are you talking about, Luther?"

He squinted. "You ain't never heard of the lost Bowie silver?"

"Can't say I have. You talking about Jim Bowie?"

"That's right. They say he was big around here. Folks say he came back from Texas with some Spanish silver, buried it up in the hills somewhere."

"And Jacko found it?"

"Dunno. But Jacko sold a map to it once." Luther giggled. "Fella from Jena, over in LaSalle Parish. Fella dug a big hole

63

until he was run off on account of it turned out to be land owned by International Paper."

"Imagine that." I opened the passenger door and then went around to the driver's side. "You think Jacko was carrying silver to lure suckers?"

"Could be. Or he may've really found it, Mr. Alan. Course, he wouldn't sell the *real* location to nobody, but where else would he get silver from?"

I started the engine. "You tell *me*."

Luther looked around and then leaned close, as if someone might hear. "There's another possibility, Mr. Alan: I knowed Jacko, knowed how his mind worked. Didn't go straight from A to Z like other folks; he always took the crookedest path."

"What are you getting at, Luther?"

"If there really was a hoard up there and Jacko figured where it was, he was too lazy to want to dig it up hisself. He'd make some other poor bastard pay *him* to dig it up."

"But what would stop the other fellow from keeping it when he found it?"

"Jacko. He was mean enough to break somebody's head and leave 'em up there for the buzzards."

I started the engine and eased out into the street.

"Mr. Alan, I know where that hole is. I could take you."

"Luther, I don't know what good it would do to trek around in the hills looking for a hole in the ground."

"It ain't that far. But if you ain't interested . . ."

The image of the empty display case flashed into my mind: What was it Jeff had said was missing? A plat map of the town and a Bowie knife?

*Bowie* . . .

"How long would it take?"

"It's just off 621, outside Stanton, maybe fifteen minutes to drive, another half hour to walk."

"I don't want to go on a wild goose chase."

"No way, Mr. Alan. I can take you straight there. You can see for yourself. You're an archaeologist: You can tell if it looks like there's something really buried there or not."

"Sure I can."

I made the circuit around the courthouse.

"Can you go by my place?" Luther asked. "I need to get my jacket. It's gonna be cold in the hills."

I waited outside the old double-wide on the outskirts of town while Luther went inside.

I told myself I was doing something crazy.

But the thought of discovering where the silver piece had come from was too tantalizing to give up. And besides, I needed to get out into the open air and work off my feelings about what had happened between Pepper and me.

A minute later Luther came hurrying out of the house, clad in an old army field jacket and a hat with ear flaps. He climbed in, and a minute later we were headed up over the bridge.

"So this is where it happened," he said, gazing out through the girders.

"That's right."

"Damn."

"You were friends with him?"

"Jacko?" He snorted. "He was one of the meanest bastards ever lived. He even tried to get his hands on Alice Mae, sweet and simple like she is, if you can believe that. I could've killed the son-of-a-bitch myself."

"But you didn't, right?"

"Couldn't. He disappeared around Thanksgiving. I was locked up in jail for most of November, ever since that state trooper stopped me." He shook his head. "Two drinks I had, and that bastard said I was driving drunk. Now I ask you, Mr. Alan, is two drinks of vodka enough to get *any* man drunk?"

"Depends on the size of the drinks and the size of the man," I said.

The little man chortled. "Goddamn, Mr. Alan, if you ain't the funniest fella I ever met."

Ten minutes later we reached Highway 621, which headed north around the corner edge of the hills that formed the wild-life preserve. We passed a scatter of houses, and three miles later I saw a gravel road on the left.

"Go there," Luther ordered. "That takes us into the hills."

I slowed and went left onto the gravel. Ahead, the road rose up, with the steep hillsides closing on either side of us.

"I think this is the right one," Luther said, as we reached the top of the hill and started down. "I recognize the trees."

"Christ, Luther, they're all pines. You mean to tell me you aren't sure?"

"Course I'm sure," Luther declared, indignant. "I remember that tree right there."

I glanced over but I couldn't tell what tree he was talking about and wondered if he wasn't making it up, anyway.

"If you get us lost . . ." I started.

"Mr. Alan, now, that hurts me. I know these woods like I know my own face in the mirror. If you think . . ."

A mile and a half later we came to a fork in the road.

"Which way?" I asked.

"Left. No, right."

"Damn it, Luther . . ."

"No, I'm telling you, the right one's the way to go. Half a mile and the gravel gives out to a dirt track."

I crept forward, aware that the road had narrowed and that there were ditches on either side of the gravel track.

"Luther, listen . . ."

"Half a mile, Mr. Alan, you'll see."

And to my surprise, he was right. At exactly half a mile the gravel ceased and the road became dirt, and a quarter mile after that, water filled ruts.

"Here's where we get out and walk," Luther proclaimed.

I cut the engine and reached into the back for my boots. I slid them on and then rummaged in my pack for my compass, trowel, camera, a roll of bright pink surveyor's flagging tape, and GPS. With the GPS, the Global Positioning System, I could use satellites to give me a reading on my location anywhere in the world. The trouble was that without a topographic map, which I'd neglected to bring, I wouldn't be able to pinpoint where I'd been until I got back to town. Finally, I reached into the glove compartment and took out my notebook and cell phone.

Luther opened his door and got out, and I felt a cold blast. I put on a baseball cap and then got out, taking my quilted jacket with me. It was cold, with a strong smell of ozone from the pines.

"Damn, but don't this smell good," Luther declared. "Especially after the stink in that jail. Place ain't fit for humans. Give me the pine woods any day."

"Which way, Luther?"

He scratched his grizzled jaw. "Well, let's see . . . Straight ahead."

"Are you sure?"

"Trust me, Mr. Alan." And with that he was bounding away down the trail.

Graham, you really are a fool, I told myself. But there's nothing to do now but follow.

I trailed behind him for a quarter of a mile, the sound of him always ahead of me on the trail, and then the sounds died away.

"Luther?"

No answer.

"Luther, where the hell are you?"

Then I saw him, just off the trail, standing under a big loblolly, furtively trying to stuff something back into his jacket.

"Luther, what are you doing?"

"Nothing, Mr. Alan, just . . ."

I walked over to him and halted as the fumes enveloped me.

"What are you drinking?"

He shrugged and tapped his jacket pocket. "Just a little something to keep the chill out." He squinted up at me. "Want some?"

"No, thanks. Now put that stuff away and let's find this place, if you remember where it is."

"Remember?" His face took on a hurt look. "Mr. Alan, you think I'm some kinda numb brain? Course I remember. It's right . . ." There was the barest hesitation and then his finger shot out like an arrow: "Right through there."

I followed him off the trail and realized, as I started to slip and slide with him down a slope, that we'd been on a ridge.

I caught small bushes to slow my descent and, puffing, reached the bottom.

A thread of water trickled along the bottom of the valley, between ridges, and I hopped over, careful not to slip.

"Up there now," my guide said, nodding at the steep incline above us.

I gritted my teeth.

"It's the onliest way," Luther said.

I flagged a tree at the bottom and started after him, my feet sliding on the slick pine needle surface of the slope, and dragged myself up with the help of small trees until I reached the top, where Luther stood grinning down at me.

"Kinda steep, ain't it?"

I started to answer and noticed that Luther was standing in a dirt rut.

"Luther, there's a road. We could have *driven* here."

"Not from where we were, Mr. Alan, trust me."

He was pulling at the whiskey bottle again.

"Hot damn but there ain't nothing like a little gut burner for a cold day."

It seemed to me the temperature had dropped ten degrees since we'd been out here, despite my sweating under the jacket.

"Where now?" I asked and Luther's grin widened.

Down the other side, of course. Why had I even asked?

I watched him pick his way down the slope like a goat and took out my compass for reference. We were heading roughly north, for all the good knowing that did. I flagged another tree and followed him once more.

This time, at the bottom, he followed the valley, where a trickle of water ran between quartzitic rocks and when the ridges on both sides died away, we followed the larger valley in a direction my compass said was east. There was a larger stream here, fed by the runoff from the ridges, and we kept to the banks, following the twists and turns. When I looked back over my shoulder, I saw a monotony of brown forest. How many ridges back to get to the vehicle? Two? Or was it three?

I was glad I'd brought the flagging with me because backtracking using the flagged trees would be the only way to guide us back if, as seemed increasingly probable, Luther turned out to be incompetent.

A half mile later we came to a place where the water rushed between boulders and I watched Luther tiptoe across the wet rocks. I followed, aware that a slip would make me a candidate for frostbite.

"Now let's see . . ." Luther began. "Yeah, it's right up there."

I gazed upward and saw a ridge whose top seemed to melt into the sky.

"Jesus," I groaned.

"Ain't far now," Luther declared and, after a quick swig of whiskey, started upward. I flagged another tree and then, taking a deep breath, began to edge up the slope, pulling myself a few more feet with every sapling I came to. Midway up I paused and looked down.

Not a good idea: If I slipped now it would be a long slide and I wouldn't be able to stop before I ended up in the water.

"Just a little more," Luther called back down to me "It's right up here."

I started again, panting, and clawed myself up the rest of the way, until I was able to stand, wavering, on the vast pine-covered plateau that was the top of the ridge.

I leaned against a slash pine, breathing hard.

"Luther . . ."

"Just about there," Luther pronounced, grinning.

I flagged the tree and started after him as he headed back along the ridge. I checked my watch: We'd been slipping and sliding for an hour and a half. The thought of having to retrace our steps to get back to my vehicle was not a reassuring one.

I was counting my paces now, flagging at hundred-foot intervals, but the little roll of tape I'd started with had grown alarmingly small.

Suddenly I saw what appeared to be a clearing ahead.

Luther was standing at the edge of the open space, pointing.

"Just like I told you," he said, nodding at a hole in the ground.

I stood on the edge of the pit and looked down. Maybe

ten feet deep, the cavity was at least thirty across, and resembled a volcanic crater, with back dirt and rocks thrown up along the sides. I bent over the back dirt and picked up a stone.

Quartzite, a common rock in these hills. Below I could see bits of sandstone and the brown subsoil of the area.

"Pretty good hole, ain't it?" Luther asked, as if proud of what the poachers had accomplished.

"How many people dug this?" I asked. "It took more than one man."

"Four or five, I hear. Till they got run off by the sheriff."

I took out my trowel and scraped at the back dirt. More gravel and quartzite, with no indications of anything worth digging for, not even a salted coin or piece of gold.

"Course, after they got run off, other folks come up here and went through the dirt to see if there was anything they missed."

"Of course." I stood up finally. It had been idiotic to let Luther talk me into coming here. There was nothing that could have anything to do with Jacko Reilly's death. Unless . . .

"Luther, who was this man from Jena that Jacko sold the map to?"

"Fella named Berry Capshaw. Always looking for a way to make money easy."

"Where is he now?"

"Last summer a man in Urania told him he'd pay him a hundred dollars to haul his chipping machine up to Little Rock. Berry got drunk and run his truck into Bayou D'Arbonne. Chipper ended up on top of him." Luther spat. "I can show you his grave in the cemetery back in town."

"I thought you said he was from Jena."

"Was. But his parents are from here and they had a space in the cemetery. You gotta take what you can git, Mr. Alan."

I looked back at the hole and thought about the four or five treasure-crazed men who'd come up here to dig it.

"Luther, there's got to be an easier way to get to this place than the way we came."

"Oh, sure, but it ain't the *best* way."

"The best?"

"You got to cross other folks' land, and I ain't about to trespass."

"Of course not."

I started around the hole. If getting back to the Blazer meant slipping under a couple of fences when nobody was around to see us, I wasn't going to be picky at this point.

"Wait up, Mr. Alan."

He came hurrying after me.

"Don't you wanna dig in that hole?"

"How would I ever get out? Besides, all I have is my trowel."

"But what if there's real treasure? What if they didn't dig far enough? Or what if they dug in the wrong place? Ain't you gonna look around, like?"

"Luther, all I want to do is get the hell out of here."

I came to a place where the trees had been marked with bright yellow paint slashes and knew we were at the end of the property. On one of the trees was a metal sign: NO TRES-PASSING.

"Mr. Alan, we better turn around."

"Let's go down the trail a little ways. There may be a better way out of here."

We walked for a half mile and all at once the trail spilled into another clearing, with a log cabin in the middle. I looked for smoke from the chimney, but there was no sign of anyone inside and no vehicle in sight.

"You want to go back now?" Luther whispered.

"Luther, there's nobody there."

I was studying the cabin carefully. It was from a kit, the kind you build yourself, and somebody had done a good job. But it wasn't the logs that got my attention but the telephone and power lines. They went to the other side of the clearing, and I guessed there was a road that led down to a highway.

"If we can get to the highway I'll call somebody on my cell phone and have them pick us up," I explained. "Then they can drive us up to where the Blazer's parked."

"Yes, sir." But Luther didn't look at all reassured.

I walked out into the clearing, aware that the other man was lagging behind me. I came to the side of the house, where an aluminum cover sheltered a stack of firewood. Suddenly my senses were on alert. Maybe it was Luther's hesitation, or maybe it was something else, the smell of something sweet that contrasted with the ozone of the pines and the background odor of burned wood.

I turned toward Luther in time to see him step out of the trees, testing each step like a deer aware that a hunter is near. There was a look on his face I hadn't seen before, one that could only be described as true fear.

"Mr. Alan . . ." he began, and the sun flashed on something in the corner of my eye. I wheeled toward the far side of the clearing, where the electric line led, and before I could react, I glimpsed a second flash, but this one was accompanied by a loud crack.

I fell to the ground and in my peripheral vision saw Luther fall, too.

Then I heard tires spraying gravel and I got onto my hands and knees. All at once I wasn't aware of the cold, only of the sweat drenching my body. I pulled myself to my feet and realized my legs were shaking.

"Luther, you can get up. They're gone."

I saw with horror that there was no movement from the form on the ground.

I ran to the prone man.

"Luther . . ."

"Bastard shot me, Mr. Alan."

"Where?"

"I dunno. I think my shoulder."

I helped him up and saw a dark red splotch against the olive drab of his field jacket, just to the left of his neck. I unzipped his jacket and then unbuttoned his shirt.

"It looks like it just scraped the top of your shoulder," I said. "Lucky it missed the subclavian artery."

"Yeah, well, it feels like it hit the jackpot."

I pressed a handkerchief against the angry red furrow and helped him rebutton the shirt and zip up the jacket.

"Luther, I'm sorry. You told me not to come this way. I should've listened."

He nodded like a kicked dog. "Yes, sir."

"Believe me, if I'd had any idea . . ."

"Yes, sir."

"Can you walk as far as the paved road?"

"I reckon."

"I'll call now on my cell phone, except I'm not sure where to tell them to come."

Luther gave me a sideways look.

"Just tell 'em to come to Sheriff Scully's cabin off 913."

# ▰NINE

Jeff Scully listened silently, staring out his window at the courthouse lawn. A deputy had picked us up and Luther was being treated by the nurse at the parish health unit. I was just beginning to thaw.

"It was probably somebody meaning to break into the cabin," Jeff said at last. "I don't keep a lot there, but I do have a few guns and a stereo system. I use the place to get away sometimes."

"Have your deputies look for an ejected shell," I said.

Scully gave me a pitying look. "These woods are full of ejected shells. I'm sorry Luther got grazed. Believe me, I am, because now we'll never hear the end of it. But I think we better just write it off unless something else happens. I'll have the deputies drop by a couple of times a shift and check the place. That's all I can think to do."

"You don't seem very upset."

He shrugged. "Some hunter with too much whiskey under his belt. Happens all the time. And that *was* a pretty damn fool thing, if I do say so, letting Luther lead you off into the hills. You're lucky you didn't both freeze up there."

"I guess so," I said. "I just thought maybe something would turn up."

"And?"

"Nothing really." I considered for a moment. "By the way, you know this Berry Capshaw, who bought the map from Jacko Reilly?"

"I had to run the idiot off the land." My friend shook his head. "Sometimes I wonder why I bother. We should just let the idiots and the tetched run loose around here."

"I understand his parents are from Lordsport."

Scully shrugged. "Calvin and Myrtle Capshaw. What of it?"

"I dunno. Just thought I might ask them what they know."

"Good luck. You'll get an earful from Calvin, I'm sure."

"Oh?"

"Tell me what you find out."

Instead of finding Calvin Capshaw, however, I went back to the camp. I was shaken and didn't feel like confronting a man who sounded difficult. The crew had just arrived from Baton Rouge and was unpacking David's Land Rover and the small pickup the company owned. When I explained what had happened, David just threw up his hands.

"Maybe you can use all this as a reason to keep Pepper from killing you. She's pretty upset."

I groaned. I'd meant to try calling her again and had been caught up in events.

"I won't be much good in the field," I told him. "Not after this morning."

"You haven't been any good in the field since you met Pepper," David said, sighing. "But I can handle things—as usual."

I went outside, got out my cell phone, and punched in my home number.

"Alan?" It was Pepper's voice and I took a deep breath.

"I'm sorry," I told her. "I meant to call sooner . . ."

"But you just didn't get around to it, right?" There was ice in her voice.

"Things happened . . ."

"Sure. You take off without a word and I'm supposed to just wait here by the phone until you get tired of playing with the boys and decide to call. Well, let me tell you—"

"Pepper, listen, I admit I jumped the gun leaving, but I was upset and—"

"—and I *wasn't?* But I didn't leave. I wouldn't pull a stunt like that on you. I have a little more concern for your feelings. I should've known—"

"Known what?"

"That you were just too unstable to—"

"Unstable? *Me?*"

"Who else?"

"Have you ever looked in the mirror? Have you?"

"I don't have time for this. I have a class to teach." I'd never heard her voice that cold, not even when we'd first met.

"Pepper . . ."

"Goodbye . . ."

"Wait."

"We don't have anything more to say."

"Yes, we do: The librarian disappeared. And somebody took a shot at me and another guy this morning up in the hills. They're patching him up now."

There was a long silence.

"You're all right?"

"More or less. Look, I'm sorry, I shouldn't have left like that. I was upset. Insecurity or whatever you want to call it. I've been worried ever since you went to Mexico last summer. Maybe it's been building up. I needed to get away. But I was going to call as soon as I got to Lordsport. And I did, only nobody answered. Then, last night, somebody knocked me on my tail outside the camp and this morning I almost got shot and—"

"Alan, you fool, get out of there before somebody kills you!"

"I can't just leave Jeff."

"Of course not. You wouldn't leave a *friend*. Just . . ."

I groaned again.

"Look," she said. "When my last class is over today I'm driving up."

"What?

"Yes. I found somebody on the Internet who deals in colonial coins. He's in Port Gibson, Mississippi. I'm bringing the silver piece up to show him." Her voice softened. "Besides, somebody has to look after you."

All my anxiety turned to relief. "When will you get here?"

"If I leave at five I'll be in Natchez by seven, depending on traffic. Give me another forty minutes to get to the camp."

"No."

"What?"

"I've got a bad feeling about this place. Let me drive out and meet you somewhere in between, so we can talk and make plans. I may have more information by then."

"Okay, we can meet for supper in Natchez. Or better, on the Louisiana side, in Vidalia. Remember that restaurant, the Sandbar?"

"I'll be there at seven," I said. "I'll keep my phone on in case you need to call."

"Alan . . ."

"Yes?"

"Be careful. If anybody's going to kill you, I want to be the one."

"I'll try to remember that."

I was just putting my cell phone back into my glove compartment when a white Forerunner pulled into the driveway and a beefy, gray-haired man in a plaid lumberjack's jacket got out. The jacket was unzipped and there was a bulge under the left arm.

I heard Digger start to growl and the man reached inside his jacket.

"It's okay," I told Digger and leashed him to the pump.

"You're Alan Graham?" the man growled.

"That's right."

He held out a credential case and I saw a card that said "Private Investigator." "My name's Chaney Reilly. I used to be sheriff here." He squinted at me through rimless bifocals. "There's those who say I may be sheriff again."

"Well, I'm not a registered voter in this parish, Mr. Reilly."

"Not here for that. I've been hired to look into Jacko Reilly's murder."

"I'm sorry, Mr. Reilly, but I'm a little worn out right now, and I gave a statement to the sheriff's office, so . . ."

I turned to go in but he put a hand on my arm.

"It won't take long. It's cold out here. We can sit in my car."

Reluctantly, I let him guide me to the Forerunner and took a seat next to him. It was warm inside, a welcome respite from the cold. I noticed a pair of handcuffs dangling from the mirror and blue and red flasher lights on the dash and wondered if you got to take your official car with you when you were booted out of office in this parish.

"There's a story you have evidence from the crime scene where they found Jacko," he said.

"I think you ought to talk to the sheriff about that."

"I'm talking to *you*, Mr. Graham. I don't think you understand just what you've got yourself into here. This is a small parish. Things aren't always done the way city folks expect. I was sheriff here for twelve years. I know people. Your stay here can be either pleasant or not so pleasant."

"You sound like a warden," I said.

"May be." He ran a hand through his longish gray hair. "Some might say the parish needs a warden. 'Cause they sure ain't got one now."

"Save it for the stump," I said. "The election's a year away."

"A year can go by pretty fast. You're a smart man, Mr. Graham. They say you've got all sorts of college degrees. Seems like you might want to come back here and do some more work sometime. Mr. Thomas Jefferson Scully may not be there then. It'd be nice to have friends."

"Who hired you?" I asked.

"That ain't information I usually give out but in this case I'll let you in on it: It was the widow of the deceased. She just wants to see justice done and she doesn't figure she'll get it so long as that horse doctor's the man doing the investigating."

He reached into the pocket of his jacket, took out a briar pipe, and began to fill it: "Look, Mr. Graham, I got nothing against you. You do your thing, that's fine. But try to forget Scully's your friend and look at it from Mrs. Reilly's point of view: Would you feel good knowing the investigation of who killed your husband was in the hands of somebody whose training was curing sick horses?"

"I'm sure there are competent people in the sheriff's office."

He laughed. "There used to be. But Scully fired 'em all

when he got in. Hell, he even let 'em rob the courthouse."

I thought about the empty display case, and there wasn't anything I could say.

"By the way, any news on who shot at you?"

"How do you know about that?"

Another chuckle. "Little place like this, you can't keep nothing secret. I was you, I'd watch out. It sounds like somebody's already gunning for you."

"I don't know they were shooting at me. They hit Luther Dupree."

"But they were warning *you*."

"More small-town rumor?"

"Call it what you want. You give any thought to *why* they were shooting at you?"

"Somebody was trying to break into the cabin. Or maybe they were trespassing and didn't want to be found out. Or they could have been illegally cutting timber."

"Find any broken windows? Any cut stumps?"

"I didn't look."

"Might want to. Or you might want to ask your friend Scully what all goes on up at that cabin."

"What?"

"Just ask."

The house door opened then and David came out. He saw the car and started toward us. I opened the car door and got out.

"It's okay, David, Mr. Reilly was just leaving."

"Just ask," Reilly said, leaning across the seat toward me. "Ask him what he does in that cabin."

I slammed the door and the car started backward as David approached.

"What's going on?"

"Just another happy local. Well, I guess I better drive down to Simmsburg and get some provisions if Alice Mae's going to have anything for the crew to eat tonight."

# ■■■TEN

All the way to Simmsburg, a distance of ten miles, I imagined that I saw Reilly's Forerunner behind me. I'd called Jeff, of course, and after an oath, he'd told me not to worry about Chaney Reilly and asked me what my plans were for the rest of the day.

"Well, take care of your shopping and check with me before you leave to meet Pepper. Reilly won't bother you, though."

Now, as I pulled in at the grocery in Simmsburg, I hoped I could count on my friend's judgment.

I didn't like what the ex-sheriff had said about the cabin, as though Jeff was using it for some unholy purpose. But I didn't feel I could pry into my friend's private life.

Half an hour later I'd stocked up and was out of the store. It was almost four and the temperature had reached its apogee for the day. In another hour it would start to drop again, and the thought of snuggling in next to Pepper was a welcome one.

I retraced my route north on Highway 12, an elevated two-lane that ran through an expanse of lowland used mainly for catfish ponds. They'd built this road after the flood of '27, so the people of Simmsburg could flee to the hills above Lordsport if it ever flooded again. The road was straight and narrow and I didn't see anything in my mirror to suggest I was being followed.

When I reached the camp, the crew was still in the field and there was a note on the counter from Alice Mae:

*Dear Mr Graham,*

*I've went to check on Paw who was shot at the health
unit but I will come back in time to make supper.*
    *God bless you for helping him your a good Christian
man.*

*Alice Mae*

I called for Jeff but he wasn't in the sheriff's office so I
tried his house. No answer. I thought of calling his pager number, then decided against it: He'd asked me to call him before
I left and I had, but there was no emergency. I'd changed into
a clean pair of jeans when I heard the crew coming in. I told
David where I was going and that I'd probably be back tomorrow. His brows went up suggestively and he shrugged.

"Just so we don't have to come bail you out."

It was dark by the time I got to Ferriday, a town whose claim
to fame was having produced the cousins Jerry Lee Lewis and
Jimmy Swaggart. My stomach was in full growl, and even
Digger was looking longingly at the beaneries we passed.

"Soon, boy," I told him.

I'd just left town and was on the busy four-lane that connected with Vidalia when I realized I was being followed.

There were plenty of trucks on the nine-mile stretch and I
was used to being tailgated, but this guy was inches from my
bumper.

I gunned my engine and whipped past a pickup.

The other car sped after me, as if he were glued to my rear.

His lights were blinding me and I tipped my mirror down,
to get the glare out of my eyes.

There were no State Police or sheriff's substations on this
highway. Just a lot of people who wouldn't be able to see
much if I stopped by the side of the road in the darkness.

I tried to remember: Was this somebody I'd cut off by mistake, or who'd taken offense at the make of car I was driving?
Somebody who hated people with Baton Rouge plates and a
big dog in the front seat?

That bothered me: Digger would scare off most would-be robbers. If this guy wasn't scared of a dog the size of a horse, it meant he had firepower.

It wasn't somebody with a case of road rage.

I reached into the glove box for my cellular phone.

The headlights behind me blinked from low to high beam and back. He wanted me to stop.

The hell I would.

I was fumbling to turn on the phone, so I could punch in *LSP, the emergency number of the State Police, when the lights behind me blazed into blue and red and a siren wail caused me to swerve across the center line.

A cop had seen us, was calling for him to pull over . . .

No. *He* was the cop . . .

If I stopped, who knew what might happen? And if I kept going I'd get slammed for trying to escape.

Digger was growling nonstop now, and I had a vision of Chaney Reilly explaining how he'd been confronted by a vicious dog, and how he'd had to shoot to protect himself.

I eased off the accelerator.

"It's okay, boy. I can handle it."

Digger didn't look like he believed it and I didn't, either.

I glided onto the shoulder, shifted into neutral, and waited.

A shadow passed over my outside mirror and I tensed. Whoever it was had gotten out of the car.

Headlights whipped by on the highway and I wished someone would pull over, anybody who might be a witness, but they kept going, giving us a wide berth.

I slowly rolled down my window and then placed my hands on the steering wheel, in sight.

"Steady, Digger."

Footsteps crunched on the shoulder and I turned my head. He was standing just left of the driver's side, but I couldn't make out his face.

Now he was coming forward again.

If he was from Lordsport he was outside his parish. I could tell him he had no jurisdiction.

Sure.

He stopped beside my open window and bent down.

"Alan, you're a hard man to catch."

I looked up, saw Jeff Scully's face, and slumped back against the seat.

# ☰ ELEVEN

"You son-of-a-bitch," I said.

"Yeah, I know. They told me you called and I saw you as you were leaving town just now. But I didn't want to stop you in the parish because somebody would see it."

"And tell Chaney Reilly."

"He's got eyes everywhere."

"So what's going on at your cabin?"

He looked surprised. "Nothing. The man's full of crap. I hope you don't believe him."

"No."

"Good."

"Is there anything else?" I asked. "Or am I just supposed to sit here like a criminal the rest of the night?"

"I was hoping there was some word on the coin."

I told him what Pepper had said. "We're going to talk to a dealer in Port Gibson. He may have a line on collectors in this area. Or if anybody bought some silver pieces lately. Collectors tend to network. In the meantime, why don't you go back over all the bulletins you've gotten in the last year or two for burglaries in other parishes? It may be listed as part of some haul. You might not have paid any attention to it at the time."

Jeff nodded. "True. And the chief deputy usually checks those, anyway. I'll go over them myself this time."

I reached for the hand brake. "I'll let you know what we find out. If you want the piece back . . ."

He shook his head. "No. Keep it for now. I don't trust it not to get lost from the property room."

"Things that bad?"

He nodded. "Chaney wouldn't think twice about getting something out of the evidence room if it suited him."

"Don't you keep the room locked?"

"Alan, I've got fifteen deputies. It's not hard to get a key."

"Okay. We'll hold it a little while longer."

"Thanks."

I released the hand brake and put my hand on the gear shift.

"Alan, there's one more thing."

I groaned under my breath. "What?"

He was shoving an envelope in my direction. "Keep this," he said. "Use it if you have to."

"What is it?"

"Look inside."

I did.

"No way," I told him. "I don't even know if this is legal."

"It's legal," he said.

"Jeff, I'm an archaeologist . . ."

"And you know how to dig things up. Including historic facts. You can check court records, do interviews, put things together."

"That's different." I thrust the envelope back at him but he held up his hands, palms outstretched.

"You have to," he said. "Please."

I shook my head. "This is the damndest thing I ever saw." I dropped the envelope on the seat beside me.

"I need you," he said.

"Good night, Jeff." I eased out onto the highway, leaving him standing there in the glare of his own lights.

When I reached the Sandbar her white Integra was already in the lot. The restaurant was located a block off the four-lane, in sight of the bridge, and I found a quiet place to leash Digger. I opened a can of dog food for him and dumped it into a small plastic dish I carried.

"Guard the vehicle," I said.

I went up the steps into the wooden building. The smell of

fish frying hit me like a club and I felt my salivary glands go into overload. I told the receptionist I was there to meet somebody and she showed me through the mostly empty dining room to a second room on the left.

Pepper was smiling at me from a booth, a plate of fried onions in front of her.

"Draft beer, seafood platter," I told the receptionist, who smiled and hurried off to get a waitress.

"Don't I get a hello?" Pepper asked as I slid into the place opposite her.

I reached over and took her hand. "You get whatever you want," I said. "Now or later."

"I'll settle for doing what's on your mind later," she said. "If you're over your mad."

"You're a hard woman," I said.

She reached under the table. "And you're a hard man."

"I'm a hungry man," I said, grabbing an onion ring. My beer came and I took a deep swallow, savoring the taste.

"Well, the place hasn't changed," I said, stretching. "Even down to the placemats. Is that why you wanted to meet here?"

The restaurant was named after the Vidalia Sandbar, an island on the Mississippi side of the river where duels had been held in the last century. The most notable had been in 1827, between two Louisiana factions from Rapides Parish, and in the melee a knife fighter named Jim Bowie had made a name for himself by stabbing a man called Norris Wright to death. Now you could dine in elegance and read about the famous brawl on the placemats.

"Seemed appropriate," Pepper admitted. "By the way, what's the situation with the librarian?"

"Still missing," I said and told her about Jeff's stopping me on the highway. "I have a funny feeling about the guy."

"Stress," Pepper said. "Plus, you're special to him. He probably really doesn't know how to deal with you."

"What do you mean?"

"You know how you are with Sam? You're friends but he's also your mentor. You joke with him but you really look at him more as a father. I imagine Jeff feels that way about you."

"Father?" I snorted. "I'm not that much older than he is."

"It's enough," she said. "He probably feels he has to please you and at the same time he needs your help, because you're the guy who can do anything, fix anything."

"That scares hell out of me," I said, grabbing another onion. "By the way, how's Sam?"

Pepper hesitated.

"What is it?" I demanded.

"Libby put him in the hospital," she said.

"She *what*?"

Her hand came over to hold my own. "They're doing some tests. She thought he needed to rest anyway. I'm sure it's all right."

"I ought to be there."

"What could you do?"

"Just be there," I said. "In case."

"What about Jeff?"

"Jeff can handle himself. I got taken in at first by the good old boy act, but he's not nearly as helpless as he's tried to make me believe. Sometimes I think he's really pulling all the strings himself. Now, Sam . . ."

"Sam's being taken care of. I'll check on him tomorrow. Besides, he'd want you to see this through."

Our plates came and I grabbed a hush puppy.

"Jeff asked about the silver piece," I told her between bites. "Do you have it in your car?"

She shook her head. "No. It's right here."

She glanced around the room to see if anyone else was looking our way and opened her handbag.

"So who's our expert?" I asked.

"His name is Hightower. He runs an antique gun, knife, and coin store in Port Gibson. I e-mailed him a scan of the thing and he said he'd look at it if we could come up and see him. I thought we could drive up tomorrow morning."

We took a room at the Natchez Ramada, on a high bluff overlooking the river. I closed Digger in the bathroom and then turned toward the bed.

"You don't want to go down to the riverboat and play

poker?" Pepper asked coyly, standing in the half light, hands on her hips. "I thought we could take a tour."

"Around the world," I said, reaching for her.

"You're ambitious." She came into my arms. "But, like they say in poker, put up or shut up."

"Enough about poker," I declared.

"Then will you settle for poking?"

I did.

The next morning, after a breakfast of waffles and eggs, we made arrangements to leave Pepper's car in the motel lot, checked out, and, with Digger in the backseat, drove up to Port Gibson. A quiet, shady little town with almost as many historical plaques as people, Port Gibson didn't seem to have changed much since Grant had shelled it in the Civil War. The streets had been paved, there were electric lines and cars, but gentility still suffused the place like an after-bath lotion.

The shop was one street back from the highway, a pecan tree–shaded house in the Greek Revival style with a hanging wooden sign that said ANTIQUES. We left Digger in the Blazer and went up the walk to the front door, which had a sign that said OPEN.

The interior had been turned into a series of showrooms, with one holding antique pistols, rifles, and lead balls; another holding knives and swords; and one containing ancient coins, all in polished wooden cases with clear glass. On the walls were oil paintings of men in martial regalia and several old flags from different periods in the short history of the Confederacy. As I took it all in I half expected Jefferson Davis to step out of the hallway, but instead the man who came out was slight, beardless, and completely bald. He wore a maroon vest and a dark red tie with a ruby stickpin. He smelled heavily of cologne and had lively brown eyes that seemed to be assessing us.

Pepper told him her name and he smiled.

"So good to meet you both," he said, offering me a soft hand with three rings on the fingers. "I'm Clovis Hightower. May I offer you some tea or coffee?"

Pepper smiled. "That would be nice."

Clovis Hightower showed us down the hallway into what had once been a parlor but was now clearly a room for entertaining his clients. He gestured to a sofa that I guessed was Queen Anne.

"So what will it be?" he asked.

We gave him our orders and he returned a few minutes later with a silver service and let us each sweeten our coffee and add cream. Then he set the tray down and took a seat opposite us, carefully hiking up his pants legs.

"I was very interested in your coin," he said. "Weapons are my special hobby but I also collect coins from the colonial and antebellum eras. I've been in this business twenty-one years. It started as a hobby, metal detecting for Civil War relics and then trading at shows and on the Internet." He handed us his card. "Do you have the artifact with you?"

Pepper nodded, delved into her bag, and placed a small tissue-wrapped object on the table. Hightower leaned over, and I thought of a spider about to spring on its prey. He whipped on a pair of latex gloves, and then his thin fingers shot to the tissue. He unwrapped and lifted the tiny wedge.

"Ahhh," he sighed, turning it over in his hands. "You found it in an archaeological excavation?"

"In a river, actually," I said.

"Really. A pillar peso, no doubt about it. Mexico City mint. Too bad it was cut up. It might have been worth something."

"You've never seen this particular piece before?" I asked.

The dealer frowned. "Not in this condition. There's no market for quartered silver pesos."

"Are there any people in Cane River Parish, Louisiana, that you've dealt with?" I asked.

"Cane River Parish? You mean over near Simmsburg?" He shook his head. "No. Now, I bought a Confederate sword from a man in Alexandria a few months ago. And I sold a Schively Bowie to a man in Winnsboro—no, I take that back, it was Winnfield."

"A Schively Bowie?" Pepper asked.

"Yes. Henry Schively was a cutler in Philadelphia during the antebellum period. Jim's brother, Rezin, had Schively make several fancy Bowie knives to his own specifications and gave them to his friends."

"But no coins. Nobody came in and bought, say, a handful of silver coins."

"I don't sell coins by the handful. And I can't say that I would sell to someone who approached me in that manner." He sniffed. "Can you be more specific about what you're trying to find out? I could help you better if you explained."

"This was found at a murder scene," Pepper said. "It may have been part of a fake treasure trove. We thought you might know where a person could buy a bunch of these if he wanted to run a scam."

"Ahhh. Now I see." Hightower scratched an ear. "Well, I don't know of anyone in that geographic area. But you know, there is another possibility."

"Yes?" I said.

"People *do* find treasures. This could be a part of a *genuine* treasure trove."

I nodded. "Well, thank you for your time, Mr. Hightower."

He gave a quick little smile and followed us toward the door.

"I'd give you twenty dollars for it," he said. "If you're inclined to sell."

"I think we'll hold on to it," I told him, shaking his hand.

"Fifty," he said. "But that's as high as I can go."

"Thanks, Mr. Hightower."

We left him tisking and walked back to the Blazer.

"Do you think he's telling the truth?" Pepper asked.

"About what?"

"Anything. He seemed pretty eager to get his hands on something he said was worthless. Do you think he could be lying?"

"That's stretching it," I said.

"I agree." She got in and I slid behind the wheel. "But I was watching his eyes when he saw it. There was something there, almost like, well, lust . . ."

"Sure he wasn't looking at you?"

She jabbed me with an elbow. "You know what I mean."

"Sure," I said, releasing the hand brake and starting the

engine. "The man's a collector. It's called enthusiasm."

"I'm not so sure."

She had the coin fragment out now and was turning it over in her hands as if an answer might emerge if she turned it just the right way.

"Well, take it on back to Baton Rouge with you and lock it up," I said.

"I'm surprised you trust me to take it back by myself." She laughed.

"You aren't going to be by yourself," I said. "I'm sending along a guard."

"What?"

"Digger," I said. "He's better than Brinks Armored."

"And more personable than some archaeologists I know," she said.

I couldn't argue with that one.

# ≡TWELVE

We had lunch in Natchez and then parted, she taking Highway 61 back down to Baton Rouge, and I heading back west over the river into Louisiana again. The sky had cleared somewhat, showing patches of blue, but the air outside was still as sharp as a knife blade.

I wasn't sure I wanted to return to Lordsport. I was out of my depth, trying to wend my way through small-town politics. And something told me that things could get worse.

As I approached the parish line, just south of Carter Crossing, I saw a sheriff's cruiser parked under a pecan tree. Five seconds after I passed he slid out onto the road and came up behind me with his flashers on.

Now what?

I didn't know the deputy but he greeted me by name.

"Dr. Graham, sorry to have to stop you, sir, but Judge Galt asked if you could come talk to him."

"Judge Galt?"

"Yes, sir. He lives just right up here in Carter Crossing."

I shrugged. "What the hell?"

Carter Crossing is a dome of rock from the last ice age that thrusts out of the surrounding lowlands. In its forests, in 1731, the Natchez fought a last, losing battle against the French. Since then, the forests had been felled and the area used for cotton and cattle. The owners now were old aristocracy. Men like Judge Galt.

The deputy led me right at the caution signal in the center

of the tiny settlement and up Highway 15, toward Winnsboro, but five miles on, at a crossroads that wasn't much more than a convenience store and a cotton gin, we turned left, onto Highway 621, and headed southwest. Ahead were the green hills of the game preserve and I realized that if I kept going, I'd pass the place where Luther and I had turned off into the hills; the road connected with Highway 20, the main route between Lordsport and Carter Crossing, and Luther and I had approached it from the other end.

We hadn't quite reached the hills, though, when the deputy turned left onto a dirt road that led back through pasture land. After half a mile a white board fence appeared on either side of the road. In the distance a house loomed against the fields, its classical columns and elliptical arches hinting at a bygone way of life. On one side someone had added a tower that stuck up like a phallus.

The cruiser pulled into the little turnaround close to the house that was the parking area. A dark blue Saturn was already there and the deputy halted behind it. I stopped behind him and got out. In the center of the turnaround was a small pond, with a concrete black boy, eternally fishing. I was still looking at it when I heard the front door open behind me. The deputy cleared his throat.

"Is something the matter?" I heard a woman ask.

I turned and saw her standing in the doorway, a woman in her early forties, with short blond hair and a refined face. She was wearing designer slacks and a wool sweater, and from the glasses dangling from a ribbon at her neck I got the impression she'd just put down a book.

"Judge is on his way," the deputy said. "He asked me to bring Dr. Graham here to meet him."

The woman nodded slightly.

"Of course. Won't you come in, Dr. Graham?"

She had just enough of a drawl to let me know she'd been born hereabouts, and the formality that said she was gentry.

When I reached the porch she held out a hand.

"I'm Tally Galt. You're the archaeologist, aren't you?"

Her hand was soft and she withdrew it after two seconds.

"Do you know why your husband wants to see me?"

She shrugged and led the way inside. "With Arlo you never know. Can I offer you something? Hot tea or coffee? I'm allergic to chocolate, so I can't offer cocoa."

"Tea will be fine," I said, my eyes wandering past her to the walls. There was a nude study, in an expressionistic style, a blond woman with two blue eyes on one side of her face and small breasts. On the other side of the door was another painting, but this one was a Brahma bull.

"They're Arlo's paintings," Tally Galt said, reappearing with a tea tray. "The blond woman is supposed to be me. He had me pose for it right after we were married. He paid a famous artist more money than most people around here make in a lifetime."

"And the bull?"

"That's his prize, Buster. He's taken all kinds of medals."

"He's big," I said, unsure what else to say.

"That's Arlo," his wife said. "He always has to have the biggest, the most expensive, the first, the . . . prettiest."

I stirred a spoonful of sugar into my tea.

"Archaeology is fascinating," she said, blue eyes on me. "I'm interested in history. I'm a genealogist."

"Really."

She nodded. "Have you ever tried to trace your family, Dr. Graham?"

I smiled. "The Yankee side is kind of murky. I think one of my ancestors was a merchant who got run out of Scotland for cheating the king."

"Not a good idea," she said. "And on your mother's side?"

"Alsatian. A bunch of them came over in the last century and settled in Louisiana."

I watched her fingers play with her teacup and I thought she was about to say something else, but then I heard tires crunching in the drive and Tally rose.

"He's here. I don't know what he wants with you, but good luck."

Arlo Galt, all two hundred fifty pounds of him, appeared in the doorway, overcoat open.

"Dr. Graham. I've been wanting a chance to sit down with you ever since I heard your people were starting to do that work outside town." He turned to his wife: "Did you offer him something stronger than tea?"

"Tea's fine," I said and heard Tally murmur her excuses as she melted away.

"Then I think I'll indulge." The big man went to his bookcase and pulled out a false set of legal volumes, revealing a bar. "Tuesday's criminal day in this parish. Jesus, I don't think there's a new kind of crime under the sun. Always the same old crap: stealing cars, switching inspection stickers, assault and battery, wife beating, manslaughter . . ."

"You wouldn't call Jacko Reilly's death manslaughter, would you?"

The judge leaned back on his bar. "Don't know yet."

"Or Miss Crawford?"

"Don't know that she's dead."

I put my teacup down on the coffee table. "So what can I do for you, Judge? You didn't have a deputy bring me here just to talk about your day in court."

He regarded me through close-set eyes and sipped his whiskey.

"I asked you here because you're a friend of Jeff's."

I nodded in acknowledgment. "I've known him a long time."

"And so have I. Hell, that's why I wanted him to run for sheriff. A breath of fresh air. An educated man. Not one of the old courthouse crowd. Of course, as district judge, I had to be careful. Not supposed to mix in these things. But when you sit in court as many days as I do, you get to be a pretty good judge of people. I picked Jeff for a winner."

"And now?"

Galt shrugged. "Time will tell."

I kept quiet, waiting for him to make his point.

"I understand he's got you helping him," Galt said finally. "That true?"

"As an expert witness, you might say."

The judge fingered his beard. "You mean in archaeology?"

"As an expert on certain artifacts," I said.

"Ahhh. You mean that doodad."

"That's right."

He ambled over with his drink in his hand and plopped onto the couch next to me, and I felt the structure sag.

"So what did you find out about it?"

I told him what Hightower had said. "My guess is Jacko stole it somewhere."

Galt nodded gravely. "Sounds like it." He shook his head again and squinted at me. "I think I know this Hightower. He's an expert on guns and knives. Especially Bowie knives."

I nodded.

"You know," Galt went on, "Rezin Bowie owned hundreds of acres in this parish and he and Jim even had a mulatto half cousin named James who lived here. The Bowies were big land speculators. They always said Rezin, the older brother, was the cooler head." He got up and went to the bar, where he poured himself another drink. "They say the Bowies used to stay at the old Morgan house in Lordsport. It wasn't the Morgan house then, of course. They called it by another name. It's on the National Register, you know."

I'd seen the old building, which had been a hotel when the town had lived off the river traffic.

"I think Jacko Reilly belonged back in those days, when there were highwaymen and steamboat gamblers. He would've been at home with old Jim Bowie." He sighed. "Well, maybe we'll find his killer one of these days. Meanwhile, I asked you here to talk about Jeff. Even before this there was concern about him among some folks. Oh, I've tried to reassure 'em. They say he's not a politician and I tell 'em that's why they elected him. But this is a rural parish. A sheriff has to be a man of the people. Jeff tries, but sometimes it just plain don't come through."

I knew what he meant but I wasn't going to agree.

"Why are you telling me all this, Judge?"

"Because you're his friend. Just like I am." He set his glass down on the bar. "Don't you have a feeling, Alan, that there's something mysterious about Jeff? That's what bothers people. A sheriff's supposed to solve mysteries, not be a mystery himself."

I thought about the cabin and what Chaney Reilly had said.

I wondered now if he'd just repeated what the rest of the parish was already saying.

"When people give folks the impression they're hiding something, then folks take 'em at face value. That can be dangerous. And, what the hell? Sometimes they act that way because they really *are* hiding something."

The judge was moving me toward the door now. He'd delivered his message: I would repeat the conversation to Jeff Scully and Jeff would get Galt's warning.

Except that I wasn't going to do that. Judge Arlo Galt could deliver his own threats.

"Nice of you to come, Alan." We shook hands. "I may drop by that dig of yours one of these days. I've always been interested in archaeology, and we have a lot of archaeological sites around here."

"Come ahead, Judge. But I hope you won't be disappointed."

"Why should I be?"

"People expect archaeologists to make spectacular discoveries. Sometimes they get surprised when they see that all we're really after is flakes of stone and broken pieces of pottery."

"Goes to show how much I know about archaeology," the judge said as I stepped out onto the porch. "Reminds me of the time Percy Grayson came up for burglary. He said, 'Judge, I oughta get a break because I'm not a professional.' I told him a man oughta not mix in something he doesn't know how to do. Five years. That's a good policy, I think: Leaving something you don't know about to the experts." He tried to wink at me but it came across as a grotesque twitch.

"Goodbye, Judge."

# ▰ THIRTEEN

The old bridge hovered in front of me like a phantom as I approached Lordsport, and off to the right I saw Jeremiah Persons's wooden shack. It appeared tightly shut, no smoke issuing from the chimney, but on a hunch I turned and stopped in the muddy front yard.

I went to the front door and knocked but there was no answer. Then I walked around the side. The yard melted away into a field overgrown with weeds. I looked toward the river. Someone had fashioned a rock path, with sandstone boulders on the side, in an attempt at landscaping, and the steps vanished at the stone paving. I followed the path to the water's edge, where a skiff floated, tied to a small willow.

Then I heard a cough from the willows a few feet away.

"Goddamn, it's cold out here," a voice said, and I saw a little man in a windbreaker, with a stocking cap, zipping his pants. "I was just in the bushes, taking a leak, when I saw you come along. Figured I might as well stay till I was finished. Wouldn't do for the mayor to go around exposing himself."

"Mr. Stokes, isn't it?" I asked.

"That's me." He rubbed a hand on his pants. "Won't shake with you, considering what I just had in my hand. But the sentiment's there."

"You looking for Jeremiah Persons?" I asked.

The mayor spat onto the ground. "Yeah, old Hawkeye was supposed to cut me some firewood. Said he'd have it for me Saturday. This is Tuesday." He squinted at me through his glasses. "So, was he supposed to sell you some wood, too, Mr. Graham?"

"No," I said, "I just wanted to talk to him about the car we dragged out the other day."

"Figure he might know something he ain't telling?"

I shrugged. "He lives down here. If anybody saw something, he would have."

"Hawkeye's not what I'd call a real good witness, know what I mean. I just buy wood to help him out. Folks around here do that sort of thing. He has a mama somewhere, Winnfield or maybe Tallulah. Can't recall just now, but Miss Ethel used to drive him up to see her every few months. Neighborly, like."

"Do you think he went there?" I asked.

Stokes shrugged. "If he could find a way. And he'll come back when he figures nobody'll bother him. All that UFO stuff made him real nervous and then, when that car came up out of the river . . ."

"I hope you get your wood, Mayor."

Stokes spat again. "It ain't hard to find. I don't get it from him, there's others."

"Nice talking with you, Mr. Stokes." I started away, but his voice stopped me:

"Be careful, Mr. Graham. I hear you got shot at yesterday. Killing somebody like Jacko Reilly's one thing, but it's bad for the town if they start killing visiting archaeologists. Be sort of like the old days, when the Jamesons and Lyles were feuding. Do you know Colonel Lyle and his son were killed right inside the old Morgan Hotel in 1870? And it all started over a woman."

"I hear the Bowies came through here a lot, too."

"Lot of famous people come through here. Jeff Davis stayed here, and so did Grant on his way back from the Mexican War. There's even a story about Jesse James, when he was in hiding. What we got now?" He dug out a cigarette and sniffed. "Jacko Reilly, and he's dead." He gave a raucous laugh. "Talk to Calvin Capshaw if you're interested in the history. He collects historical facts. Don't do anything with 'em, but he collects 'em."

"I think I've heard about Mr. Capshaw," I said.

"Probably. Couldn't *not* hear about him around here, know what I mean."

"Where do I find him?"

"Fourth house on the left when you turn onto Ouachita Street."

"Thanks."

"Meanwhile, if somebody wants to put up a sign that says UFO capital of the state, I wouldn't be against it. There sure ain't gonna be no signs after they build that bridge south of town."

"No."

I drove past the courthouse. They were breaking for lunch, and the parking lot of the food mart was full of milling people. I realized I was thirsty and stopped. On the way back into the parking lot with my fountain coke, I felt a tug at my sleeve.

"Dr. Graham? I've been looking for you. Remember me, Tim Raines?"

I recognized the young newspaper reporter and looked for a means of escape.

"I hear somebody shot at you yesterday up near Sheriff Scully's cabin."

"It may have been an accident," I said.

"That's not what Luther's saying. He's saying somebody was trying to kill him and you both."

"Sounds like he knows more than I do."

"Mind telling me what you were doing up there?"

I took a deep breath. "I already gave a statement to the sheriff's office."

"How about telling the press?"

"I'd rather not. It's cold out here, anyway."

"Damn it, Mr. Graham, don't you see? If I can get this story out to the big papers, it may be my big break. What's so bad about that?"

"Good luck," I said, putting a hand on my door handle. "Now . . ."

His head was close to my own now and he lowered his voice.

"Look, you know how these people are: Half of 'em think

the old lady was beamed up by a spaceship. They think there's something down there in the river, that there's some kind of force field, and it killed Jacko, too. They'll be wondering who's next. There could be a panic. All I want to do is get out the truth."

The wind gusted, bringing tears to my eyes.

"Tell you what," I said. "I'll help you if you'll help me."

"Fair enough." His voice rose an octave in excitement. "What kind of help do you need?"

"What's the story on Chaney Reilly? He says he was hired by Jacko's wife. Is that true?"

"That's what I hear. She and Jacko fought a lot but Jacko was hers. She's about as mean as he was."

"What about Chaney? Is he likely to beat Scully next election?"

"Most around here think Scully's honest but inept. There's something about him that just doesn't mesh. Not everybody feels comfortable with him. He's not a good old boy."

"No." I thought of the mounted animal heads on Jeff's living room wall, the hound dog he kept, and the boat in his drive. All valiant attempts to convince, and yet even I had felt it. As if he tried a little too hard . . .

"So I've answered your questions," the reporter said. "How about answering mine?"

"I honestly don't have any answers at this point."

"But they found some silver with Reilly's body, didn't they? That's all over the courthouse, how there was a treasure in the car with him and maybe he was making off with it but somebody followed him and killed him. What's the truth?"

I managed a chuckle. "No treasure," I said.

"Then what was it?"

"That really ought to come from the sheriff."

"Damn, you're a hard man," Raines complained. "Okay, try this then: Do you really think the shooting yesterday was an accident? Look, I'll keep it out of the story if you want."

I shrugged. "I don't know. I figure somebody was trespassing and we surprised them."

"Was anybody in the cabin?"

"I didn't see anybody, but I guess I didn't look very hard. I assumed it would be vacant. Why?"

"Just a question."

"But you had something in mind."

It was Raines's turn to shrug. "Folks say the sheriff's gone a lot. I figure he spends a lot of time at the cabin. It's a good hideaway."

For some reason the memory of the night before last surged into my consciousness.

"Think back to Sunday night," I said. "Was there a pile-up on Highway 20?"

"Highway 20? No, everything was quiet, why?"

"No reason," I lied. "Just a miscommunication."

Calvin Capshaw's house was a white frame two-story a block from the river. An American flag projected from his front porch like a warning finger, and even in winter the front lawn was trimmed as close as a recruit's head. The white Lincoln Towncar in the driveway was ten years old but had been polished to a high sheen. I went up on the porch, knocked, and waited, enjoying the smell of woodsmoke that drifted down from the chimney.

The door opened and a burly man with white hair and thick glasses stood looking out at me as if I might be bringing him the plague.

"Mr. Capshaw? My name is Alan Graham." I handed him my card. "I was told you're the town historian and that maybe you could help me."

The man stared at me for a few seconds, nodded, and held open the screen door.

"I'll do what I can."

I followed him into a living room dominated by a grate with a roaring wood fire. A warm breeze rubbed my face, and I realized there was a central heating system, too, making the air inside oppressive. A tiny woman with black hair got up from her knitting. I introduced myself and she smiled.

"I'm Myrtle. Calvin here knows everything about the history of this town."

Capshaw showed me to a stuffed chair and sat down close

to the fire, near a standing lamp and a small table with a pack of cigarettes.

I explained about our excavations and the need to know as much as possible about the background of the place we were working. Capshaw listened, face impassive.

"I was interested in the legend of a lost silver mine in the hills," I said finally and held my breath.

Calvin Capshaw frowned. "Who told you about that?"

His wife shook her head. "Calvin, everybody in town knows that story."

"Was it Dawson Stokes, that so-called mayor?" he demanded, leaning forward. A bony finger came out to push down against my knee. "Do you think this town will ever get anywhere represented by a man like that?"

"Now, Calvin . . ." Myrtle Capshaw began.

"The man's a laughingstock," her husband proclaimed. "All you have to do is look at him."

"I'm not sure where I heard the story about the lost mine," I said quickly.

"You probably heard about my shiftless son, too," Capshaw said. "Went up in the hills looking for it."

"I heard," I said.

"Digging that hole was the most work he ever did in his life."

Myrtle Capshaw's face twisted in pain. "Oh, Calvin, that's such a terrible thing to say. Berry was such a nice young man . . ."

"Nice and worthless, like most of the people in this town," her husband thundered. "Not to mention stupid. You can lead a horse to water, but you can't make him drink. My son was a draft dodger during Vietnam. What do you think of that?"

"It was a long time ago," I said.

"Yes, it was," Myrtle said. "I keep telling Calvin that."

"Now hear me," Calvin declared, pressing my knee again. "I served for four years, in North Africa and Italy, and then in Europe. Our young people today don't know what sacrifice is about. It's get-rich-quick. Gambling, the lottery, lost silver mines."

"I hear he bought a map from Jacko Reilly," I said.

Calvin Capshaw snorted. "Then you got it all wrong. Although it was Jacko that swindled him, not that it's hard to swindle a fool."

Myrtle shook her head. "Jacko Reilly hurt so many people. That boy was just plain bad."

"What happened?" I asked.

Calvin reached for the cigarette pack on the table. "Berry got the notion of a mine from me. Read about it and got greedy."

"That was when Calvin gave his talk," Myrtle explained. "It was to the Daughters of the American Revolution down in Simmsburg. There was a nice little article in the paper."

"Berry read where I said there was a legend about this mine in the hills and he went out and spread it to the heathens he was running with," Calvin explained. "Told the Reilly boy."

"It was just a shame what that Reilly boy did," Myrtle tisked.

"Hell, it was Berry's stupidity," Calvin said. "Jacko Reilly was smart and Berry was dumb."

I waited.

"Once Jacko heard the story he knew he had a live one on the line," Calvin said. "He asked Berry where this mine was supposed to be and when Berry told him, Jacko told him his family owned the land."

"Imagine," Myrtle said. "As if Jacko Reilly's family ever owned anything at all."

"It was slick, is what it was," Calvin went on. "Jacko knew nobody'd believe him if he just up and claimed he owned the land. What he did was let poor dumb Berry know that he had a claim on the land and couldn't do anything about it because he couldn't hire a lawyer to fight International Paper. Said if he could just hire this lawyer in Baton Rouge, they could get the land from I.P. and find the silver. Got Berry to fork over three thousand dollars. Sold his car, the fool. All for a half interest in land somebody else owned. Naturally, Berry couldn't wait for the paperwork—as if there was any. Went out on his own and started digging and was thrown off the land by the sheriff."

"What did Berry do when he found out he'd been cheated?"

"What could he do, the fool?" Calvin leaned forward again. "Hear me now, I'm not one to say there ought to be laws to protect fools from themselves. He whined a lot and finally left town and got a job over in Jena. There's probably a bigger market for fools over there."

"What's the truth about the silver mine?"

"The truth?" Calvin Capshaw sat back in his chair and drew on his cigarette. "Mister, the only man who knows the truth is dead. He died at the Alamo in 1836."

"You mean Jim Bowie."

"That's who. The Bowies were landowners in this parish. They settled here before they moved down to Opelousas in what was called the Atakapas country, and then, later, they moved up to Rapides Parish. But Bowies always owned land around here and James Bowie had land in those hills. There aren't many Bowies in the parish now, but once there were a good many."

"The silver mine story started with Jim Bowie, then?"

"Probably. He was a big land speculator, you see. Today people remember him for that knife he carried—the one the story says was made out of a meteorite by the blacksmith James Black of Washington, Arkansas—but back in his lifetime he was better known as a land speculator. He sold thousands of acres in Louisiana and Arkansas, mainly Arkansas, and almost all on Spanish land grant titles he forged himself."

"You mean Jim Bowie was really the Jacko Reilly of his time?"

"That's a way of putting it. Man was out to get rich, all right. But it didn't work and so he abandoned Louisiana and went to Texas. That was in 1830, year all his land schemes fell through and his hopes of being elected to Congress along with 'em." Calvin Capshaw picked a piece of tobacco off his tongue. "But Bowie wasn't ever one to stay down. Texas was the place to be then, with land for the taking. All you had to do was comply with some Mexican formalities. Bowie did more than that: He married the daughter of the vice governor of the province. He was on the way to becoming a power in Texas when it all started to go wrong again: She died of a fever in '33, while he was back in Louisiana, settling his affairs. That included selling the two hundred acres he owned in the hills above town."

"Calvin's researched it all," Myrtle said with pride. "He used to teach at the high school."

"I retired when we started to get students who didn't care about learning," he said. "But then why should they? I ask you, look at the kind of people they elect around here. That judge who sits there and pretends to be better than other people: It's his wife who has the money, he doesn't need to put on airs."

"Now Calvin—"

"And a sheriff who's a horse doctor. Is that the kind of person you'd vote for?" he asked me, and I stuttered.

"Not that he's much worse than that drunk and bully we had before. I tell you, sir, this country is headed straight for ruin. The past is dying and nobody cares."

"So there never was any silver," I said.

Capshaw blinked, as if taken aback. "Well, there were rumors about silver in the hills in the early days, when this land was first settled. James Bowie played on that. He spread the notion that there was silver in the hills after he bought the land. It made it easier for him to make money when he sold the tract."

I tried to imagine the Jim Bowie I'd seen in the movie *The Alamo*, cunningly duping land buyers. It didn't jibe well with my memory of Richard Widmark valiantly plunging his big knife into a Mexican as the invaders broke into the room at the Alamo where Bowie lay ill . . .

Calvin Capshaw gave a bitter little smile. "Bowie was a clever man: He might have salted the tract with silver."

"Spanish silver, like coins?" I asked.

"Who knows?" He stared at his cigarette and then flipped it into the fire. "Course, there's another possibility, though I don't recommend it."

"And that is?"

"While Bowie was in Mexico, right after his marriage to Ursula Veramende, he took off for north Texas, to the San Saba area, where there was supposed to be a silver mine guarded by the Indians. He and his people were attacked by one of the tribes and barely escaped. He always wanted to go back but his little detour to the Alamo put an end to that."

I waited as he marshaled his thoughts.

"There are rumors he really found the mine on that first trip and made off with a few pack horse loads of silver bullion."

"You mean . . ."

Another shrug. "He might have brought some back to Louisiana with him, to pay off debts. He might have buried what was left up in those hills, on or near his tract."

"Then why would he have sold the tract?"

"He didn't sell it. The rumor is he lost it in a card game. Bowie was a big gambler. He may have come here meaning to sell the land after he dug up the money. But once he got into the card game, he may have ended up having to use the land to cover his bets."

"Even if he lost the land, he would have gone back and gotten the hoard, wouldn't he?"

"Who knows? Maybe he couldn't find it again. Maybe he had more than one hoard. Maybe something kept him from staying—like the sheriff. Bowie had a mean temper and he was quick with that big knife. Or, most likely, there wasn't any silver hoard at all."

"But wouldn't it be nice if there was?" Myrtle asked. "I mean, think of it, a real treasure, right up in the hills."

"That's just what we need," her husband said sourly. "One more excuse for people not to work. Not bad enough we got the lottery, promises people they'll be millionaires if they just buy a dollar ticket. Gambling casinos on the Indian reservations, where people go throw away their welfare checks. Now we need a treasure for 'em to dig for up in the hills."

"Calvin, I only meant—"

"Nobody knows how to work anymore," her husband went on, ignoring her. "And that includes our weak-minded son. Hear me, something's happened to this country. It isn't the same as it used to be."

I got up slowly, nodding. Nothing was ever the same as it used to be, but it did no good to argue the point.

"It's called the old Corvin tract," Calvin Capshaw said, following me to the door. "I.P. bought it before the war but before they got it, it was called the Corvin tract. Corvins owned a lot of land in this parish but they're all gone now."

We shook hands and I thanked him.

"I wouldn't go up there looking," Capshaw said as I drew away. "It's a fool's quest and lots of fools have been up there. There isn't any silver and never was. It's just a dream. A dream of stupid men."

"Yes, sir."

"But hear me on this: If Berry'd had any guts, after what Jacko Reilly pulled on him, he'd of cleaned Jacko's clock. That's what I'd of done if it'd been me."

For the first time I realized what a big man Calvin Capshaw was, even in the later stages of his life.

"Were you mad enough to do it for him?"

His eyes stared at me and his fists clenched. "No. I say let fools watch out for themselves. But if it had been me, they wouldn't have found enough of Jacko Reilly to bury."

# ≡ FOURTEEN

It was just before one o'clock when I left the Capshaws. I thought of stopping by the courthouse, but I was still mulling Jeff Scully's lie: There hadn't been a wreck on Highway 20, so why had he told me there was?

Without thinking I drove out Highway 20, then left onto 12, away from the brooding hills.

Was there something up at the cabin Jeff didn't want me to see? Did it have something to do with the treasure hole a dead man had excavated? Was there something to the rumors about old Jim Bowie that the sour Calvin Capshaw had recounted? Then I thought about the little piece of silver: It wasn't raw ore, or even a piece of bullion—it was part of a coin. If there was truth to the story about the San Saba mine, then the peso fragment found with Jacko Reilly could hardly be connected, because the San Saba treasure, according to Capshaw, had been bullion, not coins.

I came to the gravel road that arrowed left, toward the archaeological excavation, and kept going. I had to think it all through, try to make sense of things. Could Jeff be more involved in this than he'd let on? I didn't want to think so— during all the time I'd known him, Jeff Scully had been straightforward, but in the last few days I'd been seeing a sly side, capable of manipulation. Maybe he was just learning to be a successful rural politician, but now I began to wonder if there were other, darker aspects of his personality.

A car roared past me and I realized I was crawling at forty-five, clogging the narrow two-lane.

If I kept going I'd end up in Simmsburg. There was no reason to go there except . . .

Then I remembered that was where Jacko's widow lived. I wondered how closely she'd been questioned and whether a visit might not be of value. I took a deep breath and, to the gratification of the long stream of cars behind me, increased my speed to sixty.

I didn't know her address but I remembered Jeff telling me that her maiden name had been Fowkes and her father ran a gas station. I was betting she'd moved back in with her parents after Jacko's disappearance.

I found a phone book at a stop-and-go gas station and there was only one Fowkes listed, Kenneth. I copied the address and then asked the counter clerk where Mound Street was.

Five minutes later I stopped in front of an old white frame house on a side street. There was a tricycle in the front yard, and a little boy with an intense look and a heavy overcoat was playing motorcycle with it, oblivious of his runny nose. I wondered if he was Jacko's son and tried to put aside thoughts about what his life would be.

I smiled at him and drew a scowl. "Don't need nobody here," he said.

I went on up the steps to the porch and knocked on the door.

The woman who opened the door was in her fifties, with her hair done into a bun, Pentecostal style, and a long, plain dress.

"Yes?" Her black eyes studied me suspiciously.

"My name is Alan Graham," I said. "I was looking for Lisa Reilly."

The woman gasped and a hand went to her throat. "What about?"

"I'm the archaeologist who found the car with her husband's remains. I was wondering if I could talk with her for a minute."

"My daughter's suffered enough," the woman said. "She

made mistakes but she's been forgiven. There's no need to rub it in."

I heard movement behind her: "It's all right, Mom."

The woman stepped sideways, as if to block my view of her daughter.

"There's no need to keep raking this up," the older woman said.

"I'll deal with it," her daughter said.

"Like you dealt with everything else," her mother said. "You did a real good job, bringing that child into the world, disgracing yourself before God and your family."

"I'm Lisa Reilly," the girl said, stepping around her mother, who sucked in her breath and took a step backward.

I looked down at her: Raven hair set off a ruddy complexion that hinted of Indian blood, and her dark eyes were hard. Large breasts thrust against her sweater, and her jeans showed off her lines to obvious advantage.

"Let's go outside," Lisa said, grabbing a jacket from a chair. She slammed the door behind us and strode across the porch as if I weren't there.

"Junior, get away from the ditch," she cried. "How many times I have to tell you, damn it?"

She reached inside her jacket and brought out a pack of cigarettes. She lit one without offering the pack to me and stood glaring at her son for a few seconds. Then she turned to me: "So what is it, you from an insurance company or something?"

"I'm the man who found your husband's car. At least, it was my magnetometer that detected it under the water."

The cold eyes assessed me for a second. "You looking for a reward, then?"

"No. I just wanted to ask you a couple of questions."

"The sheriff already talked to me."

"Maybe there's something he forgot to ask."

"Maybe. Look, hurry, will you? It's cold as hell out here." She jerked her head toward the boy: "Junior, I said to get away from the goddamn ditch, do I have to come over and whip your butt?"

"Did your husband ever mention silver coins?"

"What?" Her lips twisted into a lopsided smile. "Is that what this is all about? You after his money? You're goddamn crazy, that's what you are. Jacko didn't leave a thing."

"I'm not after anything but who killed him. The sheriff asked me to look into it."

"The *sheriff*." I thought she was going to spit but she held it in. "He couldn't find his thing with his zipper open."

"Your husband had something with him when he died." I took out Pepper's color scan of the silver wedge and held it up for Lisa to see. "Recognize this?"

She squinted. "What the hell is it?"

"A piece of an old silver coin, a Spanish peso."

She looked down quickly. "I never saw it. Now is that all?"

"The last time you saw your husband, did he act normal?"

"No, he didn't act normal. He acted like Jacko. Now I'm going in." She threw her cigarette down on the sidewalk.

"Did he say anything or give any sign about where he was going or who with?"

"You just won't let go, will you?"

I waited while she fidgeted. "Hey, you got any cigarettes? That was my last one and my folks are strict . . . I'm gonna move out as soon as I got a few dollars. Look, if you don't have smokes, can you spare a couple of bucks so I can get some?"

I reached into my wallet and came up with a ten. Her hand snagged it so fast I wondered if I'd ever had it in the first place.

"So what about the last time you saw him?"

"It was night, he was getting ready to leave the trailer, go out and meet somebody. I hear him talking to 'em on the phone. I didn't want him to go out. We argued. The bastard hit me."

"Any idea who he was talking to on the phone?"

"No. But whoever it was, Jacko was pissed. I heard him say something about the wrong one. That was what had him jacked."

"The wrong one?"

"That's what I said: Jacko said, 'We got the wrong one.'"

Didn't make any sense. When he saw me listening he cussed me."

"You don't know who he was talking to?"

"No."

"The sheriff said he ran with a group of men. He gave me their names."

"He wasn't running with nobody that night. They'd all split. His cousin Skeeter was in jail in Alec for stealing a John Deere. Presley Hobbs was working offshore. Fact is, Jacko was all sad and depressed without his little gang to boss around. That's why he was so ready to beat up on me."

"Did he ever say anything about going up into the hills?"

"The hills? Jacko would just as soon be caught dead as go out in the woods. His idea of going into the woods was sitting behind the trailer with a case of beer, bullshitting about how to score some jack. One bug bite and he was ready to come in. Jacko was good at convincing other people to go get bug bit. He was a real shithead, my Jacko."

"But you hired Chaney Reilly to find out who killed him."

Her eyes darted away, to the empty cigarette pack, and then she cursed under her breath as she realized it was empty.

"It didn't cost me nothing. Sheriff Reilly come and stuck some papers under my nose, said maybe there'd be something in it for me if he could find out who killed him. Jacko didn't leave me a goddamn thing but a four-year-old kid I can't feed. Thanks to him, I gotta live with my parents. Do you know what it's like living with people like that? All day Sunday in church, no smoking, no drinking, not doing nothing, for Christ's sake. That's why I left to start with. Now I'm right back. It ain't fair, damn it."

I thought she was going to stamp her foot but she didn't. Then her eyes nailed me with a sly look.

"You think there's a chance Jacko may have left something, is that why you're here? I got the first right. I was his wife. I got a right to anything that belonged to him, you hear?"

"I'm sure the sheriff will make sure you get what you deserve," I said.

"Sheriff Reilly promised . . ."

"Sheriff Scully, I mean."

Her guffaw was a harsh sound, like bones being scraped.

"I told you about him," she said. "He ain't good for nothing. He's too busy with his own little goings-on."

"What do you mean?"

"You don't know?"

"Know what?"

"About him and his girlfriend."

"He's not married. Why shouldn't he have a girlfriend?"

"Oh, sure, a man his age with a girl what? Sixteen? Seventeen?"

"What are you talking about?" My mouth was dry and I had trouble getting the words out. "I don't know about any girlfriend."

"No? Well, I do, 'cause I seen 'em together in Natchez one day, only they didn't see me. I seen 'em coming out of the dining room right after breakfast, Mr. Thomas Jefferson Scully the high-and-mighty sheriff, and a girl half his age, who could get him chucked out of office if her old man knew."

"Who?" I demanded. "Who was he with?"

Lisa Reilly sneered and cocked her head back, as if she was proud of what she was about to say: "It was Carline Flynn, Mr. District Attorney Flynn's daughter. It wasn't enough she was sneaking down from that girls' school in Jackson, Mississippi, where her old man sends her, not enough she was after my Jacko, who wasn't much, but he was mine. She was after the sheriff, too."

I left Lisa Reilly screaming at Junior and drove back to the archaeological camp, morose at what I'd just heard. Jeff had lied about where he was Sunday night and now I was being told he was seeing a girl who, if not underage, was close enough to it to ruin him with the powers of the parish. That was plenty of reason for him to lie to me. I thought of driving over to his house, laying it on the line, but decided against it.

Who was I to be holier-than-thou? Last year, while Pepper had been in Mexico, I'd come close to having an affair with an attractive widow. I knew how things could get out of hand when a person got lonely. But I hadn't lied to my friends.

Still, it was political suicide, if it was true, and it didn't make sense to waste my time on somebody with a death wish.

The crew was still in the field but Alice Mae was inside the house, cooking, and to my surprise Luther was outside, skinning some kind of animal.

"Howdy, Mr. Alan." He grinned toothlessly. "I made 'em let me go. Told 'em I had better things to do."

"Is that a deer, Luther?"

"Best venison you ever tasted," the little man bragged. He had an ancient butcher knife with a wooden handle and he was sharpening it on a whetstone. "I get this thing sharp I'll show you how to dress a hide."

"Where did you get the deer, Luther?"

"Now, Mr. Alan, don't worry about that. There's plenty of deer in the woods, ain't nobody'll miss this one." He held the blade up, inspected it, and handed it to me: "Try this and tell me if that ain't sharp now?"

I took the knife and touched the blade to my thumb.

"It's sharp," I said, handing it back. "And I didn't see a thing, if the game warden asks."

I went inside and was just pouring myself a drink when the phone rang.

I picked it up and heard Pepper's voice.

"Alan? You'd better come home."

I felt my stomach go weak. "What happened?"

"It's Sam. He had a heart attack a few hours ago. He's in the coronary care unit at Our Lady of the Lake. It doesn't look good."

# FIFTEEN

It was just before seven and already dark when I reached my house on Park Boulevard. Pepper's Integra was on the street outside and she flew into my arms as I opened the door.

"Have you heard anything more?" I asked.

"No. I guess that's good."

"Was it a bad attack?"

She shook her head. "I just know his heart stopped at one point and they had to resuscitate him."

"Damn."

I ate a quesadilla, washing it down it with a glass of milk as Digger yapped from the backyard. I told Pepper about my interview with Calvin Capshaw and the trip to Simmsburg. And I told her what Lisa Reilly had said about Jeff. "I don't know where to go from here."

"Maybe you need to let Jeff handle it," she said.

I nodded. She was doubtless right. I changed the subject: "When can I see Sam?"

"Next visiting hours are at nine," she said.

I checked my watch. "I can't sit around here. I'm going to the library. I need something to take my mind off things."

"Sure. I'll meet you at the CCU," she said.

I drove out to the university, parked behind the office, and set out on foot. In my mind I could see Sam lying in the sterile cubicle, hooked up to the monitoring machines, eyes half closed . . . He was an old man, and old men died, but I'd already lost my parents and I didn't want to go through this again. What would the world be without Sam?

I checked the computerized card catalog and went to the third floor, then sat on the floor between the shelves.

I skimmed the books, made notes, and at eight I walked out of the library. I was anxious to see what insights Sam would have.

And then I remembered.

I got out of my car in the hospital lot at eight-forty and threaded my way across the four lanes of the boulevard into the hospital. I went up the escalator in the lobby and down a long hall, following the signs, until I came to a clutch of people huddled outside a set of heavy, gray swinging doors. A sign said visiting hours were nine A.M., one P.M., five P.M., and nine P.M.

Libby and Pepper disengaged from the others, and Libby hugged me. "It's good to see you."

"How is he?" I asked.

"Holding on. The next few hours are critical, they said."

"He'll make it," I told her, as much to reassure myself. She squeezed my hand.

The swinging door opened and the nurse stood aside as the visitors threaded their way in.

It was like the command center of a missile battery, all computer screens and beeps, except that instead of consoles around the perimeter there were smaller rooms. Some doors were open, others closed. Each had a big window, through which a person outside could see the bed and the person in it, except for a few where the window was covered by a curtain.

We followed Libby to a room in the middle.

I let Libby and Pepper go in first. Maybe, if I took my time, I wouldn't have to go in at all. Maybe I could hang on to the illusion that Sam was still the vigorous man I always remembered, a perpetual sixty, with hair just going silver . . .

Then I forced myself into the little room.

The walls were white, like the sheets, and the man in the bed was white, too, as if all the blood had been drained out of him. There was an IV drip going, and a wire ran from under the sheet to a green oscilloscope. Oxygen tubes led from a clip under his nose to a breathing apparatus.

Libby bent to kiss him and I hung back, wondering if he even knew we were there.

Then I heard his voice.

"Can't you get me out of here?" he begged.

Pepper pecked his cheek and then I moved toward the bed.

"How are you?" I asked and felt silly as soon as I'd said it.

"I don't like it here very much."

"They'll let you out in a day or two," Libby assured him.

"I can go home?"

"They'll send you to a regular hospital room."

"I want to go home. People die up here. Besides"—his eyes rolled around to see if he was being overheard—"that last nurse that came in here was ugly."

"We'll get you a pretty one for downstairs," Libby promised.

"There was a pretty one when I woke up. I thought I'd died and there really was a heaven. But I never saw her again."

"We'll come back next visiting hour," I said.

But he was already asleep.

We went back out into the hallway.

"I'll be back in the morning," I promised Libby. "Call me if there's anything . . ." I halted, not sure how to finish the sentence.

She touched my arm fondly. "Thank you. They tell me he's stable for now."

I nodded, not saying what was on my mind, which was that *stable* just meant nothing was happening right now. He'd been *stable* right before he'd had his heart attack . . .

We ate at the Ground Pat'i on Jefferson, because I didn't know if there was enough food in the house to fix a meal. She ordered ribs and I had a hamburger with cheese, and, to compensate, a Diet Coke.

"He'll be okay," she said, taking my hand under the table.

"Yeah. But it's the future that bothers me."

"You mean the damage to his heart?"

"I mean nobody lives forever. Other people, even my parents, died. Classmates died, were killed, committed suicide.

But there was always Sam. Now I have to admit he's not immortal."

Her hand squeezed mine.

"Tell me about your research," she said, and I knew she was trying to get my mind away from Sam. "I have the feeling you're onto something."

I shrugged. "I don't know. I was reading about old Jim Bowie, the knife fighter. His name keeps popping up through this whole business. It's almost like Jacko Reilly was his reincarnation."

"But Jim Bowie was a hero," she said. "He was killed at the Alamo with Crockett and Travis."

"That's how he ended up but before that there was a lot about his life that was pretty shady. Slave trading, forging land titles, brawling. He had political ambitions, and in 1828, the year after the famous Vidalia knife fight, he was, on paper at least, one of the richest men in the country. Then his land schemes came to light and even though he and his brother, Rezin, went to Washington to try to pressure the authorities into accepting his forged land papers, everything fell apart. He ended up in Texas looking for new wealth."

"But what's this got to do with Jacko? You don't really believe in reincarnation."

"No, of course not. But I believe an old story everybody up there seems to know may have something to do with what happened to the town's bad boy."

Pepper smiled. "It's tough to lose your heroes."

I nodded. "Yeah, everybody thinks of Jim Bowie as the hero in *The Iron Mistress*."

"I've heard of that. Wasn't it a movie?"

"With Alan Ladd, in the early 1950s. Paul Wellman, the Western historian, wrote the book. I loved that story when I was a kid, though it's been years since I've seen the movie. In *The Iron Mistress,* Jim Bowie goes to a blacksmith named James Black with a wooden knife model and tells him to use it to make the knife. And the blacksmith looks it over and shakes his head, because he knows this is a knife design like no other he's ever seen, and then—and this is the part I love— he goes into the back of his shop and comes out with a box, and he opens it and takes out this piece of meteorite. He tells Bowie he's going to put a piece of a star into it."

"Nice touch," Pepper said, stealing one of my fries.

"So Bowie rides away, tells him he'll come back in a week or two, and Black promises to have the knife ready for him. You see Black heating his forge and melting the steel and then he takes out the little box and drops the piece of meteorite into the molten metal. Then you see him hammering the steel into shape and, finally, putting on the handle. When Bowie comes back—and this is the part I like—he says, 'Here's your knife, Mr. Bowie. It's got a little bit of heaven in it. And a little bit of hell.' "

"I think I remember that part," she said. "Well, it makes a nice story."

"Yes, but there was fact in it. There really *was* a James Black. He lived in Washington, Arkansas, and years later he told about how Jim Bowie showed up one day in 1830 with a wooden model for a knife."

"I thought the sandbar fight was in 1827."

"It was. In Black's version, the sandbar and a few other scrapes convinced Bowie he needed a better knife than the one he'd been using up to then."

"And that was the real origin of the Bowie knife."

"The origin of the myth, anyway."

That night I slept fitfully, half expecting the phone to ring with Libby's trembling voice on the other end. I drifted in and out of dreams. I saw Jacko in his submerged Firebird but water kept washing in and floating him out of it and turning his body over and over. I was looking at his face and suddenly I realized it was Sam's and I started upright in the bed.

Pepper turned over and mumbled something in her sleep. Looking at her, I felt a calmness descend over me, as if, with her just being here, everything would be all right. I lay back and closed my eyes.

This time a scene from an old movie flashed in front of me. I was watching a man on the deck of a riverboat, standing at the railing. Like me, he was in love, and he was on his way to meet his woman. Thoughts tumbled through his mind, memories of a past life filled with duels and romances. And he was leaving all that.

Without thinking his hand reached down to his belt and drew his great knife from its scabbard. He studied the blade for a moment, thinking of the men it had killed and the piece of star that had been used to make it, and then, with a flick of his wrist, he dropped it over the side.

I saw the final scene of the movie, as the blade sank down into the depths, coming to rest on the bottom.

Except that in my dream a skeletal hand—Jacko Reilly's—reached out to grab it.

# ■ SIXTEEN

I caught Libby outside the CCU just before morning visiting hours began, and she told me there'd been no change, that Sam had been asleep when she'd visited last night. I told her Pepper had class or she would have come with me, and then the big door swung open and we went inside.

This time he was propped up with a pillow behind him, and when he saw us he smiled.

"You look a whole lot better," Libby said.

"I *am* better. They got rid of that ugly nurse." He squeezed my hand. "You didn't bring me a little Dant, did you?"

"They'd throw us all out if I did," I told him, "but when you get out of here I'll buy you a gallon."

"That's a deal." He coughed. "It's so damn boring in here. I can't stand to just lie here. What's going on in the real world?"

Libby looked over at me and I shrugged. "Still working up at Lordsport."

"That place has a fascinating history," Sam said. "You ever been to the Morgan House, that old hotel from the last century? And there's a bunch of Cunys buried on top of that Indian mound right inside the town itself."

"Who?"

"The Cunys were a big family in the first part of the last century. Dr. Richard Cuny was the brother of General Samuel Cuny. The general was killed in the Natchez Sandbar fight, but Richard was there, too. Treated some of the victims."

"Interesting you should mention that. I was doing some reading about old Jim Bowie," I said.

"That rascal," Sam wheezed. "He made a fortune running slaves up from Galveston Island. Bought 'em from Jean Lafitte. Jim Bowie would do anything for a dollar. Only one in the family with any character or brains was his brother Rezin. But Jim got all the glory because he was hot-tempered and didn't mind cutting folks with that big knife he carried. He'd have gone down as just a brawler and a land speculator if it wasn't for the Alamo. He was stupid—or lucky—enough to end up there. Jim Bowie owes his legend to the Alamo."

"You don't think he killed a dozen Mexican soldiers on his sickbed?" I asked.

"Man was dying of typhus. He couldn't crap without help. A lot of nonsense has been written about Bowie and his knife."

"You don't believe in Excalibur," I said.

"There aren't any Excaliburs," Sam pronounced. "And there aren't any King Arthurs. I shouldn't have to tell you that."

"It's nice to believe," I said.

"Then get religion."

I caught Libby's eye and she was smiling in a way I hadn't seen since Sam had had his attack.

"Now calm down," she said, smoothing his sheet. "You don't want to get too excited."

"Hell, excitement's what I need. Send in a couple of dozen Mexican soldiers and give me a Bowie knife."

"I'll come back later," I promised him. "You take care."

"Don't forget my Dant."

Pepper would be in class all morning, so I went back to the Louisiana Room at Hill Memorial Library on the university campus and read about the Bowie brothers. I was hunting for references to silver mines, treasure, or anything that might have suggested a silver salting scheme in Cane River Parish, but I had no luck. When I couldn't justify my absence any longer, I went to the office and stoically endured Marilyn's latest lament.

"We can't go on like this, Alan," she declared, a five-foot-tall dynamo scowling up at me.

"Are you telling me our marriage is over?"

"Don't be flippant. This is serious. Unless Clarence at the bank ups our credit line . . ."

"What about the check we got the other day?"

"We had to pay bills. They were threatening to shut off the lights."

"There should be a payment from DOTD any day," I said. "They're just slow."

"They haven't ever paid the retainage from the last project. We can't survive getting paid only ninety percent of what we're owed."

"I'll see what I can do."

She spun on her heel and left. It was a routine we were both used to, but she was right: We couldn't survive without money. So far we'd been lucky, but counting on luck wasn't conducive to business longevity.

I read over a draft report we'd done for a pipeline company, signed some checks, and left for evening visiting hours, which began at five P.M. Sam informed me the ugly nurse was back. Libby told me they had an angiogram scheduled for tomorrow morning and that it would determine whether Sam would need open heart surgery. I reassured her that open heart surgery was almost routine these days and tried to make myself feel nonchalant about it. Sam was elderly but he was strong. If he'd made it this far, surgery would be a snap.

When I got home there was a message from Jeff on my machine.

I returned his call and got him on his direct line.

"I didn't know you were going home," he accused.

"Yeah, well, some things came up."

"What's the matter, Alan? Are you upset or something?"

"There wasn't any accident on Highway 20 Sunday night." There was a long silence.

"No. I lied. I'm sorry."

"Why?"

"It's kinda personal."

"So is my going up there and risking my ass for you."

"Look, it was a woman, okay? I just didn't want word to spread all over creation."

"Why? You're old enough."

"Yeah, well, there are some negatives associated with the situation. I've got to work through it all. Trust me, Alan."

"Damn it, Jeff, if this is something—"

"Please . . ."

"Do you know Carline Flynn?"

"Ross Flynn's daughter? Sure. I told you, she was getting it on with Jacko and . . ." Another silence. "Hey, you don't think . . ."

"I've heard it said," I told him.

"Well, it's a lie. I haven't seen the girl for three months— since right before Jacko went missing. Hell, she's seventeen years old. Who told you this?"

"I don't want any trouble for my source."

"Jesus, Alan, what are you, a priest? Okay, no trouble: Now who."

I told him.

"I might have known. She was jealous as hell. Look, Carline ran off from school to come see Jacko and I caught up with her and called her daddy. I kept her in the Ramada in Natchez until he could come take her back to school."

"Across a state line? Natchez is in Mississippi."

"It was what was best for the girl."

I breathed relief. I wanted to believe him and it made sense.

"Well, I can't get back for the time being," I told him and explained about Sam and his angiogram. "I've got to stick around here tomorrow."

"I understand. But Alan . . ."

"Yeah?"

"Just get back when you can."

I was at the hospital the next morning and stayed through Sam's angiogram long enough to hear there was ninety-five percent blockage of the arteries. I headed back to the CCU. Sam still wasn't back from the operating room, but Libby was in the hallway with a slightly plump, white-coated doctor.

"Sam has to have a bypass," she said. "Dr. Gomez says it's the only way to keep him from having another attack."

"When?" I asked.

"Tomorrow morning," Gomez said. "I've already called the surgeon."

"And it'll take care of the problem?" I asked.

Gomez shrugged. "A man his age, weight, I'd say the odds are about seventy-five percent the procedure will be a success."

"How long will it last?"

"The average is ten years. No guarantees."

Libby bit her lip. "Sam told me already if the angiogram showed blockage he wouldn't go for an operation."

"He has to," I said.

"You know Sam."

And I did. He was stubborn.

"When will he be back?" I asked.

"Inside the hour," the cardiologist said.

I turned to Libby. "I'll come back and see him then."

I called Pepper at the university and told her about Sam, then went to my office. In the early afternoon I went back to the hospital. This time Sam was lying propped up in bed while Libby stood beside him.

"These quacks want to cut me open," he said when he saw me.

"Then you better let 'em," I said, taking a chair.

"Not a chance. I know that surgeon, damn it. He was in my introductory physical anthropology class. He didn't know a cranium from a clavicle."

"Maybe he's learned something since."

"I'd rather just lie here and let nature take its course. Old men aren't supposed to live forever, anyway."

"No."

He looked from Libby to me and mouthed the words I'd never expected to hear: "I'm scared."

I nodded. I couldn't think of anything to say.

"Alan, I can't stand the idea of them putting that mask over my face. Even if they give me a shot first, what if . . ."

"I don't know, Sam. It would scare me, too."

"Libby says the kids are coming in tomorrow." They had a son and daughter living in far-flung parts of the country.

"I feel like a damn turkey, all plucked and ready."

"You'll be better after the operation."

"That's what they say."

I got up. "It's your decision, but we'd like to have you around for a while yet."

There was a long silence.

"You really think I ought to have this thing?"

"I do."

He turned his head to look over at Libby. "Then just this once," he said.

She squeezed his hand and gave me a smile.

"I'll be here," I said. "I'm not going anywhere."

If I'd known then what was about to happen I'd never have made such a promise.

# ≡ SEVENTEEN

I'd just come in at nine-thirty, after my evening visit with Sam, and Pepper was working at the computer she'd set up on a table next to mine, in the study. When the phone rang, my skin went cold, because, even though Sam had looked good when I'd seen him twenty minutes ago, you never could tell.

But it wasn't Libby calling about Sam. Instead, it was a man's voice, breathless.

"Dr. Graham?"

Where had I heard that voice before?

"This is Clovis Hightower, from Port Gibson. You and the lady came to see me the other day."

"I remember. How did you get my home number?"

"It's listed. And I'm very glad it is. We need to talk."

"I'm listening."

"You don't understand, Dr. Graham. There's something I need to discuss with you. I . . . I need your help. We need to meet."

"There's no way, Mr. Hightower. It'll have to be over the phone."

"Dr. Graham, please . . . I don't know anyone else. This is urgent. I have to see you tonight."

"I said I can't."

"Then first thing tomorrow morning. *Please* . . ."

"What's this about?"

"It's about a crime. A terrible crime. It's all gone too far. This has to stop before—"

"Before what?"

"Before something else happens."

"Why don't you call the sheriff?"

"No." The word emerged as a hiss. "Things have to be . . . arranged. I need someone who isn't part of the official apparatus."

"What crime are you talking about, Mr. Hightower?"

"Don't play games, Dr. Graham. You know. First there was the old man, then the other one, and if this isn't settled . . ."

"How do I know this isn't a trick?"

"A trick? My God, man, do you think I'd risk calling like this if I wasn't serious? I'm afraid, for God's sake. Things are out of hand." There was no mistaking the hysteria in his voice.

"Does this have to do with the piece of the Spanish coin we showed you?" I asked.

"Yes. No. I mean, the coin isn't relevant. It's . . . Listen, I'll explain it all, but I can't talk anymore. Meet me tomorrow at the River Oaks Motel. Natchez. As early as you can get there. I'm in room 211."

I tried to think: Sam's operation was scheduled for tomorrow morning at ten-thirty. There was no way I could be both places.

"If you don't come," the man on the other end warned, "it will be on your head. And another thing: This is between you and me. Don't tell Scully. I don't trust him."

"I'll do what I can."

I lowered the receiver from my ear and turned to Pepper.

"What is it?" she asked. "Who was that?"

I told her. "He wants me to meet him in Natchez tomorrow morning."

"But what about Sam?"

"I don't know. He says if I don't come, he'll run."

Pepper frowned. "But what can Hightower know? Unless . . ."

"Right: unless he's in this up to his eyeballs."

"Then call Jeff. Get his help."

"That's what I thought at first but I'm not sure that's the

best thing to do." I explained about Jeff's lie. "He says he and Carline aren't involved but there was something about his explanation, an evasiveness. And Hightower said specifically he didn't want Scully involved."

"Alan, you don't think Jeff is in this?"

"Two days ago I'd have said it was crazy. Now . . ."

She faced me, blue eyes earnest. "So what do you plan to do?"

"I don't know."

"Yes, you do. I can tell."

"How's that?"

"You'll agonize about it and have bad dreams but in the end you'll go. You'll tell yourself that being here isn't going to affect Sam, that I can stay and fill in for you, and that I can make apologies, and that you can't take the chance Hightower knows something important. And in the end you'll go and worry about Sam all the way."

"You've got it all figured out."

"Of course. If it seems like my idea it'll be easier for you."

I stared at her. "You're something."

"Yeah."

And she was right: I did have bad dreams, with Sam lying on a sacrificial stone slab while an Aztec priest in a white lab coat cut open his chest with an obsidian blade. I was trying to protest that it wasn't supposed to be done that way, but Sam, alert and seemingly unaffected, was telling me to be quiet, that he was the only man alive to have a chance to witness the ancient sacrificial ritual.

The memory of the dream dogged me all the way up to Natchez. Sam would be all right: They did a dozen bypasses a week in that hospital. It wasn't the experimental procedure of thirty years ago. Today it was routine. You just put the patient out, stopped his heart, and . . . I kept seeing the Aztec priest, holding the pulsing organ up to the sun god. I realized for the first time what my waking grogginess had blocked out: The sun priest had my face.

The River Oaks was one of a couple of motels on the south side of Natchez, just across Catherine Creek, as you came in on the four-lane. Once it had been a first-class establishment, but the advent of gambling and lodging closer to the river had sent it into decline. Still, it was a decent enough–looking place, two stories of faded green cinder block with half the parking lot empty.

I had no idea what kind of vehicle Hightower was driving or whether he'd registered under his own name, but he said he'd be in room 211. I parked by the waterless swimming pool and climbed stairs with flaking concrete risers. At the top, a black woman in a white maid's uniform was stuffing sheets into a hamper on wheels. The room to 209 was open and I figured she'd be at 211 in six or seven minutes. Unless she was bypassing the rooms that were still occupied; nine was a little early to roust out guests.

I knocked on 211 and waited. No answer. I knocked again.

The curtains were drawn and I couldn't tell if there was a light on inside.

"Mr. Hightower, it's Alan Graham."

No answer.

I turned to the cleaning woman.

"Do you know if anyone is still registered for 211?"

The woman gave a massive shrug. "I ain't seen nobody. He may be asleep."

"Could you open the door just enough for me to see if there's anybody inside?"

She frowned. "I don't know about that."

"I tell you what: You're headed this way anyhow. I'll stand back. Just open the door like you're going to clean the room and tell me if the room's occupied, how's that?"

She gave me a patronizing smile, sighed, and walked over to the door.

"Housekeeping," she called and inserted her key.

No answer, and she twisted the key and then pushed the door open.

"Anybody inside?"

She took a step inside and then stopped. I thought she was letting her eyes adjust to the dimness but then I heard her gasp and she said, "Oh, sweet Jesus."

"What is it?"

But she wouldn't move, just stood there, rooted, repeating "Sweet Jesus, sweet Jesus."

I gently pushed the door the rest of the way open and looked over her shoulder.

At first the room just seemed in need of a cleaning, with sheets pulled down to the rug and a valise open in the middle of the floor. But then, as my eyes took in the details, I saw the red streaks on the wall, the broken mirror, the shoe on the bureau, and, hanging over the bed with his mouth open, the half-naked body of a man I knew must be Clovis Hightower.

The maid was trembling now, too weak to walk away, and I started away, my gorge rising, then forced myself to turn back for a last, quick look at the scene before the police came and it was changed forever.

There was blood everywhere, and it was hard to tell whether the murdered man, whose head touched the floor with his upside-down face staring at us, was wearing a red undershirt or whether it was his bare torso that was painted with his blood. I glanced down and saw red tracks on the carpet, heading for the door, but they ended where we were standing. The killer must have removed his shoes.

All of a sudden I realized I was shaking and at about the time I reached for the rail behind me to steady myself, the maid let out a long, loud wail.

I sat down on the first step of the stairway to wait for the police.

The first cops were a Laurel and Hardy pair in uniform who asked me why I was there, what business I had with the murdered man, and took my driver's license as if to ensure that I didn't bolt. When I told them I was looking into a situation for the sheriff of Cane River Parish, they seemed unimpressed, and then I showed them the credentials Jeff had given me.

"He's a deputy," Hardy said to the thin one, and they both looked disgusted. I could understand their response because I didn't feel very official at that point.

They left me alone and were quickly replaced by two detectives. One, a sad-looking man with the face of a bloodhound, examined my identification card and the shiny badge

Jeff had forced on me that day between Ferriday and Vidalia, and handed them back.

"Why didn't you check in with us first?" he asked. "You're not even in the right state."

"I didn't know there was going to be a crime," I said and repeated the story of Hightower's call last night.

One of the uniforms said, "You know how these country sheriffs are, Lieutenant."

The lieutenant ignored him. "You didn't go inside the room."

"No."

He nodded, and the cell phone in his pocket rang. He listened, said a few words, and then disconnected.

"Your sheriff's in the area. He'll be here in five minutes."

I started to say something but kept my mouth shut. Jeff was in the area: Why? He was as far outside his jurisdiction as I was. It didn't make any sense unless . . .

A few minutes later I saw his Bronco swing into the parking lot below and he got out and started up the steps. The sad lieutenant met him halfway down and they shook hands and exchanged some words. Then Jeff, followed by the policeman, came over to where I was leaning against the wall.

"Rough one, eh, hoss?"

"Rough," I said.

He put a hand on my shoulder and went down the walkway and peered inside the room. Then he came back to where the rest of us stood.

"I'll have my deputy here give you a statement and any other cooperation you need," he said. "It looks like this ties in with something we're working on in Lordsport. I hope we can share notes." There were mumbles of assent. "Might be a good idea to search the victim's place of business. From what you say, he may be in the stolen antiques business." More mumbles of assent.

"Now, if my deputy can go, I think he's a little worse for the wear."

We were back in the parking lot, standing beside Jeff's Bronco, before he spoke again.

"Goddamn, Alan. I gave you the credentials to get Chaney

off your back. I didn't know you'd start pretending to be a *real* deputy."

"I didn't plan to."

"You should've called me when Hightower called you last night. You know that, don't you?"

"Bad move," I agreed. "Lucky you were close enough to come here and bail me out."

"Damn straight," Jeff swore. "Well, what do you make of it?"

"Sounds like Hightower was involved with Jacko in some kind of antique stealing ring," I said. "And Jacko's killer decided it was too dangerous to leave him alive."

"That'd be my guess, too. That's why I want to be at Hightower's place when the locals search it. So where to now for you?"

I looked at my watch. It was barely eleven and the crew would be finishing up the week at the dig. Sam's operation was already under way. There was nothing I could do back home, and I dreaded the wait at the hospital.

"Maybe I'll drive over to Lordsport," I said.

"Okay. I got a few more things to do here with these boys and I'll be along. But Alan . . ."

"Yeah?"

"Keep all this under your hat for now. And for God's sake try not to find any more bodies."

I ate at the Sonic in Ferriday, in no hurry to get to Lordsport. My mind wasn't on archaeology and I knew that if I went to the excavation I'd only blunder around aggravating the ultra-meticulous David. Better to stay out of the way.

I approached the bridge and slowed as I saw a line of cars waiting. The middle of the bridge was lifted to allow a barge through, and I gazed absently at the little square bridge tender's cabin nested among the girders. It was the first time I'd seen the bridge raised and I hadn't realized what a traffic jam it created. As I waited my eyes wandered over to the lonely little shack of Jeremiah Persons. If I could find Jeremiah, maybe he'd have some ideas. Where had Mayor Stokes said he was from? Winnfield? Tallulah? The mayor hadn't been sure but something stuck in my mind, if I could just get it free . . .

The center of the bridge began to go down and two minutes later the cars ahead of me started forward. I saw the bridge tender coming down the ladder as I passed and wondered idly if he got paid by the barge.

I rolled down the west side of the bridge, passed the old white Methodist church on the left, and slowed for the curve by the courthouse. A couple of orange-suited prisoners were picking up trash from the courthouse lawn, and I involuntarily slammed on the brakes as I recognized Luther Dupree.

I pulled in at the food mart and walked over.

"Luther, what in hell?"

The little man shrugged: "It's that game warden, Mr. Pope. I told you, he's been after me ever since I beat him in court on that fishing thing. This time he's claiming I poached a deer from the preserve. Hell, I don't have to go to no damn preserve for a deer; they're all over the place. Look, Mr. Alan, if you could talk to the judge . . ."

I threw up my hands and walked away. Now I especially didn't want to go to the excavation. I'd hear enough when I got back to Baton Rouge. I felt sorry for Alice Mae, but I could only go so far . . .

I looked at my watch again. Just after noon. Maybe I could get Pepper at the university. I punched in the number on my cell phone, but after four rings the departmental secretary came on and told me Dr. Courtney wasn't in. I tried my own office then and Blackie answered.

"Anything happening?"

"No, the firemen did a good cleanup."

"What?"

"Joke."

"Asshole. Any word on Sam MacGregor?"

"I heard he was sick. Is that true?"

"Where's Marilyn?"

"At lunch. Oh, there was one call for you."

"Yes?"

"David. He was pissed. Something about a game warden taking away last night's supper before they could eat it."

"Goodbye."

I put away the phone and sat quietly in the Blazer, thinking. I had time on my hands. Jeff Scully was headed up to Port Gibson, and that would take the rest of the day. I wondered what I'd find if I went back to his cabin?

# ▆ EIGHTEEN

I drove back over the bridge and turned onto 621 at Stanton, winding along the side of the game preserve until I reached the narrow gravel road that led to Jeff Scully's cabin. A mile off the blacktop was an iron pipe gate, and I parked at the side of the road.

On Monday, when Luther and I had come through on foot, the gate had been open. I hadn't asked Jeff about that. I examined the heavy lock, then climbed over the bars and dropped into the drive.

The cabin looked the same as it had before, only then I'd been too shaken to examine it. I had only impressions, and I wasn't sure whether coming here now would reinforce or destroy them. In fact, I wasn't sure what I expected to find here at all.

I went up the drive toward the porch, acutely conscious of the fact that anyone with a rifle could pick me off from either the house itself or the sides of the clearing. But there was no sound besides my feet crunching the gravel. I stepped onto the porch and bent to look in through one of the front windows. My breath fogged the glass and I wiped it with my hand. The interior was dark and all I could see was a couch, some chairs, and a fireplace. I went to the front door and tried it but it was locked.

I straightened and walked around to the back, studying the ground. There'd been no rain in the last few days, and in the bare spot behind the woodshed I saw the marks of raccoon, deer, and a wolf or large dog. But there were no shoe prints.

That meant that when the deputies had come to check out the shooting, they hadn't looked too hard behind the house. Maybe, because the land belonged to the sheriff, they hadn't looked too hard anywhere.

I tried the back door but it, too, was locked. I went to each window in turn, and on the north end of the house I found that when I pulled up on the windowpane, the window moved upward, leaving a space just large enough to slip through.

I reached inside, then stopped: What was I thinking? This was Jeff's house and he trusted me. What kind of a friend would I be to break into his place in his absence? Guilt flooded me and I eased the window back down.

Without going through the contents of the cabin, there wasn't likely to be much to find up here. Unless I went back to the hole that poor Berry Capshaw had dug in the hills.

I walked to the rear of the clearing and found the trail Luther and I had used. A few minutes later I was passing the POSTED signs that indicated Jeff's property and confronting new ones that said INTERNATIONAL PAPER.

It was chilly, though not as cold as the first time I'd been here. The sky was light gray with scudding clouds, and when I sniffed I thought I could smell rain.

I hurried my pace, wondering what excuse I'd give if somebody surprised me back here.

But why did I have to worry? I had the credentials Jeff had given me. I was a duly appointed officer carrying out an investigation.

*Okay, Graham, just keep believing that and see how long you stay alive.*

The clearing was just ahead and I made my way to the edge of the hole and looked down into the pit.

Calvin Capshaw had been right: His son had been a fool. Only a fool would troop up here with a shovel and dig a hole that yielded nothing but gravel. All for the mythical Bowie silver.

I stepped back and walked around the clearing, eyes on the ground. Maybe someone had dropped something. Maybe I'd find another peso fragment. Maybe . . .

But after ten minutes of searching I turned up nothing but a cellophane cigarette pack cover. I went back to the hole and stared down again. I wondered how far Berry Capshaw would have dug if he hadn't been run off. How far is far enough when your head's filled with dreams of wealth?

A branch cracked behind me and I turned. As I did, my foot slipped and I felt myself tottering on the edge of the hole. Earth and gravel cascaded away under my feet and I reached out, barely righted myself, and managed to leap away from the edge.

I looked in the direction of the sound but there was only a squirrel, complaining noisily from a limb ten feet up.

I was sweating now, and I realized I was in no state to be walking alone in the woods. Finding Hightower had unnerved me, and though I'd come here to try to clear my head, I was still too jittery to know what I was doing. And falling into a ten-foot hole was the last thing I needed.

A raindrop spattered the ground in front of me, and I felt another on my arm. In the distance I heard the rumble of thunder.

I hurried back down the trail, aware that the air was growing darker. Jeff's cabin watched me with hollow eyes as I passed. The rain was driving now in a steady patter. I came to the gate and pulled myself over, feet slipping on the steel bars. I dropped safely onto the other side and grabbed the top of the gate for support. My eyes settled on the gatepost, where a smudge of blue paint overlay the aluminum, waist high. I hadn't noticed it before and now, despite the rain, I considered it for a long ten seconds. Then I went back to the Blazer, backed up far enough to turn around, and headed back to Lordsport.

By the time I reached town there was a full scale thunderstorm under way, with yellow bolts of lightning forking overhead and leaves flying by on the wind. I pulled in at the courthouse and ran in the back way, past the sheriff's office, taking the elevator to the second floor. I went into the clerk's office, where the conveyance books were arrayed on tables to the left,

with a counter to the right. The young black woman on duty
smiled as I came in shaking off the raindrops.

"Nasty, isn't it?" she said.

I smiled back, nodded, and went to the books.

By the time they closed I had the chain-of-title for the land
where Berry Capshaw had dug his hole.

I thanked the attendant, who asked if I was really going to
leave in this storm. I told her I was that crazy and took the
elevator back down. Five minutes later, with my clothes dripping, I stopped in the camp drive and ran inside.

The crew was gone for the weekend and I had the place to
myself. For a long time I sat quietly in the dark, listening
to the thunder crash outside. Finally, I reached for the phone
to call Pepper. There should be definite word on Sam now.

I tried my house in Baton Rouge. After four rings I heard
my own voice saying to leave a message so I said where I
was and asked Pepper to call with a report as soon as possible.
I apologized for staying over, but explained that I didn't want
to drive in a storm, after dark.

I turned on the light, got out my notebook, and began to go
over what I'd found out.

The land in question was part of a four-hundred-and-thirty-
five acre tract owned by International Paper. In 1940, however,
two hundred acres had been sold to I.P. by one Abner Corvin.
The other two hundred and thirty-five acres had been formed
from seven or eight smaller holdings bought over the years
from different individuals. Ignoring the smaller tracts, I'd followed the larger holding through a series of successions to
1870, when it had passed, at a sheriff's sale, from the widow
of a man named Harold McElwain. Like many in the aftermath
of the Civil War, she'd been unable to pay the taxes. But the
McElwains had owned the tract for over a third of a century,
ever since the day, in December 1833, that title passed from
one James Bowie to one Martin McElwain, for one thousand
dollars. And Bowie's title had been confirmed by the General
Land Office, on the basis of a Spanish grant purchased for
fifteen hundred dollars from the original grantee, a man named
Josiah Loomis.

Two things stood out: If Bowie had fabricated the title and forged the name of Loomis (or invented him altogether, which some of the records suggested he had with other titles), then the fraud had gone undetected. But secondly, if he had bought the land to salt with silver, he'd failed miserably, because he sold it for less than he'd paid.

I put aside the notebook and went back to the telephone. This time Pepper answered.

"It's storming," I said. "I can't get out tonight."

"I saw the weather on the news. Best for you to stay put," she agreed.

"What's the news on Sam?"

"He's in the coronary surgery unit now. That's where they put you after a bypass. If everything goes well he'll be back in a regular room in a couple of days. The first forty-eight hours are the most important: There's always the chance of a stroke."

"I wish I could be there. But there's been a complication besides the weather." I told her about Hightower. "Somebody must've been afraid he was going to spill his guts."

"Lord," she breathed. "I don't guess there are any suspects yet."

I thought of Jeff, just a few minutes away from the crime scene when they'd called, and thirty miles outside his jurisdiction. "No."

"Will you be okay there at the camp?" she asked. "Should you go stay with Jeff?"

"I don't think so. I'm fine here," I assured her. "Snug as a bug."

"And if the river goes over the banks?"

"Never happen," I said.

"And you once accused me of being reckless."

"That was when you wanted to take a fifteen-foot boat into the Mississippi River to look for that Tunica boy."

"Seems like a long time ago," she said.

"Yeah."

Silence, then: "I wish you were back here."

"I wish I was, too. But I'll leave as soon as it's light. The rain should pass through tonight."

"Don't leave the doors unlocked, and for God's sake don't find any more bodies."

"I'll do my best."

I hung up the phone and was wondering what there was in the house to read when the power went out.

For a long minute I sat in the darkness, listening to the rain pelt the roof. It was chilly inside the old house, so I felt my way to the space heater and then realized I needed a match. I blundered into the kitchen area, feeling my way through the cabinets until I located a box of matches. I lit one and made my way to the heater. I turned on the jet, stuck the burning match into the grate, and was reassured by a *whoosh* as the heater lit. I did the same thing with the heater in the main bedroom.

I checked the bedroom window, made sure there was two inches of space between the bottom of the window and the sill, and then went back into the living room. I could call Jeff, see if he'd found anything in Port Gibson. That is, if he was back.

Or did I have another reason for wanting to talk to him? Was it to see if he said something that would put an end to my suspicions, provide some explanation for why he'd been across the river in Mississippi this morning and who he'd been seeing on the sly if it wasn't Carline Flynn?

I lifted the receiver and put it to my ear, but the line was dead.

I thought of running out to get my cell phone from the Blazer but the rain was unremitting. For tonight, then, I was isolated. I decided to turn in early.

# ▰ NINETEEN

When I awoke the atmosphere was chill, as it had been on those long-ago school mornings of my youth. As I snuggled under the covers, vaguely aware of the gray dawn pressing against the window, I had the temporary sensation that I was still in the fifth grade, in the old house on Park Boulevard, waiting for my father to come up the stairs and tell me that this was the final call. I stretched and the sensation dissipated. I sat up slowly, my skin prickling from the chill. The rain had stopped but there was still a dripping outside, from the trees and eaves. I padded over to the heater, turned it up, and then went into the front room and did the same.

I'd had strange dreams again last night, but I couldn't remember what they were. I knew I'd woken up once, sweating, and shouted into the darkness.

I washed up and found some eggs and bacon and half a carton of orange juice. By the time I'd finished breakfast and washed the dishes it was seven-thirty. I tried the telephone. The earpiece emitted a dial tone. Next I opened the front door and looked out. Water was standing in the yard but there was no sign the river had spilled over its banks. Mainly just a godawful mess for the crew when they came back Monday and had to pump out their excavation units.

If I left now I could be home just before ten. I'd have most of my weekend in front of me and I could check on Sam at the hospital. I threw on my jacket and was starting out the door when I heard the sound of tires on the gravel drive, looked up, and saw Jeff's Bronco. He got out, clapping his hands together and blowing out clouds of vapor.

"I wondered if I'd catch you," he said. "I called last night but the lines were down."

"I'm headed back to Baton Rouge," I said. "Unless there's something up here I'm supposed to do."

Jeff shook his head. "Nothing that comes to mind. Look, Alan, I appreciate what you've done so far. If I'd known what was going to happen with Hightower, I wouldn't have involved you."

"A typical day in the life of an archaeologist," I said. "It's just that the dead people I generally deal with have been dead a little longer."

"Right." He shook his head. "I was looking at the coroner's preliminary report on Hightower. Twenty-five knife wounds, nine inches deep, with a blade an inch and a half wide. Somebody did everything but skin the poor bastard."

"Well, at least I'm not the one who had to count the knife wounds."

"That's two of us." He stuck out a hand. "Well, thanks again."

"Sure. By the way, was there anything interesting at Hightower's shop?"

"At his shop, no. He was pretty careful. But at his house there was a shitload of stuff from burglaries all over the place. He may even be connected to a murder—besides Jacko's, I mean."

"Oh?"

"Old man in Columbia had his place broken into, his guns were stolen, and he was beaten to death. Happened last October and it never was solved. Now it looks like Hightower may have put Jacko up to it, because we found one of McElwain's rifles in Hightower's house, and I've had it on my stolen list ever since the sheriff at Columbia sent out the bulletin three months ago."

"What was the victim's name?"

"Tom McElwain." He shook his head. "I knew Jacko was a bastard but not that much of one."

"Have you talked to the people in Columbia?"

"No. I'll call them later to tell them what we found. But right now I'd just like to nail down whoever killed Jacko Reilly and Clovis Hightower. That would wrap the whole thing up."

"Maybe you will," I said, shook hands with him again, and watched him get back into the Bronco.

When he was gone I went back into the house.

McElwain. Where had I heard that name?

I looked in my notebook and there it was: A McElwain had bought the two hundred acres in the hills above Carter Crossing from Jim Bowie in 1833. Of course, there might be a lot of McElwains in these parts but it seemed a coincidence worth noting.

I looked at my watch. What would it cost me to drive up to Columbia and talk to a few people? I still had my credentials and Jeff hadn't explicitly ordered me off the case.

And if I was headed up in that direction, there was something else I wanted to check out at a certain estate in the area.

At just after eight I pulled into the judge's driveway. Tally Galt's Saturn was there and I was glad there were no other cars. I walked over to it, inspected the mirror on the right side, where it had scraped against something, and then started back for my vehicle. But as I walked across the drive I saw someone coming toward me on horseback, from the field behind the house. I waited, hands in the pockets of my jacket, as the horse and rider drew slowly nearer, coming toward me on the other side of the white board fence. At first I thought it was a man, but there was something in the form itself, and I realized the rider was Tally Galt.

I walked over to the fence to wait but she was taking her time.

"Beautiful horse," I said as she approached, nodding at the chestnut with a star on its forehead.

"Two years old," she said. "His name is Crash. Ironic name considering that he's the gentlest horse we own."

"Up early," I said.

"Arlo likes to sleep late," she said. "But I like to be up at first light. Comes from a country upbringing."

She reached down to pat the horse's neck. "Was it Arlo you came to see or me?"

"Actually it was your car."

"Really." She patted the horse again, her eyes on its neck, as if she were blocking me out. "All the way out here on a weekend to see a car?"

"Actually, I'm on my way somewhere else but this seemed like a good time to stop."

"Did it? All right, I'm listening."

"I was up at Jeff Scully's cabin just now," I said. "I saw some paint on the gatepost that matched that scrape on your mirror." I nodded my head at her car. "The other day when somebody shot at Luther and me they were in a hurry to get away afterward."

"I've had that scratch on my car for a long time."

"I don't think so. I figure you just haven't had a chance to get it fixed. And you knew the sheriff wasn't going to press the issue so there wasn't any hurry."

"Is that what you think?" Her voice was toneless and her eyes held my own.

"Yes. I don't know why you were up there. Maybe you forgot something and just happened to be there when we came along. You weren't really trying to shoot anybody, were you? You were probably shooting up in the air. You just didn't aim high enough."

"If I wanted to shoot you, you'd be dead," she said coldly.

"Anyway, Jeff told me he was seeing someone but he didn't want to talk about it. I thought it was a younger woman at first, but putting it all together I figure it was you."

"You'll never prove a thing."

"I don't need to. It's not a crime—except the shooting and I figure that was an accident. It was, wasn't it?"

"Do you have a recorder?"

"No."

Her head dipped slightly in acknowledgment. "My foot slipped on the gravel. When I saw Luther fall down I guess I panicked. Are you going to report it?"

"No, Luther's okay. I'm not interested in what you or Jeff

Scully do after hours. I'm more interested in where you were yesterday morning."

"Yesterday morning? Why?"

"Were you with Jeff?"

"Mr. Graham, this conversation is becoming distasteful."

"I'm sorry. I understand it might be."

"How could you *possibly* understand?" she said, looking past me then at the fields beyond. "Look around you: What do you see? Galt land, Galt horses, Galt cattle, Galt women. Do you see that Brahma bull in the field out there? That's Buster. Arlo bought him at auction in Baton Rouge for twenty thousand dollars. It's his prize possession. He has an old Colt pistol, too, one of the first they ever made. It's worth thousands. But he didn't buy it for an investment. He just likes to hold it because it's his. I married Arlo after his first wife got tired of being a part of his collection. I took her place. And my money took the place of the money he'd spent."

I waited.

"But I don't have to explain myself to you," she said, shifting slightly in the saddle, and for a second I thought she'd lost her balance, but then she recovered. "You have no business prying into my private life. If Arlo knew . . ."

"If Arlo knew he'd what? Or does he already suspect?"

She glared at me and I thought for a second she was going to bolt, but she kept herself under control.

"What the hell do you want? You see all this, you see *me*. I'm human, I'm not some butterfly on somebody's collection board. What right do you have to judge me?"

"I'm not judging you. I'm just saying Jeff Scully's a decent man, who worked like hell to get where he is, and never let up enough to enjoy the friendship of women. Now I think he's in over his head and I hate to see it ruin him."

"And I'm a man-ruiner? I'm going to ruin your poor, helpless little friend the sheriff?"

"I don't know, because I don't really know you. I just know Jeff."

"Do you? Get out of here, Mr. Graham, and don't come back."

I nodded. "However you want to play it, Mrs. Galt."

\*    \*    \*

I took the long way to Columbia, swinging out wide into the floodplain and then coming in from the northeast and crossing the old bridge into town. It was sixty miles going this way but I wasn't in any hurry.

Once at the courthouse, I found the sheriff's office and asked to see the detective who'd handled the McElwain murder. Two minutes later a tall man with gray hair, glasses, and a lumberjack shirt came out to the counter and introduced himself as Chief Deputy Forbes.

I told him my name and said I'd been asked to come to Columbia by the sheriff of Cane River Parish. Forbes gave me an appraising look.

"You got identification?"

I showed him the identification card and badge.

"I'm a Cane River deputy sheriff," I said, swallowing hard.

Forbes picked up the ID card, read it, looked at me, and then examined the badge. Finally, he put it down.

"So you are." He leaned over the counter. "I heard your sheriff's got his hands full down there."

"It's not as bad as it sounds," I told him. "Now about McElwain."

"Burglary that turned into a murder," the chief deputy drawled. "Screwed up from the get-go. Old man didn't have nothing worth stealing, much less killing for."

"Can I get a copy of the report?"

"Sure." His eyes narrowed. "But you don't mind telling me why, do you? If you got something on this, we'd like to know."

I told him about Jacko's murder and the killing of Clovis Hightower.

"Damn." He was already delving through a stack of papers on his desk. He brought out a circular and shoved it across the counter. I saw a list of guns, knives, and serial numbers.

"How did you get the list?" I asked.

"McElwain's nephew gave it to us. The nephew's the one that found him. Only relative."

"No clues?" I asked.

"Clues?" The deputy screwed up his face. "You mean evidence?"

"Right, evidence."

"No. Figure there must've been a couple of 'em. Real nasty bastards, too. They trussed up old Tom McElwain and beat him until he was almost dead. Then they left him in his own blood."

He went to a filing cabinet and came back with a folder. "I'll make a copy of this for you."

Five minutes later he handed me a new folder of papers.

"You think whoever killed this Reilly fellow killed McElwain?" he asked.

"I wouldn't be surprised. Where can I find this nephew?"

"Charlie?" Forbes laughed. "Probably still in bed. Working ain't his strong point. Do you know where the old drive-in used to be in Grayson?"

"More or less."

"It's a street back, wood frame house with a Galaxie on blocks in the side yard. He's been working on that damn car for two years. I guarantee you won't miss it."

He was right. As I got out a small spotted dog came racing up to yap at me. A radio was blasting loud music from the side of the house and I saw a car on blocks, under a hickory tree whose overhanging branch had been converted into a derrick for a pulley and chain. There, bent over the open hood, was a man in camouflage hunter's garb and a green hunter's jacket.

"Hey," he yelled when he saw me. "Come here."

I walked toward him and as I approached I saw he had a wrench on one of the motor mounts.

"You got a metric wrench?" he demanded in a loud voice.

"Sorry," I said.

"What you say?"

"I said I don't have one," I yelled over the radio.

"Oh." He looked back down at the engine and rubbed a greasy hand across his forehead. In his late thirties, he was already nearly bald.

"Some jack-leg rebuilt the motor couple years ago and used metric bolts when he put it back. Bad idea. Now I got to go down to Wal-Mart and get a new wrench."

I waited.

"You selling something?" he asked.

"Not me," I said. "I'm a sheriff's deputy."

"What?" He straightened up slowly.

"From Cane River Parish," I said. "I came to ask you about your uncle."

"My uncle?"

I told him about Jacko's murder and then about Hightower's. "They found some of your uncle's guns in Hightower's house."

Charlie McElwain wiped his nose with the back of his hand and squinted over at me.

"So the ones who done it are dead?" he asked.

"Two of them, I figure. But there's at least one left."

He nodded and bent back over the engine. "Hey, hold this."

I moved over beside him.

"Take this wrench and hold it here while I twist."

I took the wrench, fitted it around the nut, and held it while he applied pressure to the bolt head.

"Piece of shit bolt," he said and wiped his hands on a rag.

"Can you tell me about your uncle's murder?" I asked.

"What?"

I gestured for him to turn down the radio and he complied.

"Your uncle's death," I said.

"What about it?"

"Tell me what happened."

He stepped back from the car and spat on the ground.

"Somebody killed him. I come in and he was laying on the floor, beat to shit, everything all pulled out and all over the place. That's all there was to it." He shrugged. "They was from out of town."

"How do you know?"

"Shitfire, man, ever'body in town knew Uncle Tom wasn't worth nothing. Anyhow, he used to keep his money buried in the yard, under this tree. Ever'body knew that. Anybody from around here would've dug under this tree first, but they didn't. All fifty dollars was right where he buried it."

"But they took some guns . . ."

"A Winchester shotgun, a .22 rifle, a lock box."

"A lock box?"

"That's right."

"Do you know what was in it?"

He shrugged. "Couple of old coins and pieces of coins he said were Spanish or Mexican. A couple of old papers. A gold wristwatch, I guess belonged to his daddy or somebody. A picture of him with some girl when he was young. And a butcher knife and a pistol."

"A butcher knife and a pistol?"

"Yeah. One of them little .22 Derringers without no trigger guard, cast metal with aluminum barrel insets. Cheap crap like they used to send here from Europe a few years ago. I figured he kept the gun and the knife to protect the rest of the junk in the box. If the gun hung fire, which I wouldn't be surprised if it would, he'd cut 'em with the knife!" He laughed at the joke. "Whole business pissed me off."

"Because they killed your uncle."

"Hell, no. Uncle Tom was a mean son-of-a-bitch with battery acid for blood. But he was gonna leave me the Winchester."

"And you didn't see anything?"

"Just Uncle Tom. I was, well, you might kinda say, drunk that day."

I eyed the stack of beer cans on the other side of the hickory tree. No further explanation needed.

"Look, you think you can get that shotgun back?" he asked suddenly.

"Why?"

" 'Cause this ain't worth a shit," he said, throwing the wrench down on the ground and sniffing. "This house, this land, ever'thing here he left me. Ain't none of it worth a shit."

"Tough," I agreed.

I started away, but he called after me: "You find that Winchester, you let me know. You can keep the rifle and the Derringer."

# ≡ TWENTY

I came back the shorter way, driving down the east side of the river, along the floodplain, and then crossing on the ferry at Drayton, to skirt the hills, on my right. Somewhere around Paul's Creek I picked up a sheriff's cruiser, which lolled behind me for a few miles and then dropped away, gone, I supposed, down one of the side roads.

Just before Lordsport I called my home number on the cell phone but no one answered. It was midmorning and Pepper could be any of a number of places—exercising, grading papers at the university, or even visiting Sam—so I left a message, saying I'd be home in three hours and that this time I meant it.

As I came into town, arcing up through the hills and then down again, I thought of stopping by the courthouse and then remembered that it was Saturday and Jeff probably wouldn't be there. I wondered if Tally Galt had called him and, if she had, what his reaction would be. Just as well if I didn't talk to him just yet.

I headed for the camp to get a few things and this time I saw a sheriff's car parked just off the road, before the turn-in. As I passed, the deputy kept his head down as if he was reading something, and I swung onto the gravel drive and pulled in beside the house.

Halfway out of the car I stopped. Something felt wrong. I scanned the windows. Had I left the inside lights on or off? The main room was lit and I realized the shades were all up.

Then I relaxed: Alice Mae had a key and she might be inside tidying things up. If so, it had been a long walk for her, because I didn't see the truck. Maybe it was broken down. I knew she'd come to work afoot if necessary just to make up for Luther's misdemeanors.

I went up the steps, saw the front door was open, and stepped inside.

"Alice Mae?"

Then I froze. The room was deserted but the furniture was upended and dishes had been pulled out of the cabinets and littered the floor. I stepped across the shards, eyes on the hallway.

"Alice Mae?"

A groan issued from one of the bedrooms.

I hurried into the hallway and stopped in the doorway to the main bedroom, where I'd slept last night.

Alice Mae Dupree lay on the bed, eyes half open, with only her long hair to hide her nakedness. As I watched she turned her head to one side and groaned again.

I rushed to the bed and bent over her. "What happened? Are you all right?"

Another groan. I was reaching for the blanket, which had been thrown on the floor, when I heard the screeching of tires outside and heard doors opening and feet racing on the gravel. The front door crashed open and as I turned toward the hallway a deputy burst into the room.

"Freeze," he commanded. "Put your hands up and turn around, real slow."

I realized as he cuffed me that he was the same deputy who'd escorted me to Judge Galt's place.

"Look, I just got here," I said. "I passed you on the road. I—"

"Shut up," he commanded, shoving me into the hallway and prodding me out into the living room, where I saw three other men, one in a deputy's uniform and two in plainclothes.

"Caught him in the act," he said. "Somebody better get Doc Carraway. Looks like the Dupree girl's been beat up and raped."

"This is ridiculous," I said. "Reach in my shirt pocket.

You'll find a deputy's commission, signed by the sheriff, and a badge. I just got here, and if this man didn't see me pass by two minutes ago he has his head up his ass."

Something shoved me from behind and I hit one wall. The other men looked away, as if embarrassed. One of them was already talking on his portable radio and I heard him saying something about a doctor and getting an ambulance.

"Take him out and sit his ass in the car," the deputy behind me said. "I figure if we search this place real good we may find some party powder."

"I want a lawyer," I said.

"I bet you do," the deputy said and one of the others smirked.

He led me outside, put me in the back of his cruiser, and shut the door. I was still trying to make sense of it when a white Forerunner pulled up behind the other cars and Chaney Reilly got out. He walked past me as if I didn't exist and went into the house.

Now I understood.

They took me to the courthouse, hustling me through the basement door directly into the sheriff's office. They uncuffed my hands, but before I could take it as a hopeful sign, they cuffed them in front of me and sat me in a chair in a small room with green cinder block walls and left me by myself. I smelled disinfectant and wondered how many times they'd had to clean up after incontinent prisoners. My watch told me it was after one when the door finally opened and Jeff came in, followed by Ross Flynn. Jeff wore jeans and a windbreaker, and Flynn was dressed in camos and boots and I figured they'd gotten him off a hunt, which accounted for the sour look on his face.

"I'm glad to see you," I said as Jeff came in. "How about getting these cuffs off?"

"How about you tell us what happened first?" Jeff said. "And you know you're entitled to a lawyer."

"I asked for one, damn it, but your men out there wouldn't listen."

"Just following procedures," Jeff said, his face deadpan. "You want a phone so you can call your lawyer now?"

"No, not now that you're here, I just wanted to get those monkeys off my ass. This is a put-up job. Didn't you see Chaney Reilly out there?"

The sheriff and D.A. exchanged looks.

"Chaney Reilly isn't out there," Ross Flynn said, his voice raspy. "Now listen: I got other things to do, but since they called me in, I'll lay it out for you. The sheriff's office got a call that somebody heard screams from the archaeology camp. When the first unit responded they found you leaning over Alice Mae Dupree, who was naked on the bed, and half conscious. Blood tests are being done but the best bet is that she was drugged. Maybe that date rape drug. And some white powder was found at the camp. That's the long and the short. If we charge you, it'll be with attempted rape. If the tests show she had intercourse, it'll be rape. If you want to make a statement we'll listen."

I half rose from the chair. "This is insane. Jeff, what is this? Tell him this is crap. Your deputy out there saw me turn into the camp. He didn't answer the damn call—he was waiting for me to get there. I was set up. Besides, a blood test will prove I'm innocent."

Jeff stared at me, his face giving away nothing.

"Your credentials as a deputy of this parish are revoked," he said. "Effective immediately. Until the district attorney decides what to do, you'll be held, and if you're charged, I think Judge Galt is the duty judge this weekend. I'll see if he wants to order a blood test. May take a while to get the results, though."

I kept listening for some indication that this was a joke but his voice was level, and I even thought I detected a hint of anger.

"Jeff, you don't believe this?"

He said nothing, just stood there, arms crossed.

"I think I want to call my lawyer now," I said.

I made a long distance call to Stanley Kirby, AKA Dogbite, in Baton Rouge. If I was lucky, the rain had reached Baton Rouge last night and made it too wet for golf, but you could never tell. I listened to the fourth ring and was about to give up when I heard his voice on the other end.

"Stan, this is Alan. I need your help."

"If it's a traffic ticket, pay it. I have a recital to go to."

"Listen, Stan, this is serious. They're saying I raped a girl."

"I thought you were tight with Pepper these days. Why would you want to go and do that?"

"Damn it, Stan, I didn't. It's phony. I need to get out of here."

"That could be hard. Jeez, Alan, why couldn't it just be something like drunk driving?"

"Stan, this is life or death."

"For me, if I don't make it to my daughter's recital. Actually, she's pretty good. Have you ever really listened to the French horn?"

"Stanley . . ."

"Okay, who's the ADA? Have they assigned one?"

"ADA? The D.A. himself is handling this."

"No way. He hasn't handled a case since Noah started his zoo. Wait a minute . . . Where the hell are you?"

I told him and held the phone away from my ear as he swore.

"Cane River effing parish? That's the asshole of beyond. I'm not going up there. That's one of those country places where they make it up as they go along. Look, you'd do better to get a local lawyer."

"I don't know any local lawyers."

"Well, there was a fellow named Quigly, over in Simmsburg. He might . . . No, he got disbarred over that vote-buying business. Well, hell, I dunno."

"Stanley . . ."

"I'll see what I can do. Were you going with this girl?"

"She was the cook, damn it."

"Oh, Alan . . ."

"Get me out of here."

"I'll be in touch."

I didn't like the sound of that but there wasn't anything I could do. They took away the phone and left me in the little green room for the rest of the day and I wondered what was going on. The deputy who brought me a tuna sandwich for lunch wasn't informative, just left the sandwich on a paper plate with a soft drink in a paper cup and went out again.

Just after six another deputy opened the door and handed me an orange jumpsuit. "Put this on and hand out your clothes," he said.

My heart sank.

"Has anybody called for me?" I asked.

"Quiet as a graveyard," the man said, waiting. He watched me strip and don the jumpsuit with CPP on the back for Cane River Parish Prison.

"You'll get your stuff back when you leave here," he said, and I tried to tell myself it was a good sign, because he was broaching the possibility. "Come on, time to take some pictures."

"Pictures?"

"Pictures and fingerprints."

I followed him to a camera and a background. He turned on a bright light and handed me a menu board.

"This is ridic—" I began and realized he'd already taken the picture. He asked me to turn profile and I did so: I never realized before how being stripped of one's dignity and clothing also stripped away the will to resist.

"Now we're gonna have to find a safe place for you," he said, pointing toward the hallway. "Don't want to put you too close to Luther, on account of what you did to his daughter. But I think we got a free cell on the end."

He led me through a big steel door and into a corridor with cells on either side. Some of the cells were occupied and faces looked up in curiosity as we passed. I didn't know any of the faces until we got to the last occupied cell and saw him.

"Mr. Graham?" Luther cried, his knuckles white as he grabbed the bars. "It ain't true what they say, is it? You didn't do what they say?"

"No, Luther, I didn't."

We reached a cell at the end and I was glad to see it was empty.

"Don't pay no attention to Luther," the deputy said. "Still, you got to understand how he feels." He shut the door behind me. "You know, this is a first since I been here."

"What is?"

"We ain't never locked up a geologist before."

"I'm an archaeologist."

"Whatever. Sweet dreams. If you have trouble going to sleep, try counting dinosaurs." He laughed gently at his joke and walked away.

It wasn't one of the better nights of my life. After a supper of corn bread, red beans, and a couple of boiled wieners, the jailers left us alone. One of the inmates decided to audition for the Grand Old Opry but his musical talents were unappreciated by the others, who screamed and stomped their feet until the deputy on duty came and told him to shut up. There was another prisoner, fortunately at the other end of the corridor, who let out random howls, and drew admonitions to shut up until he finally went to sleep. The one thing I didn't hear, which both gratified and disturbed me, was anything further from Luther Dupree.

I settled down to the hard cot and tried to muster some self-control. I was as scared as I'd ever been. It wasn't just the momentary physical fear of death or injury, where you could lash out with at least a prayer of altering your situation: This was the kind of fear that comes from isolation and with it, helplessness. The kind of fear that grows because you have time to reflect, the kind of fear that increases every time you open your eyes and see that the stone walls and the bars and the Lysol smell and the dim glow of the neon bulbs in the center of the corridor are all still there and this isn't a dream.

It wasn't cold in the cellblock but I was shaking.

The only way to make it stop was to figure out exactly what had happened and why, and then maybe, just maybe, I'd be able to develop a plan.

It was all I had.

And, of course, it had been the work of Tally Galt. I'd scared her and she'd flown into action. The question was determining the chain: If she'd called Jeff, then it didn't explain Chaney Reilly's being on the scene, because he and Jeff were political enemies. So, unknown to Jeff, she'd probably called

Reilly. Which meant that not only was she hiding her affair with Jeff from her husband, but also her dealings with her husband's political foe. It sounded like good ammunition to use against her but it was only my word. They had the girl and I had no doubt that chemical tests would show she'd been drugged. They'd find the same kind of drugs in my Blazer, conveniently put there by one of the deputies who'd made a deal to stay on after Chaney Reilly got back in. Alice Mae, never a paragon of mental acuity on her best days, would be bluffed, threatened, and confused into saying whatever they wanted to hear. On cross-examination she might not hold up and the whole case might head south. But men had been convicted on less, especially in country towns, and besides, they didn't necessarily need a conviction: All they needed was enough smoke to get me out of the way. Ross Flynn, still an enigma to me, could impanel a grand jury and get an indictment without any trouble, since I wouldn't be able to cross-examine witnesses and have a lawyer in the grand jury room. Even if the indictment were dismissed months later, it would be an ugly cloud over my head, and my professional reputation would be ruined. The Department of Transportation and Development, hearing about it, would probably issue a stop work order on our contract and we'd never get any projects from them again.

Thinking about it didn't do much to abate my shakes.

It was Jeff's role in all this that puzzled me the most.

What had turned him suddenly against me? Was it Tally? Or was his stance a political one, born of the need to survive? If so, was he willing to sacrifice me for expediency's sake? Was he really a craftier person than the bluff, open Thomas Jefferson Scully who'd been my employee ten years ago? I recalled Tally Galt's ironic laugh when I'd told her I knew what kind of a person Jeff Scully was. She was letting me know how little I really knew him these days, and I was beginning to see she was right.

I lay back on the bunk finally and drew the thin cotton blanket over me. Things seemed bad now because it was night but I knew they'd seem better tomorrow. Or would they? I wondered what Pepper was doing now. Surely she'd made calls when I hadn't come home, been told what had happened. And she would have appeared at Dogbite's door. Nobody faced with a determined Pepper could refuse her, and she and Dogbite might be outside at this very minute, demanding a writ or whatever it took. After all, Pepper would know any kind of charges against me, especially rape, would have been trumped up. Wouldn't she? It was no use speculating, because no matter what *might* be going on outside, the fact was that I was *inside* right now.

I closed my eyes and tried to sleep, but even though the hullabaloo in the other cells had been replaced by snores and snorts, I couldn't put aside the mixture of shame, anger, and fear. Just being here made me feel guilty, as if I deserved it somehow, or else why would I be undergoing this?

Then I tried to put aside the immediate problems and think back to a hundred sixty years ago. Because I was sure now that was where the real answer lay. I tried to visualize Jim Bowie, the hero of a hundred cheap novels and films, riding into town one day on his way to Mexico, dressed in buckskins, two pistols in his belt and the big knife in a scabbard at his side. At least that was the way he was represented in fiction. But from what I'd read about him in the last few days, the heroic figure of legend didn't jibe with history. He'd been a brave man, surely, but his bravery was often a form of recklessness, as if he hadn't thought things through. He'd been ambitious, but without the patience to carry a plan to completion. Instead, he'd looked for shortcuts. Even his land dealings had suffered from a failure in thoroughness, for the Spanish grants on which the titles were supposedly based had been so clumsily forged that their fraudulence was self-evident. Patriot, knife fighter, hero—none so aptly described him as the simple word *adventurer*. And after a lifetime of adventures that he had lived through due to his brashness, he'd at last met the final one at the hands of Santa Anna's army.

He'd bought the land adjacent to Jeff's cabin in the hills, legally or illegally—it probably didn't matter now. On his way out of Louisiana for his fatal rendezvous in Texas, he'd sold it to a man named McElwain, and it had stayed in the McElwain family for thirty years. Then, a hundred thirty years after the McElwains had lost the land at a tax sale, another man named McElwain, living forty miles away, had been brutally beaten to death, and a catchall of his property had been taken. Some of the property had turned up in the house of another murdered man, a few months later. And a fragment of coin that came from old Tom McElwain's lock box was found with the corpse of the man who'd probably headed the break-in gang.

But what among Tom McElwain's possessions could have been so valuable that it was worth murdering for? What item or items might connect McElwain to the man his distant ancestor had bought some land from over a century before?

The stolen guns couldn't have been the object of the burglary. That left the lock box. I tried to remember what it had held. A picture of Tom McElwain with a young woman. Was the object some kind of blackmail? It seemed unlikely. An old gold man's wristwatch. It didn't seem the kind of thing to kill for on the face of it, but you could never tell and I wasn't an expert on watches. Some silver coins. Well, they'd wanted the coins, all right, because part of one had showed up with Jacko. I was assuming all the coins were Spanish pesos, but I'd only gotten that from Tom McElwain's nephew, who probably knew as much about coins as he did about fine wines. If one of the coins was a rarity, such as a Brasher doubloon, that would be plenty of motive for murder, and Clovis Hightower was the kind of man I could see coveting a rare doubloon. Jim Bowie had been a treasure hunter—could he have won a valuable coin in one of his famous card games in Natchez Under the Hill? Maybe used the coin again in a card game with the original McElwain? It made sense, except that if Hightower had set up the burglary, it was an aberration for him to have used a bunch of bunglers like Jacko and his crowd.

What else was in the box, then?

Some papers. That was all young McElwain had said. Papers. That could mean anything. Deeds, a will, a notarized statement, a birth certificate. Even a treasure map.

Had he been holding back a map to the place on the old McElwain property where Bowie had buried some Mexican silver? A treasure trove was a pretty good motive for murder.

Yet no map had been found in Hightower's possessions, or if it had, it hadn't been recognized. But that didn't mean anything: Jeff had only been there for the initial search. If the paper had been especially valuable, Hightower probably would have put it in a safety deposit box, and maybe it was there still, to be found when the box was opened under court order. Or maybe he had his own hiding place somewhere on his property. If that were the case, it might never be found. Or, most likely of all, maybe Jacko and his henchmen had decided not to give the map to Hightower and had held it out for themselves. Maybe that was why Hightower, too, had been killed. But if that were the case, the map might be lost, because Jacko's crowd didn't keep things in deposit boxes. They hid them under mattresses or in tin cans buried in the backyard. And old papers didn't stand up well to that kind of abuse.

The only other two items in the lock box had been a butcher knife and a cheap import Derringer, and there, alone, I was willing to take the younger McElwain at his word when he'd said his uncle had put the pistol in to protect the other things and the knife in case the pistol didn't work.

Eventually I went to sleep. I even dreamed, though the dreams were even more confused than usual. In one I saw Jim Bowie, standing on the famous sandbar, blood streaming from the knife and bullet wounds in his chest and shoulder. Sun glinted on something in his hand and I saw it close up, the famous blade, gleaming Damascus steel a foot long, with a guard of brass, as it began its deadly work, welded to its master's hand . . . Except that when I looked, the face of the man with the knife was not that of Jim Bowie, whose portrait I'd seen in books, but, rather, that of the man I'd seen a few days ago in a sheriff's office photo—Jacko Reilly. And I was the man on the ground, who'd just been savaged by the blade. I realized then I was dying and yet I felt nothing, and I decided that dying must be an illusion, and soon now I would awaken from the dream.

Until I saw Luther Dupree standing over me, my cell door open, his eyes staring down at me on the bunk. As I watched he hawked and spat, and the gob landed on my chest, striking like a bullet, and I screamed soundlessly, wondering why I couldn't make any noise, summon any help, until I saw the bubbles around me and felt the current cold as death itself and far above me saw the tiny blur of light that was the surface, dimming now even as my lungs burned for air . . .

Someone was shaking me and I opened my eyes.

"Get up," the deputy was saying and I roused myself to a position on the edge of the bunk. My mouth was sour and my eyes burned. I didn't know if it was still night, but I pulled myself upright and followed him out, down the corridor. As I passed Luther's cell he rushed forward.

"Mr. Alan, listen, I knowed you didn't have nothing to do with what happened . . ."

I ignored him, just shuffled forward like an inmate being led the last mile, except that when the big door opened I didn't see a gallows but Ross Flynn, standing with his arms crossed. He regarded me for a long second and stroked his drooping mustache. "All right, you can get your things. My office isn't going to prosecute the charges. But if you're smart, you'll go home right now."

Before I could say anything the deputy led me back to the green room, where my clothes sat on the table. "Just leave the jumpsuit there," he said.

When I'd dressed, the same deputy handed me my keys.

"It's seven-thirty. You can get breakfast at Brocato's in Ferriday. That's in Concordia Parish. In case you don't know how to get there, one of our cars will follow you to the parish line. Have a good day, now."

As we walked out into the hallway I noticed the display case on the right, the one that had been empty before, now held the big Bowie knife that had been stolen.

"When did you get your knife back?" I asked.

"Yesterday," the deputy said. "The sheriff brought it back from Mississippi. They found it in the house of that antique dealer that got murdered."

# ▰TWENTY-ONE

The cruiser followed me all the way to the Tensas River, at Guyton, which was the parish line. And at the parish line, to my surprise, a Concordia Parish cruiser took over.

Ross Flynn's work, I told myself: The two parishes were his district. Also Judge Galt's.

I kept going at Ferriday, and it wasn't until I was on the four-lane stretch into Vidalia, with the bridge to Natchez in sight, that I called home on the cell phone. To my relief Pepper picked up immediately.

"I meant to come home but there was a little complication," I explained. "Did Dogbite call you?"

"Yes, he did, Alan, and I was frankly, well, shattered. To find out you'd been charged with, well, with molesting that poor young woman, after all we had together, and I thought I knew you . . ."

"It isn't funny, damn it."

"I didn't laugh when I heard it. How do you think it feels to learn that the man you've given your most intimate secrets, shared a bed with, loved, has this, this hidden vice, this—"

"Enough. You could at least have come up."

"Why? Jeff said it was under control."

"*Jeff?*"

"Sure. He said it was a put-up job by Chaney Reilly and Jeff was using it to smoke out the disloyal people in his own department. He figured they were doing it to embarrass him and he couldn't intervene directly on your behalf so the best thing he could do was let you sit in jail overnight while he talked to the D.A. He said the D.A. knew it was all a sham. Besides . . ."

"Yes?"

"Jeff said you'd been taking that badge he gave you a little too seriously and he wanted to teach you a lesson."

"Did he? And did he say anything about a woman named Tally Galt?"

"The judge's wife?"

I told her about my conversation with Tally. "I don't think Jeff's being completely honest," I said. "I think he doesn't dare get too close to me because he's afraid his affair with Tally will come out."

"Well, he's your friend. Or was."

"Yeah." I drove on for a while. "So how's Sam?"

"Asking for you. When I told him you were in jail he said he'd trade his hospital room for your cell."

"Sounds like he's better."

"We'll see."

"You sound doubtful. Is there something you aren't telling me?"

"Well, they'd kind of hoped he'd bounce back a little faster, but he's still in bed, won't let 'em raise him up at all. And he gets a little confused sometimes."

I didn't like the sound of it. "I'll be back soon," I said, as if my being there would change things.

"I hope so," she said. "Seems like you get in trouble when there's nobody to look after you."

"Yeah." I was rising up onto the bridge now and the Mississippi was below. The phone transmission changed to static as the bridge girders flew past. I sneaked a look down at the river, wondering if any of the Vidalia sandbar was still left.

"Are you still there?" Pepper asked as I came down the other side, into Mississippi.

"Yeah. I was just going over the bridge."

"Something wrong?"

"I was thinking about something. You remember the display case that was burgled in the courthouse?"

"You told me about it."

"Somebody stole some old artifacts connected with the Morgan House hotel. One of them was a replica Bowie knife."

"And?"

"When they let me out just now I passed by the case and the knife was back. The deputy told me it was with Hightower's things."

"So?"

"Why would anybody steal a replica knife worth twenty bucks?"

"Are you sure it's a replica?"

"Why?"

"I've been doing some reading about Bowie and the Bowie knives. Did you know it was really invented by Jim's brother, Rezin? He got a blacksmith over in Avoyelles Parish to make it for him. It was just a plain butcher knife, nothing special—a wood handle with a nine-inch blade, one to two inches wide. Rezin used it for hunting but when Jim got at cross purposes with Major Wright and his faction, Rezin insisted Jim should have it to protect himself, and that's the knife Jim used in the sandbar fight in 1827, and the knife he always carried after that. But between 1830 and 1841, when he died, Rezin Bowie kept improving the design, and all kinds of blacksmiths and cutlers and surgical instrument makers got into the act. Some of the Bowies that were turned out on Rezin's design were pretty elaborate, Spanish notches in the blades, coffin-style handles as they were called, initials on silver plates in the handles. Did you know there was even a famous knifemaker in Baton Rouge at the time, a blacksmith named Daniel Searles? His shop was where the Centroplex is today. He made a Bowie knife to Rezin's special order. It was the first one with a guard on it and all the Bowie knifemakers after that adopted the design. So your display knife could really be *one* of the originals."

I shifted the phone to my other hand and pulled into a gas station on the right.

"Not exactly," I said, stopping beside one of the pump islands. "The maker is Western. It says so on the blade. If you look through my old chest in the attic you'll probably find one just like it. I bought it when I was about eighteen. They used to sell them in sporting goods stores. It's really a short sword, and it fits what everybody's idea of a Bowie knife should be. But old it ain't."

"So maybe it was stolen by mistake. It doesn't sound like Jacko's crew knew what they were doing."

"Yeah, by mistake." The words resonated in my memory. I told her what Lisa Reilly had told me, about how Jacko had been talking to someone on the phone the night before he disappeared; that there was some kind of argument; and that she'd heard Jacko say something about the wrong one.

"So maybe they were arguing about the courthouse knife," she said.

"Seems likely. Hightower would have recognized that it wasn't genuine."

"So it wouldn't have had anything to do with the McElwain killing."

"No." I reflected for a moment. They were close, but somehow the pieces didn't quite fit the holes . . .

"Well, maybe it'll make sense when you've gotten a chance to rest," she said.

"Yeah. Look, I've got to pump some gas now."

We signed off with expressions of mutual affection and I turned to the gas pump.

Home was less than two hours away. That was where I ought to be. It was where my duty lay. Sam was sick. I could do more good there than blundering around in a place where I was no longer wanted.

All at once I realized my head was aching. Probably hunger, I told myself. Shoney's was five minutes ahead, on the south side of town, on Highway 61, and its breakfast buffet would still be open. I might as well eat there. There was no way I'd ever figure this one out because no one was talking and the only people who might know the truth had dropped out of sight.

Miss Ethel and the odd recluse she'd befriended named Jeremiah.

The only reason for them to have vanished was that one or both of them had seen something. But nobody seemed to know where to look for them, and I almost had the sense that people were just as happy for them to stay in hiding.

What had Snuffy Stokes said? That Jeremiah had relatives in Winnfield or Tallulah? The two cities were in opposite directions, one sixty miles to the west, and the other at least that far to the north. Obviously, Stokes had no idea.

My head started pounding again. I went into the station to pay and picked up a small bottle of aspirins and a bottle of water. I went back out into the parking lot and started to open the aspirin bottle. And stopped . . .

All at once I remembered the medicine bottle Jeremiah Persons had shown me that day by the river, the medicine the doctor had prescribed for Jeremiah's headaches. I tried to visualize the label. It was from a chain discounter. Wal-Mart. That was it. The Wal-Mart in Winnfield . . . No, Winns*boro*. Of course. The first major town north of Carter Crossing, just twenty-five miles up Highway 15, in Franklin Parish . . .

I swallowed two aspirins with a gulp of water and climbed back into the Blazer. There was a map on the seat beside me.

As far as the deputies were concerned I was safely in Mississippi now, headed home. If I made a U-turn, crossed back into Louisiana, it would be just twenty minutes to Carter Crossing and ten minutes beyond that to the Franklin Parish line.

Maybe I should call Pepper, though. She'd try to talk me out of it, and I wasn't sure I didn't want her to succeed. Yes, at the very least I ought to give her a chance . . .

I reached back into the glove compartment for the cell phone and my hand touched something I hadn't noticed before. As I drew it out I recognized it immediately and my hand started to shake.

The credentials Jeff had handed me. He said he'd revoked them, but somehow they hadn't searched my vehicle. Or maybe they had and someone had replaced them where I'd see them when I left town.

Someone . . .

## TWENTY-TWO

I grabbed a bag of Trail Mix for breakfast and headed back over the bridge into Louisiana. This time I didn't see a police car the entire time, and fifty minutes later I was entering Winnsboro, a cotton center with a four-lane that hooked around the west side of town. I found the Wal-Mart on Highway 15, on the north outskirts, went to the pharmacy, and showed my deputy's badge.

"Did you fill a prescription in the last month for a man named Jeremiah Persons?"

The druggist went to his computer, input the name, and then came back to the counter.

"On January fifth. Motrin 500 milligrams. That's a formulation for arthritic pain. It's like regular Motrin except in a stronger dose."

"Do you have an address for Jeremiah Persons?" I asked.

He went back to the screen. "Yes, it's in Lordsport."

I tried to hide my disappointment.

"Do you have anybody named Persons in town?" I asked. "I understand he has kin here."

"Let me see." The fingers played on the keyboard again and he came back with a sheet of paper. "Tawanda Persons lives out on Highway 15, about a mile south of town, it looks like. That's the only Persons I have in the computer."

I took the paper. "Thanks."

"Is this Jeremiah wanted for something?"

"Just for questioning," I said.

He squinted over the counter: "Are you sure you're a deputy?"

"Don't I look like one?" I asked and left before he could answer.

The home of Tawanda Persons was a white frame house half a mile from the main road. It was hidden at the end of a gravel lane and I wouldn't have known it was there if I hadn't asked first at a house close to the highway. Even then, I had to show the badge to get the woman who came to the door to point out the way. And I was sure that by the time I was back to the Blazer she was already on the phone to people in the house at the end of the lane.

I was even more sure they'd been warned as I approached and saw a thin haze of dust over the lane, which did not end at the house itself, but seemed to stretch out into the fields beyond.

As I got out a hound rushed out to bark at me but when I raised my hand it slunk away, growling.

The house looked deserted but a thread of smoke from the brick chimney told me otherwise. I looked around the yard. There was a garden plot to one side with a scarecrow and a well with an iron pump handle. A couple of chickens pecked halfheartedly at the short winter grass and I suspected that there were more chickens nesting in the barn.

There was no car in the yard but plenty of tire tracks and a spot of oil on the hard ground.

I went up onto the porch, between a pair of rocking chairs, and knocked.

The weather had turned cooler during the night and I had my jacket zipped to my chin. I knew that if they wanted to play a waiting game they could probably wait me out.

I knocked again. Still no response.

With the woman in the house on the highway watching for me to leave, there was no way I could drive partway down the lane and wait for them to come back. And if I went as far as the highway, the woman in the first house would be watching to see if I tried to double back.

Good system. You could almost disappear out here.

The only thing to do was take the field road. It might wind around and eventually come out on the highway but I knew it was more likely it would dead-end in a field.

I followed the road to the end of the tree line and when I turned left I saw a white Chrysler, caught in a slough, its rear wheels spinning futilely.

I got out slowly and walked toward it, keeping well to the side as the rear wheels threw up a fine spray of mud.

"You're going to ruin your tires," I said, but the windows were up and she couldn't hear me, just kept trying to drive the car out of the ditch until she looked over, saw who I was, and then gave up.

I waited while she opened the door.

"Well, you don't have to just stand there, Dr. Graham," Ethel Crawford said. "Can't you see we're stuck in this hole?"

"I have a come-along," I said. "Just stay where you are to guide the wheel and I'll pull you onto the dry ground. Then we'll sit down and talk."

"Jeremiah got out at one of the hedge rows back there," she told me as we sat under the tree in her car, with the motor running to keep the heat flowing in. "He doesn't like commotion. Besides, it's really me you want to see, I imagine."

"I imagine," I said.

"When you wouldn't come up after I called you, and the deputy treated me like I was senile, I didn't know what to do. I had nowhere to go. I went to see Jeremiah and he told me he'd bring me here, to his mother's."

"He has family, then?"

"Oh, yes, but Jeremiah's independent. He likes to be alone. It's something he says happened as a result of the war."

"Vietnam?" I asked, and she nodded.

"They used to send him on missions in the jungle. I think he suffers from that stress business. Being around people for too long makes him nervous. But I guess I don't threaten him and I don't talk all the time when I'm with him so we get along fine."

"He's been hiding you."

She nodded. "I've been treated very well."

"But you can't stay here forever."

"No."

"There's still a killer at large." I told her about the murder of Clovis Hightower. "We need to stop it. Now."

"Well, it might never have gotten this far if people had listened to me to start with."

It was my turn to nod. "You're right. But I guess it isn't too late to start." I shifted in the seat to face her: "You found out something that frightened you. Maybe it's time to tell me what it was."

There was a long silence while she thought and finally her head gave a tiny dip of acknowledgment.

"It was that night, I think it was a Friday, after you left. I couldn't sleep so I got up. Sometimes I walk at night. Lordsport's a small town, you can do that at night without having to worry about getting robbed or worse."

I waited while she found the right words.

"It was later than I thought. After one. I bundled up and walked around the block and I didn't see a car pass. And I guess I was thinking about all that had happened and about finding the car with that Reilly boy in it and I just sort of naturally walked down past the courthouse and up and over the bridge."

I tried to visualize it, the plump, little librarian hurrying along the silent streets and then up, over the ancient structure with the skeletal girders, and the little bridge tender's box with black windows like hollow sockets . . .

"I stood in the middle of the bridge, looking down and trying to remember, but nothing came. Everything was quiet and all I heard was the water against the banks and the wind in the trees. Then I thought, 'Well, maybe I need to go down to the water's edge and look out from there. Maybe I'm in the wrong place.' I mean, the bridge is all iron and there are those that say metal can interfere with brain waves and I thought maybe I should go to where there wasn't any . . . metal, I mean."

I didn't say anything.

"So I walked to the end of the bridge, away from the town, and then I went down the little hill, to where you put the boat in the other day and I stood there for a minute. I was thinking about that night, driving back from Ferriday, and hearing that splash in the water, and how if I'd just had my head turned a little differently, well, maybe I'd have seen what it was and maybe that dead Reilly boy would have been found a little sooner. And I was thinking, too, that maybe whoever had killed him had been there that night, when I crossed, and that if I *had* seen and stopped, well, maybe it wouldn't have just been the Reilly boy who was murdered. It gave me the chills to think about and it was already a cold night."

She pursed her lips slightly, as if trying to repress the thought, and went on: "And it was while I was standing there, by the river, that I heard it."

"Heard what?" I asked.

"What sounded like a pebble rolling down the bank from under the bridge and falling into the water."

I tried to imagine it as she spoke, the old woman standing at the river's edge, the few lights from the town's street lamps dusting the far side of the water white, and then a sound from the blackness to her right.

"At first I thought it was an animal but it stopped as soon as I turned my head and I had the strangest feeling somebody was watching me. So I took a step toward it and called out to ask who was there."

She took a deep breath and I waited.

"When there wasn't any answer I decided to press the issue, you might say: I've dealt with too many children in the library to let somebody get away with bluffing me. So I said, 'I see you, come out of there this minute.' And that's when it happened."

"What happened?"

"Somebody came running at me out of the dark."

"Man or woman?"

"A man, I imagine. Tall and wearing a jacket, because it was cold. I couldn't see his face, but I knew he didn't mean me any good, so I turned and ran. I heard him right behind me but at the last second, right when I was sure he was going to catch me, he must've tripped on something and fallen because I heard a thump. Naturally, I didn't stop to help him. I just kept going to the road and then turned back and started across the bridge, toward town. But I'll never forget, when I got to the end of the bridge, I turned around, and there he was at the other end, standing there, almost like a scarecrow, staring at me."

"But you couldn't see his face."

"No. It's like I told you before, there was almost no light. About all I could see was his dark jacket, dark pants, and some kind of baseball cap, I think."

"Baseball cap," I said. "What color?"

"I don't know. Black, blue, brown . . . It was so dark and I just wanted to get out of there, because for all I knew he was coming after me, so I went to the sheriff's office and woke up the deputy and he told me to go home and said he'd send somebody to check it out but I don't think he ever did."

"And that's when you called the sheriff the next day," I said.

"Yes." She sighed. "But Jefferson didn't want to listen to the babbling of an old woman. And as for you, Mr. Graham . . ."

"I know," I said. "And we were both wrong."

She smiled with satisfaction.

"Yes. But I suppose one can't be right all the time."

"No, ma'am."

"And, naturally, since nobody wanted to believe me, I went to the only person I could rely on, Jeremiah, and he let me stay with his mother's family here in Winnsboro. They're lovely people and I'll never be able to repay their kindness."

I sat back against the seat, trying to put it together.

"I imagine the killer must've thought there was something still at the scene that could incriminate him," she said. "That's the only reason I can think of that he'd have gone back there."

"Makes sense," I agreed. "But we still don't know who it was."

"I'm very sorry. I simply didn't think it made sense to let him catch me." She sniffed.

"Of course not." I started to open the door and stopped: Something had flashed in the passenger side mirror and I tensed, letting my eyes wander down to the oval of polished glass. Slowly, a form appeared, not walking so much as gliding toward us, in a partial crouch, and after the initial shock I realized the form was that of Jeremiah Persons.

"We're about to have company," I said. "Jeremiah."

Miss Ethel gave a little cry of surprise. "Where?" She turned around slowly and her eyes widened in alarm.

"Jeremiah . . ."

But the black man was out of hearing, standing just off the right rear, as motionless as a stone.

The librarian opened her door and got out.

"Jeremiah, what's going on?"

I waited until she was out and then opened my own door and turned to face him.

The man a few feet from me wasn't Jeremiah Persons, or, at least, not the Jeremiah Persons I knew. His face was expressionless but there was something about his eye, a coldness, that I hadn't seen before, and it never wavered from my own. He'd frozen when I got out and I realized his stance was that of a hunter, halted a few feet from his prey. But most of all my attention was drawn to his hands: They were strong hands and the fingers were bent, like those of a strangler.

I had the distinct feeling that Jeremiah Persons had been sneaking toward us for the kill.

# ▰▰ TWENTY-THREE

"Jeremiah?" Ethel Crawford took a step toward him, and for an instant I thought he was going to spring. Then he relaxed and his hands fell back to his sides. His eye shifted, focused, and a frown clouded his face.

"You remember Dr. Graham," she said. "He came here to tell us how things were going in Lordsport."

Jeremiah nodded. "Yes, ma'am."

I walked over. "I traced you through the headache medicine you showed me. How are the headaches, by the way?"

"Okay."

"You get them often?"

"Pretty much. Ever since the war."

"Vietnam?"

"Yeah."

"You were in country."

"Yeah. LRRP, they called us. Long Range—"

"—Reconnaissance and Patrol," I said.

"You got to understand," he said. "I didn't know who you was. You come asking and I told Miss Ethel to take off. I bailed at the corner so I could catch up from behind, because I knew this old road wouldn't go much further. I didn't know you weren't the one who—"

"I understand," I said.

"But I'm glad it was you."

"Well, now that we're all together and glad about every-

thing, can we go back and sit down by the fire?" Miss Ethel
asked.

I stayed another half hour, long enough to have two cups of
hot coffee sweetened with honey, and listen to Jeremiah's
story. Unfortunately, he didn't have much to relate. He hadn't
seen anything when Jacko's car had gone into the river; all
he'd heard was the splash and he'd figured it was something
big, but when Miss Ethel had called down to him from the
bridge, he'd been willing to let her notify the authorities and
go on fishing. I started to ask him how a car could have rolled
down the embankment without his hearing the tires on the
shells or, for that matter, how he hadn't heard it coming along
the road above, and how it was he hadn't heard a door opening, since someone must've jumped out before the car went
into the water. But I didn't, because what he was thinking was
clear: With Miss Ethel on the scene there was no need to mix
into somebody else's trouble.

The situation the night the librarian had been chased was
similar.

"I was sleeping, I heard somebody give out a whoop and I
got up and went outside. By the time I got to the door all I
heard was footsteps, running."

"So what do you plan to do now?" Miss Ethel asked. "Turn
us in for leaving the scene of the crime?"

I exhaled and shook my head. "I think I'll go back to Baton
Rouge, which is where I started for this morning, anyway."

"What about us?"

"I'm the only person who knows you're up here. It might
be best for you to stay a little longer for the time being. If
that's all right with Jeremiah's mother."

The mother, an ancient, stooped woman in a checkered
dress, smiled. "Don't get to see my boy that often, anyway."

As I walked out onto the porch, Ethel caught me by the
arm.

"Do you know who did it?"

I shook my head again. "No."

"Well, keep looking. I'd like to get home in time for the
DAR meeting next week."

"Good luck."

*   *   *

This time when I called on the cell phone Pepper gave me hell. What did I mean by not coming straight home? Didn't I know she'd been worried sick? I should have gotten back two hours ago and when I didn't come, she'd called Jeff at home and told him that if he'd done anything to me she'd deal with him personally, and he'd been apologetic, denied all knowledge, and now look, she'd never been more embarrassed in her life.

I abased myself. "I had to nail down Miss Ethel and Jeremiah. I thought maybe they'd seen or heard something they'd forgotten to mention."

"And did they? No. Instead, you went right back where you'd been told not to go, meddled, stirred things up, and you're lucky you didn't get killed this time."

I sighed. She was starting to sound like a wife.

My God, what was I thinking?

"I'll be home in two hours," I said. "You can slap me around then."

"It's not funny," she said and hung up.

It was just after three when I walked into the house. She wasn't there. Instead, there was a handwritten note by the phone.

> *David called and wanted to know if the project's been shut down because he heard you'd been banned from the parish. He doesn't know whether to take the crew up there or not, and if he does, who's going to cook for them?*

All good questions, I admitted.
Then I saw the rest of the message.

> *I've gone on an outing with Ellsworth Hooker, who wanted me to look at some artifacts at a remote location.*

I slammed the telephone table with my fist.
Ellsworth Hooker! Captain Hook!

I was still staring at the note when the phone jangled.

"Yes?"

"Gotcha."

"Pepper? What in the—?"

"Figured I'd get your attention with that note. I had to run out to my office for something."

"That was unconscionable."

"Yeah. I loved it."

"I ought to—"

"What?"

"Nothing. Just get on home."

"Giving orders?"

*"Please."*

"Maybe."


That evening I saw Sam for the first time in days. He lay weak and pale on the blanket, with a worried Libby hovering on the other side of the bed.

"I thought you'd packed up and gone to Alaska," he said.

"I'm sorry." And I gave him an account of what had happened. "I don't know a lot more now than when I started."

Sam shifted his position slightly. "Seems to me you know a hell of a lot, starting with old Jim Bowie."

I took a seat in a chair beside the bed. "I don't know what that land business was about. Did Bowie buy the land to salt with silver and pretend it was worth more than it was? If he did, nobody bit. Of course, by then people had probably heard of his schemes, but you'd have thought he'd have hooked a sucker early on."

Sam grimaced. "You're forgetting he had family in that parish. The Bowies were well known. It isn't smart to crap where you eat."

It was Libby's turn to grimace.

"People around there would have known the Bowies pretty well," Sam said. "I don't think he would have salted that land. But in the early days, before much was known about geology, there was a notion that there was silver up in the hills, and in a lot of other places. Silver, gold, diamonds . . . He may have bought it because he really thought there might be wealth for the digging."

"And when there turned out not to be he wanted to unload the tract?"

"Something like that." Sam shifted again. "Damn, can't somebody crank this thing up? I can't sit up if this bed's going to stay flat."

Libby and I exchanged looks and she pushed the button, raising the head of the bed.

"That's better," Sam pronounced.

"Of course, he may have used the tract to bury his own silver," I offered.

"And sold it for a song afterward? Not by a long shot," Sam said. "Look, from what you told me before, the man was liquidating all his assets, heading to Texas. The land was just something to be gotten rid of." He coughed. "But he wouldn't have sold it for a song if he could've gotten silver or gold out of it. I'm afraid the Bowie legend is overblown, all because of that damn knife. But every hero has his mystical weapon, from King Arthur on down. Magical knife, magical man. It's one of the oldest themes in Western literature."

"I'm sure Alan remembers that lecture," Libby said gently.

"Well, he can hear it again."

"Okay, Jim Bowie wasn't quite the figure of legend," I said. "Where does that get us?"

"I don't know. You started this."

Libby and I looked at each other again.

"I think he's better," she said.

"I'm afraid so."

"Are you leaving?" Sam asked.

"For right now."

"Well, what are you going to do about that business?"

I shrugged. "I don't know."

"That seems pretty clear. I can't believe I taught you all those courses and you still can't use your head."

"You're sick. I'll come back later."

"Why bother? You aren't going to do any good here. Look, what's this case about? Jim Bowie, if you look at it from one angle. But what's it about when you look at the people who were murdered?"

"I don't know, Sam, but I'm sure you'll tell me."

He managed a nod. "Damn right. Okay, I'll make it simple: What started the thing? And don't tell me the Alamo. I mean, recently? It was the killing of this old man McElwain, right? And what got stolen from him?"

"Some guns and his lock box, and I've already figured it was something in the lock box they wanted."

"And something they could sell to this antiquarian, Hightower. Does that eliminate anything?"

"Probably the watch, the cheap Derringer, and the butcher knife. The coins . . ."

"Did Scully say they'd found any of the coins with Hightower?"

"No."

"Then he either didn't get them or disposed of them. But that misses the point, anyway."

"The point being?"

"What do the coins have to do with Bowie? I read about that San Saba business, the so-called lost mine, guarded by Indians: That wasn't a trove of peso coins. Besides, if these were Bowie's coins, there wasn't enough in the lock box to be worth fooling with."

"There was a photograph . . ."

"Forget that."

"And a paper. A map, maybe."

"Which, again, wasn't found with Hightower."

"He could have sold it, buried it, or put it in his safe deposit box."

Sam shook his white mane in frustration. "What did that woman say, Jacko's widow? About the wrong one?"

I repeated Lisa Reilly's words.

"Well, that's the key to the whole business, of course. You figure that out and you'll have it."

"Thanks, Sam."

As I went out I ran into his son, a wiry young man with Sam's smile but his mother's brown eyes.

"Any change?" he asked.

I nodded. "Oh, yes."

"And?" Concern clouded his face.

"I think he's almost ready to go home."

When I got back to the house Pepper was there. We looked at each other for a while before either of us spoke. Finally I said, "Sam wants you to treat me better."

"Then he's sicker than he looks."

"Actually, he's a lot better. I seem to have that effect on people."

"You'd better start peeling potatoes or you aren't going to get any supper."

"I peel potatoes very well," I said and headed for the kitchen. I let Digger in, and after apologizing to him for leaving him home this time, I washed my hands and went to the utensil drawer. I reached inside for the potato peeler, felt something sharp, and drew back my hand. "Damn."

"What now?" Pepper asked from behind me.

I drew out a carving knife. "Why did you put this in here? It's the wrong . . ."

"Well, what am I supposed to do, when you leave this place in a mess and go running off to—Alan . . . What is it?"

I looked down at the knife but I wasn't seeing it. Instead, I was seeing the display case, at first empty, and then with its huge Bowie knife replaced.

The replica. *The wrong one . . .*

# ■ TWENTY-FOUR

"I have to go back," I told her.

"An epiphany?" Pepper asked. "A revelation on the road to Ferriday?"

"Don't be sarcastic. It's just that certain things seem to make sense now. Sam was right: I've been looking at things the wrong way."

"Let me record that," she declared, smiling. "I may want to play it back some time in the future to remind you."

"I'm serious."

She put an arm around my waist. "And I'm listening."

"That's better. Anyway, what I was saying, if I can remember it now, was that—"

"—you were wrong." She squeezed me. "So let me guess: You're talking about Jeremiah. He's black, he's poor, he drinks too much, and he just sort of floats in and out and nobody pays any attention to him."

"True enough. I thought he'd taken off because he was trying to help Ethel Crawford, who was his friend. But that wasn't it at all, don't you see?"

"Clearly."

"Go on and laugh. But I'm telling you, Ethel isn't the witness we ought to be listening to: It's Jeremiah."

"All right. And what will this witness tell us that she won't?"

"He may be able to tell us what he saw that night."

"You mean when Jacko Reilly went into the water?"

"No. That's the wrong night."

"Oh, I see. And the right night—"

"—was when Miss Ethel saw somebody under the bridge and ran away."

"You think Jeremiah Persons was lying about not seeing anything?"

"He said he was sleeping when he heard somebody yell and when he got up and looked out he heard footsteps. But his cabin is a hundred yards away."

"It's not impossible."

"But Ethel never said anything about yelling. She says she called out to whoever it was but she never said she yelled."

"Maybe she didn't want to admit it."

"Believe me, Ethel Crawford isn't the kind of woman to let out a shriek." I turned to face her. "I think Jeremiah was lying. I think he was protecting himself. He didn't want to offend Miss Ethel, because she's his wheels. But he didn't want to get involved in white people's business, either."

"So you think he was standing around admiring the bridge on a cold night? Or out fishing? That doesn't make any sense."

"No."

"And what about Jacko's argument on the phone, the one that Lisa overheard? How does that fit in?"

"That, I think, is the key," I said, sucking my finger. "So if you don't mind, I think I'll call the crusading reporter for the *Cane River Weekly Trumpet* and tell him there may be a story in all this if he plays his cards right."

After supper I found Tim Raines's telephone number on the Internet and called him at home. When he heard my voice he let out a low whistle.

"You must've read the story I wrote about your arrest."

"No, and I can't say I look forward to the opportunity. Look, you want to be in on a *real* arrest? Want to find out the identity of the person who killed Jacko Reilly and murdered a man in Natchez the other day?"

"What are you smoking?"

"You're the one who wanted me to share."

"Okay, I'm listening."

And I told him what I wanted him to do. Afterward, I called David and told him to have the crew stand down for tomorrow, until I could straighten things out.

"I don't suppose you have any idea where we'll get another cook," he said.

"We only have about a week to go. Maybe we can find somebody in Simmsburg."

"Yeah, and what'll you do to *them*?"

"That's a hell of a thing to say. I never blinked at the girl. This was all something Chaney Reilly put together."

"All I know is we've got another week of work and the principal investigator's spent more time in jail than he has at the site. Marilyn said she even got a call from DOTD asking if any of this was true."

"What did she tell them?"

"I think she said she didn't know."

"*What?*"

"Well, maybe not *that*, exactly."

I tossed and turned a lot that night and while I was eating breakfast on Monday morning Tim Raines called back and told me I was right.

"Now what?" Pepper asked, and I saw worry lines creasing her forehead.

"Oh, just another trip up to Winnsboro," I said. "I think I need to talk to Jeremiah Persons again."

It was just after eleven when I knocked on Jeremiah's mother's door. Miss Ethel's car was behind the house and I knew this time they were inside, waiting.

His worried-looking mother offered me a cup of coffee, which I accepted, trying to mitigate the tension in the room with small talk as I drank it. But it was no use. They knew I hadn't driven nearly two hundred miles for no reason.

I got up slowly. "Jeremiah, can we walk around in the back and talk a little, just you and me?"

His mother shot him a look.

"It's all right," I said. "I just need to get some things straight."

"Jeremiah didn't do nothing," the old lady said.

"I know," I said. "He's not guilty of anything. I just need his help."

When we were in the yard, I walked back past the chicken house. For a few seconds I watched a pair of hens picking at the ground in a desultory way, while a rooster stood to the side. Finally I summoned my courage:

"I want to talk to you about what you saw that night," I said.

Jeremiah looked away. "Told you, I didn't see nothing, just heard the splash."

"I'm talking about the night Miss Ethel got chased off the bridge."

"I said I was sleeping."

"But you woke up."

"That's right but I didn't see nothing."

"You must have. You had a view of everything, Jeremiah."

"What you talking about? That old house down in the field, the bridge up high, you can't hardly see . . ."

"Jeremiah, I don't think you were in the house. You said you heard Miss Ethel yell out. But I don't think she yelled at all. I think you were just trying to make her happy, support her story, but without getting involved yourself."

Jeremiah shrugged. "You can believe what you want."

I wasn't making any headway. I took a deep breath.

"Look, I don't want to involve you. And I won't. Unless you keep denying things and then it'll all have to come out."

His eye darted to my face. "What'll come out?"

"How you like to climb up to the bridge tender's house at night with your wine and sit up there and drink. I asked Tim Raines to talk to Mr. Peebles, the bridge tender. Peebles said the lock hadn't worked for a while and he figured somebody had been up there when he saw the bottles. He got rid of them, of course, and put a new lock on the door of the control house. I'm sure your fingerprints are all over the place, though. So if you were up there, with a good view, you may have seen a lot more than you're telling, and that makes you a material witness."

"But I didn't do nothing."

"Jeremiah, you can break the law by *not* doing something as well as by doing something. If you see something you ought to report and don't, then . . ."

"You don't need to tell me the law. I seen enough of the law when I was in the army. I seen what kind of law they got."

"Oh?"

"Law is what the officers say. You do it or else. Then, something go wrong, it come down on you, it's all your fault, you should of known . . ."

He turned to face me. "Mister, I been threatened by worse than you and in a worse place. I may not be much, but I'm a man and I ain't gonna be threatened about something I didn't do and wasn't none of my business in the first place." He spat on the ground and one of the hens strutted up to inspect it. "And don't tell me about justice and what's fair and protecting people, because that's what all that was about over there. Every time we burned a village it was to protect people and I protected people until I can't sleep no more."

I could see there wasn't anything more to say. I'd lost.

"I guess I can't blame you," I said and left him in the yard.

The two women looked up as I entered.

"Well?" his mother asked.

"He's been through a lot," I said. "I can't blame him for not wanting to take any more chances."

"You think he saw something he isn't telling?" Miss Ethel asked.

"I had that feeling but maybe I was wrong."

Jeremiah's mother shook her head and seemed to grow smaller in the chair, with the bright quilt around her.

"Boy never was right after he come back from that war. I had four boys. Lost one in a wreck, from drinking, right out there on Highway 15. Lost another one in a shooting in New Orleans. My oldest boy, he died six years ago this April from a infection. That was Jonathan. Jeremiah, he was my baby. He was so handsome in that uniform." She pointed a withered hand toward the wooden mantel and I walked over and took down a small, framed photograph. It was of a young black man in fatigue uniform. He was smiling and there were palm trees in the background. I put the photo back on the mantel.

"I don't know what happened over there," the old woman went on. "He used to be so friendly, so happy being with people, but after he come back he just kept to himself." She reached a hand up to wipe her eyes.

"It's all right, dear," Miss Ethel soothed.

I held out a hand. "I'm sorry I bothered you. I just thought it was worth the chance."

I made my way back out, zipping up my jacket, though the weather had warmed up. For a few minutes I stood in the open air, feeling the heat of the sun, and then went over to the red Blazer. I heard the screen door slam and saw Miss Ethel coming down the steps.

"What do you think he saw?" she asked. "Something I missed?"

"I think he was in the bridge tender's house," I said. "With a bottle of wine. I think he may've seen the whole thing when you went down to the river that night."

"My Lord." She clutched at her throat.

I shrugged. "I don't have any proof, though. I don't think I can get the police to sweat it out of him. He's made up his mind not to talk."

"But there's a murderer running loose."

"I know. Maybe you'll have more luck with him."

She frowned. "Jeremiah's a strange man. He doesn't talk much. It's like there's a whole world in there nobody can get to. But when he does talk he makes perfect sense. I know he drinks, but he never has around me, and I don't think he's had a drop since he's been up here."

I got into the Blazer and started the engine.

"Good luck, Dr. Graham."

I thanked her, released the hand brake, and started out of the yard.

And heard someone calling after me.

I braked and looked in the mirror.

Jeremiah's mother was standing on the front porch, waving to get my attention. I put the Blazer into reverse, returned to where I'd started, and got out.

The old woman was making her way down the steps now and I hurried toward her.

"What is it?" I asked.

That was when I saw Jeremiah on the other side of the screen door.

"It's my son," she said. "I told him he had to do the right thing, didn't have no choice. He'll talk to you now, Mr. Graham."

I went up the steps slowly, afraid the man on the other side of the screen would vanish, but he remained, not moving, until I got there, and then he spoke:

"You was right. I was there that night," he said. "I seen it. I seen who was after Miss Ethel."

# ▰▰▰TWENTY-FIVE

I met Tim Raines at the Recreation Area, just on the other side of the bridge. He drew his battered tan Tercel next to my Blazer and got out, smiling.

"We scored, did we?"

I told him what Jeremiah had said.

"So what do we do now?" he asked.

"You got a pocket recorder?"

"Just like you asked."

"Then let's see what we can do." I put my cell phone in my pocket, locked my vehicle, and got into the Tercel. "I hope you don't mind driving. My Blazer's pretty well known by now and we have to pass through the middle of town."

We crept over the bridge and I saw that Jeff's Explorer was in the driveway leading to the sheriff's office. A couple of trusties in orange jumpsuits were washing it and I had to fight the chill that came over me as I remembered my own night in jail.

We passed the Highway 12 turnoff that led to the archaeological site and Simmsburg, and kept going, the hills on our right. Just ahead, on the left, past the high school, was the gravel road that led to the archaeological camp. As we passed it I caught a glimpse of a vehicle in the woods, near the house.

"Turn around," I said.

"But I thought we were going—"

"Somebody's at the camp. I want to check it. The crew isn't here today."

Raines nodded, found a driveway, and turned around. He came to the camp drive and turned in.

"I know that truck," Raines said as we pulled up beside the other vehicle. "It's—"

"It belongs to Luther Dupree," I said. "I imagine his daughter's here, since Luther's in jail again."

Before Raines could say anything I was out of the car and on my way into the house.

Alice Mae looked up from her mopping as I came in and gave a little gasp.

"Oh. Mr. Alan. I didn't . . . I mean . . ."

"It's okay," I told her. "I saw the truck here and just wanted to check."

"Mr. Alan, I hope you aren't mad. I didn't say nothing against you, really. I mean, I don't even remember what happened. I woke up and I was here and there was all these men around and they was telling me you . . . But I didn't think you'd . . . I mean, I didn't know, and they told me I had to sign something and I didn't know what it was, but I was scared, they said my paw would never get out of jail and . . ." She twisted her wristwatch. "Then they said they'd let you go and I was glad but I figured you'd be mad and then the sheriff said you wouldn't be, on account of you weren't that kind, you'd understand, and you weren't coming back here, anyway, just Mr. David and the others, and they wouldn't hold nothing against me, he didn't think, and I thought if I cleaned the place up real good, maybe, had a good meal ready, though I'm not sure where to get the food, but—"

"Alice Mae . . ." I held up a hand. "They aren't coming today. But it's good of you to clean up here. And I don't hold anything against you. You were drugged. You weren't responsible."

"God bless you, Mr. Alan."

"But there are a couple of things you may be able to clear up."

"Oh?"

I heard Raines open the door behind me.

"Did you know Jacko Reilly, Alice Mae?"

She flushed red and started twisting at the watch again. "I reckon everybody knew him."

"But did you ever talk to him? I mean, just the two of you?"

She gave an exaggerated shrug. "I reckon once or twice. I know what folks say about him, but he was nice to me."

"He was a nice-looking man, wasn't he?"

"Yeah, Jacko was nice-looking."

"And when he disappeared you were unhappy."

"I reckon." Another shrug. "I mean, I figured he was just gone somewhere, but I didn't know he was dead or nothing, not until they found him."

"And that made you real sad, didn't it?"

"Sure. Thinking about him down there in that car, under all that water for those months, and no Christian burial or nothing. I know Paw didn't like him but he was always a real gentleman to me. Just like you, Mr. Alan." She smiled shyly. "I mean, he used to sometimes give me things. He said I was pretty. Ain't no man ever said that to me before."

"What did he give you?" I asked. "Do you remember?"

"Well . . ." She licked her lips and her hand went down to her left wrist again, and the blocky old watch. "He give me this watch, for one thing."

"It's a pretty watch," I said. "Mind if I take a look at it?"

"I reckon not." She slipped the watch from her wrist and held it out to me. I held it up for Raines to see.

"Did he tell you where he got this?" I asked.

"No."

"When did he give it to you?"

Another shrug. "Dunno. Before Thanksgiving. He said it was a Christmas present. I said it was early. He just laughed and said they had all the Christmas stuff out in the stores so he didn't reckon it was early."

"What did your father say about his giving you this?"

"He didn't like it but I cried when he said he wanted to take it away so he said I could keep it." She sniffed. "That was when Paw was in the jail. He was mad because he said while he was in the jail couldn't nobody keep an eye on me and make sure nothing happened. But then Jacko disappeared." She shook her head. "You don't know how lonely it was, Mr. Alan, with Jacko gone and Paw in jail."

"I'm sure it was. I want you to think back a week or so, Alice Mae. I want to tell you a story and I want you to tell me if it's true, okay?"

Her nod this time was doubtful. I went on:

"It was a cold night. Maybe you couldn't sleep. Maybe you were thinking about Jacko, just lying there in bed. Your paw was in jail again, so you were by yourself. And like you said, it gets lonely."

"Yes, sir."

"And maybe you got up and couldn't get back to sleep. Does that ever happen, Alice Mae?"

"Sometimes." She looked from me to Tim Raines and then away.

"Maybe sometimes at night you even take your paw's truck."

"Sometimes. I mean, he won't let me drive except just to work and back, and never no other time. Only time I get to drive it is when he ain't around. Sometimes late at night I drive it up and down through town, when it's quiet, so don't nobody see, and I go slow past the houses, all them houses dark with folks inside, and a few of 'em with little lights on, with maybe people inside can't sleep, and I try to think what it's like in there, how it'd be to live in one of them houses, maybe like if I was married and had my own kids, and how maybe those houses ain't like the double-wide, all drafty with a hole in the floor where the cold air comes in . . ."

"I understand."

"Sometimes I even look in the windows and—" She stopped suddenly.

"It's okay," I said. "I know it was you outside my window that night."

"Mr. Alan, I'm sorry, I—"

"It's all right. Alice, do you ever go down by the bridge?"

"Maybe once."

"Thinking about Jacko?"

"Yeah." She shifted her weight from one foot to the other.

"You parked and got out?"

"I went down off the road and stopped in the woods on the

other side. I got out and walked down by the water and I was thinking how terrible lonely it would be down there." She looked up at me. "I know folks said bad things about Jacko, and maybe they was true. I just know when I seen him he had nice words to say to me and no other man never did. There wasn't nothing like you think, neither: My paw was always too close for that. It was just Jacko was somebody to talk to sometimes and he was nice."

"Sure."

"And after a while I walked down under the bridge toward the other side, where couldn't nobody see from up above. Funny, I almost felt like somebody was watchin'. Then, after a little while, I heard feet walking and I knew somebody was coming down by the river and I didn't know who it was, but I knew if they caught me and my paw found out, he'd be mad as a nest of hornets and so I tried to get way back in the dark, and then somebody called out for me to come outa there, and it was a woman's voice, but it scared me, and I kinda tripped on the rip-rap and whoever it was, they give a little yell and took out runnin' and I wanted to say, 'Wait, I ain't gonna hurt you,' and so I went after her, but she kept going and when I got up on the bridge she was all the way to the other end, so I went back and got the truck out of the woods where I parked it and I drove all the way to Carter Crossing before I turned around and come back."

Raines gave a little whistle. "Well, that settles that."

"You gonna tell my paw?" the girl asked.

"I don't see any need," I said. "You didn't do anything wrong."

"Then what you gonna do?"

"Nothing," I said. "You can go on mopping. The crew will be back tomorrow."

She wiped a strand of brown hair out of her eyes. "Thank you, Mr. Alan. You're real good to me."

We stopped at the highway.

"How did you know she'd be at your camp?" Raines asked. "You said we were going to her place."

"We were but I just happened to see the truck when we passed."

"Lucky." He scratched his jaw. "Okay, so the girl was all dressed up for the cold and she scared Miss Ethel, and that's what the old lady saw, not some killer, and our man Jeremiah was sitting up there in the bridge house with a bottle and saw it all but didn't want to get involved. Fine, but does that lead us any closer to who did the crimes? Jacko killed the old man in Columbia and stole everything he could get his hands on and the piece of silver was just something he scooped up, along with the watch, right?"

"That's how I make it."

"But somebody killed Jacko and then they killed this fellow Hightower, over in Natchez. How do we find out who did that?"

"Let's see Ross Flynn," I said. "I think he can help us on this one."

Ross Flynn's office was across the street from the courthouse, on the high ground shadowed by the hills. While a chubby blond secretary worked on the word processor outside he listened to us in his private office, which had once been the bedroom of a house. From one wall a stuffed badger looked down and on the other was a mounted lever-action carbine. Flynn sat back in his swivel chair, boots on his desk, staring at the smoke curls made by his cigar.

"Why didn't you go to the sheriff?" he asked. "This is his job. I just prosecute cases."

"This is a rural parish," I said. "I've seen how things work. They work the way you, the sheriff, and Judge Galt want them to."

Ross Flynn took out his cigar and pinned me with his eyes. "You got a hell of a nerve coming back. I could just as easy reinstate those charges."

"You could," I said. "But you won't. I think you're a fair man and you want to see the guilty person caught."

"I still have to go by the law."

"But you have some flexibility when it comes to procedure. For instance, if a member of somebody's family has a problem, there are ways to handle it without going through the legal motions."

Flynn's eyes narrowed. "What are you talking about?"

"Maybe somebody owes somebody else, so if somebody gets a request to handle a case a certain way, to arrest somebody who's making trouble . . ."

"What are you talking about?" Raines asked.

"You were just repaying Jeff Scully a favor," I said. "Well, the favor's repaid."

"Hell, I thought Jeff was your friend."

"I thought so, too. And maybe he still is. But he's in too deep."

Flynn sighed. "Yeah, I guess so." He sat forward in the chair. "I hope this works." He lifted the phone, then put it down. "I guess we ought to just walk over there. No need to warn folks by calling first."

We walked across the street to the courthouse and took the elevator down to the sheriff's office.

"Sheriff in?" Flynn asked the deputy on duty.

"He's in court, I think. You can catch him there."

"Never mind." And Flynn told him what he wanted.

The deputy shrugged. "I reckon we can do that. You want to wait in the interview room." He glanced over at me. "You need security for him?"

"Not right now," Flynn said dryly. "He's in my custody."

The green room hadn't changed any and a chill went through me when I remembered my recent experience. Flynn took the interview chair but Raines and I stood up.

"I'm not sure about having him here," Flynn said, nodding at the reporter. "This ain't a public spectacle."

"You can trust me," Raines said. "All I want is first dibs."

"Yeah," the D.A. said. "Well, remember, if you screw up the investigation, your ass is mine and—"

The door opened and Jeff Scully, with his tie loose at the neck, stood staring at us.

"What's going on?" he demanded. "Ross, what are these people doing here?"

"Chill out, Jeff," the lawyer drawled. "We're just borrowing your room."

Scully frowned at me. "What do you want here, Alan? I thought I told you to go home."

"You did. And you also left those credentials in my glove compartment."

"My mistake."

"Sure. But just in case I needed to use them, they were there, and if I screwed up, you could deny everything. Jeff, you're a better politician than I thought."

Before he could answer there was movement behind him, and a small figure in an orange jumpsuit stood beside him in the hall.

"Come on in, Luther," Flynn called out. "We're having a pow-wow and you're invited."

The little man limped in, a lopsided grin on his face.

"Mr. Alan," he greeted me and looked around at the others. "Look, I ain't mad at Mr. Alan here, 'cause I don't believe he did nothin' to my little girl, and whoever said he did, well, I'll deal with 'em when I get out."

"This isn't about Alice Mae," Flynn drawled.

Scully moved into the room behind Luther and shut the door. "Well, suppose somebody tells me just what it *is* about?"

"If Mr. Pope is saying I killed more'n that one doe, he's a damn liar," Luther declared.

"This isn't about a doe," I said. "It's about a watch." I held up the old gold Bulova that Alice Mae had worn. "Alice Mae says she got this from Jacko Reilly."

Luther frowned and scratched a grizzled jaw. "That's right. I didn't want him giving her nothing. But after it was done, what could I do? Why? Did he steal it?"

I nodded. "From a man in Columbia. A man Jacko murdered."

"Damn." Luther hit his thigh with the flat of his hand. "I knowed it wasn't no good to have him around her." His eyes narrowed. "Look, you ain't blaming nothing on her, are you?"

"Well, it *is* kind of interesting isn't it?" I asked.

"What?"

"That Jacko was around her at all."

"It's a small town. I can't watch her all the time."

"Of course not. But when would she have a chance to meet him?"

"What are you saying?" Luther looked from me to the seated Ross Flynn.

"I think you know," Flynn said.

Luther's eyes narrowed and he rubbed his mouth with an arm.

"It was Jacko's own fault, was what it was," he said. "I never kilt nobody. But like they say . . ." He grinned. "Shit happens."

# ≡ TWENTY-SIX

"Do you know what you're saying?" Scully asked.

"I reckon I do," Luther said. "I was there when it went down."

"Wait a minute." Ross Flynn held up a hand. "If we're going in this direction—"

"You gonna read me my rights?" Luther asked. " 'Cause I figure I know 'em by now, but you can go on and do it again."

"Damn," Flynn swore.

"I don't need no lawyer. Except for the burglary thing. I reckon I was with Jacko when we did that one but I ain't hurt nobody, that was pure Jacko, and all I done was stay with the car, outside. It was Jacko gone inside and I reckon he was the one killed that fella. I didn't know nothing about nobody dying until later."

"What were you after?" I asked. "You went to Tom McElwain's place to get something."

"Sure did. Jacko had a deal with this fella in Mississippi that sold antiques. Fella said he'd give Jacko a lot of money to go to Columbia and bring back a certain thing, because there was somebody willing to pay top dollar. Jacko paid me two hundred to go along, and said there'd be more afterward."

"This thing McElwain had," Flynn said. "What was it?"

Luther coughed. "Well, it was supposed to be a knife."

"A knife?" Flynn asked.

"Not just *a* knife, don't you see? *The* knife."

Flynn sighed. "And what knife would that be?"

Luther shook his head disdainfully. "Well, the original Bowie knife. The one used by Jim Bowie. The one he killed them men with at the sandbar fight. The knife that was made out of a meteor, like in that movie I seen. The original Bowie, that's what knife."

The district attorney gave me a disbelieving look and I just nodded. Luther wasn't finished.

"See, somebody told this Hightower dude that old McElwain had this knife and Hightower knew it would cost too much to buy it, so he figured to just steal it. He didn't know Jacko would kill nobody. That's 'cause he didn't know Jacko's temper. That was the damn thing about it all."

"What?" Flynn asked.

"That there weren't no knife. It was all made up. You didn't have to do more than set foot in the old man's house, with all the junk in there, to see that."

"I thought you stayed outside," Scully said then.

"Well, I got tired of waiting and looked in through the window while Jacko had the old man tied up."

"Let's get this straight," Flynn said. "You say there was no knife."

"Hell, no. All that was for nothing. Oh, Jacko got some guns and a lock box that had some coins and stuff in it, but there weren't no knife, and Jacko was in there for over a hour, so I reckon he turned it upside down."

"What happened next?" Flynn asked. "What did you do?"

"Me? Two days later I got caught by that state trooper and I'm here to tell you that was the biggest goddamn frame-up that ever was, because ain't nobody can get drunk on two damn drinks and—"

The D.A. held up a hand. "Stick to the point, Luther."

Luther rubbed his jaw again. "I'm trying. Don't you see, if I hadn't of got locked up, we never would've got the *other* knife."

"*What* other knife?" the irate Flynn demanded.

"Well, the one that was in the case outside in the hall there," Luther declared.

"*You* stole the things out of that case?" Jeff Scully asked.

Luther Dupree shrugged. "We needed a knife to pass off on

Hightower. I was in jail and Jacko come and told me how easy it was to get out at night, with the deputy sleeping, and half the time they didn't even lock the cells if you wasn't in for nothing serious, and so I just took the stuff one night and snuck out and handed it all to Jacko in the street out there and went back to jail afterward."

"I'll be damned," Scully swore. "And Jacko took the knife to Hightower."

"Something like that. But Hightower wasn't stupid. He said it was the wrong one and he wouldn't pay. They had a terrible argument, Jacko said."

"The wrong one," I repeated, but nobody heard me.

"So what happened then?" Flynn persisted.

"Well, Jacko didn't have his money and Hightower didn't have his knife. Oh, Jacko give him some guns and things we stole but that wasn't what Hightower was after. But Jacko said it was his fault sending us to a place on a wild goose chase and he had to kill a man and it wasn't something he liked to do and he figured since it was Hightower's fault, Hightower owed him for the trouble."

"Of course," Jeff said.

"So Hightower said he'd come over here and they'd meet at the rec area outside town and work something out."

"Only they didn't," Flynn said.

"Not exactly."

"Hightower killed Jacko," Flynn said.

"Yup." The little man leaned forward. "I was there, see? I seen it all."

"I thought you were still in jail," Flynn said, then gave the sheriff a sour look. "Oh, that's right. I forgot. You had the keys to the place."

"You might say that." Luther shrugged. "It was late, wasn't nobody out, and Jacko said he wanted me along in case Hightower tried anything funny. I was supposed to wait in the bushes at the rec area and watch and make sure everything went right."

"But instead things went wrong," Flynn said.

"Well, Hightower didn't want to give him more than a couple hundred dollars more, said some pretty hard things about old Jacko. Not that they wasn't true. I can't say I liked Jacko all that much myself. He was always sneaking around and trying to make up to my Alice Mae, and her with no more sense of what men are all about than that table there. No, Jacko was a hard man to like."

"Exactly what happened?" Flynn asked.

"I was outside the car. All's I heard was arguing and then there was some pushing and shoving and the door opened and Hightower come out and he had a knife in his hand. He throwed it down, like it was dirty, and from the moonlight I could just barely see Jacko in there, limp as a dead otter." He licked his lips. "I don't reckon you got any water, do you? Whiskey'd be better but I'll take water."

Jeff turned and called to someone down the hall for water.

"Hightower rolled the car into the water?" Flynn asked.

"Yup. Started her up and drove outa there and I walked up to the main road and all I seen was his lights disappearing at the side of the bridge. I didn't know what he was up to, but I didn't figure I wanted to know, neither. Hightower's car was at the rec area and I knowed he'd be back, so I just waited a little while. Pretty soon another car comes down the road, slow like, from the direction of Carter Crossing, and when it gets to the bridge it slows down and stops. Then it goes on and a little while later I see somebody walking toward me up the road and I knowed it was Hightower. When he passed by I seen a look on his face like nothing you ever seen in your life. Like his face was just a mask. Like he was dead hisself. In a little while his car started up and he drove away. I picked up the knife and wiped it off and I walked on back to the jail and locked myself in. Well, can't never tell when a knife'll come in handy, in that place."

Flynn pushed back his chair. "That's all real neat, Luther. There's just one thing missing."

"What's that?"

"Somebody killed Hightower."

Jeff handed Luther a paper cup with water in it and Luther nodded.

"I was feared you was gonna ask that."

"Well?" the lawyer said.

"Hightower was running scared. He actually told me on the phone he was thinking of doing a deal with the law and him the killer, if you can believe it."

"That's why he called me," I said. "He wanted me to be a go-between, to help him plea bargain."

"And he'd of claimed I was the one kilt old Jacko, the bastard. He'd of sold his soul for six months in jail. They's some pretty low people in this world, I'm telling you."

"So you solved that problem by killing him," Flynn said. He gave Jeff a sour look. "On one of your little furloughs from the jail."

"Well . . ." Luther began and then, in a move surprisingly fast, threw the water in Jeff's face and darted out the door.

It was a full second before anybody could react, and then Jeff and I raced after him. He shot through the sheriff's office and out the door and into the parking area.

We would have caught him if it hadn't been for the mop bucket in the middle of the hallway. Somehow Luther had dodged it, but Jeff, in his pursuit, stepped into it and fell headlong onto the hard tiles. I stumbled against him, just managed to keep from falling, and then squeezed past as he raised himself to his hands and knees with an oath.

Luther was at the highway now, heading left, toward the river.

I'd never been a sprinter myself, but I figured I could catch a man with a limp.

"Luther!" I yelled but he kept going.

What I didn't see was the man coming out of the courthouse just then, a burly man with longish gray hair and glasses, and a bulge under his flapping coat.

Chaney Reilly.

He saw the pursuit and broke into a trot, heading toward Luther and the bridge on a converging course.

Behind me I heard somebody yelling and I recognized Jeff's voice: "Reilly, leave it alone!"

I was steps behind the panicked Luther, at the foot of the bridge, and I was already panting as I started up the grade.

At any second now a car might come from the opposite direction, and Luther was in the middle of the road . . .

"Luther," I called again but he wasn't listening. Instead, incredibly, he was headed for the side of the structure, and the ladder that went up to the bridge house.

"No!" Jeff yelled behind me and I started to turn around, tell him there was nothing to be alarmed at now, Luther had trapped himself, couldn't go anywhere else, but then I realized, from movement in the corner of my eye, that it wasn't Luther he was yelling at, but Chaney Reilly.

I wheeled, saw the pistol in Reilly's hand, and, as if in slow motion, saw it being raised.

"Reilly!" But he didn't seem to hear, just raised the weapon inexorably, and even as I rushed toward him I saw the gun jump in his hand, heard the explosion, and knew it was too late.

I froze and then looked over my shoulder.

Luther was halfway up the ladder, swaying now, and even as I watched he let go and plunged from the side of the bridge to vanish into the waters below.

# ≡ EPILOGUE

It was a Tuesday afternoon a week later and I'd gone to Carter Crossing to visit Tally Galt at her telephoned request. The weather for the last three days had been warm, in the sixties, and people were talking about an early spring. We walked around the covered swimming pool and stood facing the hills, as if the house had ears.

"I couldn't let this finish without talking to you," she said. "And apologizing."

I didn't say anything, just waited for her to choose her words.

"When you came here last time you frightened me rather badly," she said. "That's why I called Chaney."

"You have some interesting friends," I told her.

"He isn't a friend. I knew he'd jump at any chance to embarrass Jeff, though."

"And you were willing to sacrifice Jeff's political career?"

"What choice did I have?" I saw her fist clench and unclench by her side. "It was either that or let everything come out."

"Didn't Reilly wonder what this was about?"

"I'm sure he did. But he wasn't going to turn down something free. Here was a chance to do a favor for somebody whose husband could help him."

"And now . . . ?"

"Killing a man who was running away, even if he was an escaping prisoner, is something he's having a hard time explaining, especially since Luther didn't have a weapon. At least, that's what I hear. Maybe you hear something else from Jeff."

"I don't hear anything from him."

"Too bad. I know he's sorry about what happened, and I'm really to blame for it, not him."

"Jeff's a big boy," I said. "Like you reminded me before, he can handle himself. Or did he ask you to call me?"

"No, that was my idea. He doesn't know you're here."

"So why *am* I here?"

"Partly to watch me eat crow. Partly to hear you say you aren't going to tell anybody who shot at you that day."

"There's nothing to be gained from that," I said.

"Thank you. For your information, I was up at the camp getting some things I left after the last night we spent there. When I saw you and Luther coming I panicked. I guess I was a little paranoid. What if somebody had been following me? I was just trying to scare you."

"Is that all?"

"All?" Her dark brows rose. "You mean, may you be dismissed? Not quite yet."

She reached into the pocket of her jeans and withdrew a slip of paper. "I don't know what you think of me and ordinarily I wouldn't care, but for some reason I do. You're like a, well, conscience. Does that make sense? Don't answer. I know it's just my guilt. You can't sneak around like Jeff and I've been doing and not feel guilty. At first it's so much fun because you *are* sneaking, and it's like you're getting away with something, but after a while it's like carrying a ton of concrete."

"I've been called a lot of things," I said, "but concrete's a first."

"I'm perfectly serious. You have that effect, at least on me. But, then, like I said, it's mostly in my own head, right?"

I shrugged.

"Anyway," she went on, "when a person feels guilty about something, sometimes they look for a way to make things up. This is mine." She handed me the piece of paper. "I found this on Arlo's desk. When I realized what it was I was horrified. I didn't know what to do. You'll understand when you read it. I don't know where he got it but he buys the strangest things and trades people for old documents. Of course, this is just a copy I made when he wasn't home. He wouldn't like the idea of my pilfering his desk and his precious collection."

I unfolded the sheet of paper and looked down at a page filled with the kind of handwriting common in the last century, when people still practiced penmanship.

*April 16, 1858*

*My Dear Grandson,*

*You have often expressed an interest in our family and I have tried to tell you all I know about it. You asked recently about the story of your Uncle William and his encounter with the late Col. James Bowie, who as you know has gotten a reputation as a patriot of sorts due to his death in Texas some years ago. I think that, being a young man, you fancy a tale of romance and derring-do, as in the novels of Mr. Scott. So, as I am now not so young as I used to be, it seemed to me appropriate that I should tell you the whole story, as it was told to me by your Uncle William, my late brother, who lived in Lordsport on the Cane River at that time.*

*In the winter of 1833 Mr. James Bowie, a land spec-ulator and adventurer, rode to Lordsport from Natchez, on his way to Alexandria, where he had business deal-ings. Mr. Bowie had some notoriety as a brawler in these parts and it was said he had made and lost several fortunes through unsavory land dealings, as well as by running slaves from Galvez Town in Texas. I don't know if any of this is true, but that was the man's reputation. He also had a name as a duelist who'd killed a man in Natchez some years before. Your Uncle William always said Bowie's reputation was somewhat overblown and aside for a fondness for drink the man was mainly brag-gadocio, but I don't know about that.*

*When Bowie arrived in Lordsport in late 1833, he was*

on his way back to Texas, because certain of his schemes hereabouts had fallen through. He had lived in Texas for several years at that time & had married a wealthy Mexican woman, which would I suppose put him in the class of fortune hunters, but the word was that he really loved this woman & she died while he was away in Louisiana and Mississippi, leaving him quite inconsolable. In any case, he resolved to return to Texas and wished to liquidate whatever holdings he had in the United States.

At that time, Bowie was the owner of a tract of land in the hills, which rumor said he had acquired some years before and tried to sell for silver mining. You know as well as I do that there is no silver in those hills and so Mr. Bowie was never able to sell that land but on his way to Texas he thought that he might be able to sell it cheaply because the word, according to William, was that the Bowies were always short of cash.

He stayed at the Phelps boardinghouse, which, as you know, is still there. While in Lordsport it seems he indulged his habit for strong drink and inquired about local sporting events, all of which caused him to be directed to a card game in the home of a certain Mr. Amos Light, who was himself much addicted to racing horses and card playing.

Your Uncle William was a young man then and not at all the sober, careful man you remember. You were only eight or nine years old when he passed away at the age of fifty-two. You may recall that he married late, at the age of forty, & before that there was much in him that was wild.

Now what follows I have directly from William and as he told me the story many times & I never knew him to tell a lie, I believe that it is the truth & that you may believe this as factual.

The night after Mr. Bowie arrived William happened to attend the card game at the home of Mr. Light & it was in the course of this game that Mr. Bowie became very drunk. When he had lost all his money he put up *the deed to the two hundred acres in the hills & shortly lost that as well. Then he pulled a large hunting knife, which he used to wear in a sheath at his belt, & said it was a knife that had killed a man & would be worth something & that, by G—, if nobody would purchase it so he could continue to play cards he would as leave use the blade to cut his own throat because life was not worth living for him anyhow. His companions thought it best to humor him, because it was not safe to leave him in possession of such a weapon in that state of mind, & so they let him pledge the knife and two of his pistols & I think Mr. Light won the pistols & William got the knife and also the tract of land which, however, he never thought of much value. The next day Mr. Bowie was in a more reasonable frame of mind but there was much discussion about what to do with his weapons. It was finally decided to let him continue with several other travelers who were themselves armed, but to hold his own weapons until such time as he or a family member came to redeem them, as he was far from recovered from his intemperance.*

*I don't know what happened to the pistols. William said that for many years Amos Light had them but then they disappeared. But William was always careful about the knife, which he said had a certain history, having killed a man & been associated with Mr. Bowie. He thought someone of Mr. Bowie's relatives might come later & wish to redeem it because there was a story that it had been made at the request & order of Mr. Bowie's older brother, Mr. Rezin Bowie, but Mr. Rezin Bowie died five or six years after James, so it appears the knife is ours fair and square, such as it is. Your uncle showed it to me once. It was an ordinary-looking butcher knife with a blade about nine inches long and a wooden handle & nothing that would distinguish it from any other knife of a similar sort. After he died, your Great Aunt Sophie kept it and some of the silver pieces from that card game and the Bible our mother gave William and some of his other possessions in a locked box but I*

*talked to her the other day & she expressed a willingness
to let you have the box & its contents since you were
interested in the family.*

*I don't know if this is anything you want especially
but it is something having to do with the history of our
family & it seemed right for you to have it.*

*Your loving Grandfather,
Arthur Davis McElwain*

When I'd finished I looked up at Tally Galt.

"I *am* glad you called me," I said.

"I'm happy to hear it. But, of course, it leads to another
problem . . ."

I nodded. "Your husband's the one who went to Hightower
and told him to get the knife."

"Yes. Arlo would never have proposed anything illegal, of
course. I'm sure he just wanted this Hightower to act as a go-
between, to be sure that what he got was authentic and that
he wasn't overcharged."

"But McElwain wouldn't sell. Or maybe his price was too
high and Hightower saw his commission going down the
drain. So he sent Jacko to steal it, only Jacko being Jacko, he
killed McElwain and took everything else he could get his
hands on."

"That's what I'm sure happened," Tally said. "And my husband could have done something at the time, but he didn't.
His reputation is too precious. So he just stood back and let
events take their course and four people are dead. All so Arlo
Galt could touch and handle and caress a knife that has history
attached to it and have people admire it on his wall." She gave
a little laugh. "And it was all for nothing because Mr. Mc-
Elwain didn't even have the knife, did he?"

"I think he had it," I said. "It's just that nobody recognized
it."

"Oh?"

"They expected a knife that was like Prince Valiant's sing-
ing sword. A mystic blade. True collectors, like Hightower,
knew that wasn't quite accurate, but Jacko and Luther didn't."

"Life is full of ironies," she said.

"Goodbye, Mrs. Galt. I hope things work out for you."

"Oh, they will. As you may have noticed, your friend Jeff is a realist. He's lived dangerously up to now but I think he's had his fill."

"You don't seem very upset."

"Did you think I'd break down and cry in front of you? There's plenty of time for that when you're gone." She summoned up a smile. "Our Jeff is going to make a fine politician."

"I'm sure." I started away, then stopped: "You don't know where your husband got that letter, do you?"

"You see through me, Mr. Graham. It was mine, of course. My grandmother was a McElwain. Somehow Tom McElwain's side got the knife—one of those messy family disputes where everybody grabs things after somebody dies. But our side kept the letter. I mentioned it to Arlo one day without thinking. You know the rest."

She followed me to the door and we shook hands, and as I started down the steps I heard the door close behind me.

I drove back to Lordsport, crossing the ancient bridge, and then passing the turn in to the archaeological camp, where today there were no cars parked. I kept going out Highway 20, past the high school on the hillside to the right, past Gunn's Road, all the way to the place where a dilapidated double-wide sat in a bare space, a beaten blue pickup in front of it.

When I knocked Alice Mae came to the door. Her eyes were red and her cheeks sunken.

"Mr. Alan," she said, touching her stringy hair self-consciously.

"Hello, Alice Mae. I wonder if I could ask you something?"

"You're the first person come by here since Paw was killed. At first there was all kinds of people, ladies, who brought me things. Pies and cakes and sandwiches. I still got some of it in there. I can't eat all that. Then nobody come no more. I been sitting in there watching TV and sometimes I think I can hear his voice. But I know I don't really, because Paw's dead. He was killed by that man. And it wasn't right, Mr. Alan. It wasn't right what Sheriff Reilly done, because my paw didn't kill nobody."

"Of course not," I murmured. "Alice Mae, do you remember a knife your paw used to skin that deer with? A butcher knife with a wooden handle?"

"Sure."

"Do you know where he got it?"

"I reckon."

"He brought it home after going out with Jacko, didn't he?"

"Yeah. But—"

"Alice Mae, do you know where the knife is now?"

She stared at me for so long I thought she hadn't understood and then she broke into a laugh that lurched from mirth into hysteria and tears started to roll down her cheeks.

I grabbed her shoulders. "Alice Mae, what's so funny?"

"Do I know where it is, you asked. And the answer is of course I know where it is. I took it with me when Paw sent me to collect the money from that man in Mississippi, the money Paw said the man was supposed to give me to get Paw outa jail. When I went to get the money, the man was already leaving his shop and I followed him down to Natchez and watched him go to the motel, and I sat outside a long time, trying to figure what to do and wishing Paw was there to tell me. And finally I figured I better just go to his room and ask him. But when he saw who it was he started to laugh, said he wasn't going to pay Paw nothing. He saw he was crazy to be worried about somebody that had to send a dumb, ugly girl to do their work. And then he said if Paw didn't leave him alone he'd do him like he did Jacko." She shrugged. "That's when I pulled out the knife."

"Alice Mae . . ."

"I killed him, Mr. Alan. I stabbed him until I was too tired to stab him anymore and then I left him there and I drove back to Louisiana."

"And the knife?"

"When I was halfway over the bridge I throwed it off."

I thought of the blood-spattered young woman, the knife flying through the air and then landing in the muddy waters. Landing near the place where, in the last century, a sandbar had existed, a sandbar where there had once been a duel . . .

"Alice Mae, listen. I need to get some help for you. I'm going to call some people."

But she just kept on laughing. I figured she wouldn't stop until after the deputies got there. Then she'd tell them the story all over again. But before I called them I wanted to hear Pepper's voice, to remind me that there was still a sane world out there.

"Hey," I told her, "I love you and I'm coming home."

# ▰▰AUTHOR'S NOTE

There is a vast literature on James Bowie and the Bowie knife. These include both biographies and novels. Probably the two best-known fictional treatments of James Bowie's life are *The Tempered Blade* (1946) by Monte Barrett, and *The Iron Mistress* (1951) by Paul I. Wellman. Of the two, the Barrett book is closer to the truth, probably because his work was published two years before Raymond Thorpe's purportedly historical *Bowie Knife*, which apparently influenced Wellman by its uncritical acceptance of the James Black story.

There is no space here to recapitulate the evolution of the Bowie-type knife, but the best concise treatment this writer has seen appeared in a 1979 commemorative publication by the Commission des Avoyelles, entitled *Bowie Knives, Origin and Development*. This valuable publication, which relies heavily on collector Bill Williamson's work, establishes definitively that the knife was invented by Rezin Bowie and details, with drawings and verbal descriptions, the stages through which the weapon evolved.

More recently, the historian William Davis has published a highly readable and informative account of Jim Bowie's life and adventures in his excellent book *Three Roads to the Alamo: The Lives and Fortunes of David Crockett, James Bowie, and William Barrett Travis* (1998).

What is presented in the preceding pages is fictional, but

though place names have generally been fictionalized, it is set in a place where the Bowies once owned land and which they frequented. The author makes no claim that what is recounted herein happened. But it *could* have happened . . .

*Malcolm K. Strum*